FRESH GRAVE IN GRAND CANYON

Praise for Lee Patton

Nothing Gold Can Stay

"*Nothing Gold Can Stay* is a 14-carat gem. The characters, both major and minor, are extremely well drawn…as a work of romantic gay fiction it is absolutely priceless."—*Jone Devlin, Triangle*

Every Summer Day

"No matter where a reader lives, it's always a delight to discover a book that sets a gripping story in a recognizable ZIP code…DU alumnus Lee Patton delivers that compelling blend with his latest novel, *Every Summer Day.*"—*University of Denver Magazine*

By the Author

Nothing Gold Can Stay (as Casey Nelson)

Love and Genetic Weaponry: The Beginner's Guide

My Aim Is True

Every Summer Day

Coming to Life on South High

FRESH GRAVE IN GRAND CANYON

by

Lee Patton

2021

Credits
Editors: Jerry L. Wheeler and Stacia Seaman
Production Design: Stacia Seaman
Cover Design by Tammy Seidick

Acknowledgments

This novel began life as a late-night tale on Swamp Point above Grand Canyon. Around the campfire, Debbie Northcutt's Sierra Club volunteer crew speculated about a group of Colorado River rafters finding a dead body on a remote canyon beach, with the deceased being the most difficult and disliked member of the group. I vowed I would complete that narrative someday, and here it is.

Many thanks for the feedback on the earliest drafts to Coleen Hubbard, Sharon Wilbert, Chris Kenry, and Tom and Cathy Hand. Gratitude to diehard bookworm George Ware and fellow novelists Kristen Hannum, Jack Long, John Serini, Tracy Smelser, and Greg Francis for their close reading and suggestions on later drafts, and to Jerry Wheeler for his editorial insights and overall support.

For background on "how violent criminal behavior is connected to a combination of abusive childhoods and brain dysfunction," I'm indebted to the work of psychiatrist Dorothy Lewis and neurologist Jonathan Pincus as featured in Malcolm Gladwell's *New Yorker* essay, "Damaged."

For indispensible information on Grand Canyon's mile-by-mile geography, geology, and river lore, I relied on Larry Stevens's *The Colorado River in Grand Canyon: A Guide*, and Buzz Belknap and Loie Belknap Evans's *Grand Canyon River Guide*.

For Billy, Greg, and Dave

Thanks for all the great times on all the great rivers

MID-CANYON PRELUDE

Mile 52

On a desert delta uninhabited for centuries, a new grave appeared deep in Grand Canyon's roadless wild. Hidden behind coyote willows, the burial pit was shallow.

Uncanny silence followed the Colorado River's course. No laughter, no shouted tries at echoes, no rafting guides' monologues. Though thousands of rafters floated through Nankoweap every season, no guides led them up the trail to the ancient native granaries today. Only the lilt of a canyon wren sounded for the fresh human corpse.

As the grave festered far below, the day began as usual at Grand Canyon's South Rim Village. On the rim near Thunderbird Lodge, a twelve-year-old Texas girl, used to the featureless flats of the Panhandle, struggled with awe. On a one-hour family detour off the interstate, the girl was allowed just minutes to scan the mesas and buttes spreading to the North Rim horizon, but the brief canyon view infused her with wonder for all the secret formations the Earth's surface must hide.

Five thousand feet below the Texas girl's baptism in the sublime, another life had been buried in haste, the last rites a quick blessing muttered to the wind.

Chapter 1

Mile Zero

RAY O'BRIEN shivered from his quick skinny-dip. Face-down on a rock ledge above the swimming hole, his white butt exposed to the Arizona sun, he was glad for the desert breeze drying his skin.

Still dead tired from his seven-hundred-mile overnight drive from Denver, Ray balled up his clothes to form a pillow. He'd hoped his plunge into the water would startle him awake, but instead he kept drifting into drowsy half-dreams. It didn't matter if he napped for a while, naked like this, did it? The other volunteers were wandering downstream along the Colorado River, and the willow brush and Grand Canyon's first sandstone outcrops hid him well.

Dozing only to wake again, aware of a splash, Ray jolted up. Damn. He scanned the swimming hole bank to bank, ready to cover himself, but he didn't see anyone break the creek's surface. A small rock chipped it, though, from an unseen hand around the rocky bend. It skipped five times.

A loud splash followed the rock. Soon an arm came into view, slicing the water with a powerful stroke. Then he saw the rest of the swimmer, an elongated mass of tanned skin, naked as Ray was. His kick was strong enough to echo up the side canyon's walls.

The skinny-dipping man's sidestroke roiled dolphin-like, that hard kick propelling him across the swimming hole. He halted in the sandy shallows. Wavering off balance, the man stood sideways.

Ray was sure the swimmer didn't notice him on the rock ledge above. Too astonished for lust, he studied the swimmer's naked profile, a glimmering physique almost unreal in its beauty. This intruder must be a dozing hallucination.

Yep, take a long look, then say goodbye to all that. Tomorrow morning, when this Wildlands Society expedition started down the Colorado River with the canyon's entire three hundred miles off-limits to other rafters, Ray knew he must brave a three-week spell of celibacy. No cohort on Earth was more heterosexual than environmental volunteers.

The intruder was smiling now, offering a slight wave as he glanced up at Ray. Losing his footing in the sand, he pivoted face forward, his waving fingers now a grasp across empty air. He couldn't counter the wobble with his other arm.

He didn't have one. Like a marble Adonis posed in a Greek temple, the swimmer was perfect in form except for that missing limb. Hoping to appear unfazed, Ray waved back.

The intruder recovered his balance, gave Ray a brief salute, and waded under the bank. He disappeared behind the shallow bend's willow shrubs. Ray leaned over the lip of rock to see where he'd gone but couldn't spy anything behind the screen of streamside shrubs.

In a short while, the coyote willows parted and the man appeared, climbing up the rock ledge on the same faint trail Ray had taken. He'd put on his boots and dirt-caked khaki pants but was still bare chested. His muddy shirt dangled over the shoulder of his missing arm. He stopped short a few yards from where Ray still lay, frozen now in the warm sun, belly down and butt up.

"This is interesting..." the man muttered.

"What?" Grand Canyon? The swimming hole? The stark-naked guy perched over it?

"Didn't expect to see someone else here, among all this naked...rock."

Now it felt weird to be bare assed like this, undefended, so Ray reached for his shorts, pulling them on with a fake casual, locker room ease as he turned over to face the man. "Is this your first time in the canyon, too?"

"No. I live in the area."

"Then you must be used to naked rock."

"That doesn't make it any less interesting." The intruder looked younger up close, dark forelocks dripping down his forehead. "Tourists don't usually bash through the willows to find this place, so I didn't expect to see anyone else at the swimming hole. Especially with the river closed to rafting."

Ray stood, surprised to realize the man was so tall, having a few inches on Ray's six feet. The big local guy might not be well disposed to a skinny out-of-state *tourist* sunbathing on his own special Arizona rock. Plus, though he was one-armed, the intruder still possessed another arm whose mighty biceps might overpower both of Ray's.

The dark-haired man kept staring, serious. What happened to that smile, that wave? When Ray caught his eyes, though, he looked away, putting on his shirt without buttoning it.

"I heard about this swimming hole from a friend of mine, our group leader," Ray told him. "I needed to wash off after a long road trip. Sorry if I'm trespassing."

"Hey, it's cool. It's public land, man. It's a free country." The guy half smiled, still reluctant to meet Ray's eyes, and gestured downriver. "I'm on a job today, eradicating invasive trees. I was taking a break and trying to wash off the day's grime myself. But now I've got to get back into these filthy clothes. Anyway, just wanted to say howdy, to a fellow, you know—"

"Skinny-dipper?"

"Yeah. See, I'm trying to rejoin humanity."

Humanity could use him, Ray thought. He really did look Greek, with his olive skin and dark, soulful eyes. The man extended his hand to Ray.

Ray clasped it, doing his best to match the man's muscular shake. Without another word, the howdy-sayin', tree-rustlin' guy vamoosed down the trail. His mud-caked work shirt flapped outward from his shoulder as if he'd grown a stiff appendage to make up for the one he'd lost. Then he disappeared into the brush.

When he was sure the guy had vanished, Ray shucked his shorts again and dove into the pool. When he came up for air, he kept one arm fixed to his back, trying to power forward with the other, the way the one-armed swimmer had done. But no roiling dolphin, Ray could barely wobble forward, gulping great strangled breaths. Kicking hard, though, Ray managed to stay afloat until he reached the other shore.

❖

JENNY BRIDGER passed Ray the bottle for another swig. He had just joined her on a smooth boulder overlooking the Colorado River. "Nothing like a cold beer on a hot desert afternoon." The beer wasn't that cold, having been stashed in Jenny's daypack for a few hours, but she relished every sip. The late afternoon had ripened into sweet, early summer indolence. For the first time in memory, she had what people called time to kill.

But why kill time, of all things? Jenny wanted to savor each minute of the hours before the river guides arrived for their first camp dinner. After that, the volunteers' time would be consumed by braving the river to reach the research sites in two small wooden dories and a supply raft, then by taking measurements and collecting data along the riverbanks. Jenny's time would be used in overseeing the five Wildlands Society volunteers—two female students, a Texas couple, and family friend Ray, a last-minute substitute for a cancellation. Meanwhile, she would be coordinating all logistics with the three river guides—an oarsman, an oarswoman, a young guide in training—plus the Park Service ranger assigned to the project and the cook, who happened to be Jenny's mother-in-law. *Ex*-mother-in-law.

Ray still looked dead dog tired after his long night drive from Denver. He'd arrived at their Lee's Ferry camp so late, Jenny and the other volunteers were already asleep. Now he rested his head on Jenny's shoulder and muttered, "The swimming hole was great. Beautiful. I'd completely forgotten real life could be so compelling."

Coaxing the beer bottle back from Ray's grip, Jenny looked downriver toward the small boulder that marked River Mile Zero, the official entry into Grand Canyon. She realized she'd already lost her own compelling moment in mulling over her leadership of the whole cast and crew and the hundreds of river miles of responsibility she'd taken on.

Jenny tuned back in as Ray roused himself enough to tell her everything he'd just escaped in Colorado to join her in Grand Canyon at the last minute. Just as his high school drama students had started their final projects, he'd started a summer gig as literary advisor for a play being developed in Denver, a documentary theatre piece based on a study of neurological damage in killers' brains.

"So, before you could even erase the chalkboard one last time for the summer," Jenny asked, "you decided to jump into the company of mother killers, father rapers, and chainsaw-wielding nutcases?"

"I'm mostly reading about them, Jenny."

"So, as you raft the canyon for your first time ever, you'll be obsessing on some psycho who cracked his foster parents' skulls with a skillet? I worry, okay? It's my prerogative as a wise, slightly older woman."

"Just because my stepfather was a twisted son of a bitch, I'm supposed to spend my whole life avoiding stories about sons of bitches?" Ray accepted the bottle for the final swig. "I could've easily cracked his skull with a skillet. The real miracle is that I didn't."

"No. Even as a little boy, you were too morally evolved to kill *that* son of a bitch."

"Faint praise, Wise Older Woman."

"Not really." Jenny rose. "I'm not so sure if my wisdom is always going to override my worst impulses. During my divorce, when the battle got too ugly one night, I actually searched Google for poisons that might go undetected in my ex's scotch. I just couldn't decide which was best, suicide or homicide. Or both." She patted Ray's head. "Now, look alive. Let's start exploring *my* research subject—mud, which never murdered anyone. Look at all that perfectly innocent, sticky mud down there!"

Jenny dropped the emptied bottle into her daypack before she whacked into the brush. Mud flattened and clogged the coyote willows here, still damp from the Glen Canyon Dam flood release two days before. Jenny and the first batch of volunteers had stood on that concrete crescent above Lake Powell the morning of the flood release. Mere citizen Jenny Bridger joined the Secretary of the Interior, Arizona's governor, and a battalion of state officials to witness the largest ever release of water through the dam's spillways. This would be the greatest effort yet to recreate Grand Canyon's pre-dam natural river surges.

Though the Colorado River had already retreated to its normal flows here at Mile Zero, muddy seeps stretched more than thirty yards from the riverbank. That mud was to absorb Jenny's attention in the weeks to come as she supervised this party of Wildlands Society volunteers to investigate the artificial flood's impacts through the entire length of Grand Canyon.

"Come on, Ray!" Jenny called, loud but unseen down in the willows. "You gotta see this."

Carol Carne, the Texan volunteer who'd been strolling the river road nearby, suddenly heeded Jenny's invitation. She hopped from the road into the brush below with a whoop. "Show me!"

"Okay, but I've got a lot more than mud to show you," Jenny told Carol. "First thing tomorrow, it's gonna blow your mind. We vanish downriver, beyond the reach of society, down through the geologic layers of time itself."

"It *is* kind of overwhelming," Carol Carne drawled as they sauntered forward. "Having the whole canyon to ourselves. The first ordinary folk to witness everything this flood release transformed."

"Yeah," Jenny said, "I feel like a little kid today. My tummy's actually fluttering. If soils really are restored, think what that'll mean for plant life on the banks and deltas."

"Maybe a cure," Carol said, "from the cancer of the planet."

"Like healing herbs?" Ray asked, having bashed the brush to join them. "Some uncovered native roots?"

"No. I mean maybe we'll help cure the human urge to

dam and divert and poison every watershed." Carol smiled at Ray, then danced forward, arms out to welcome the river breeze. "Human beings, Ray, *we're* the cancer."

"For somebody who's so easygoing," Ray told Jenny, voice low as Carol twirled ahead, "she sure has a grudge against the human race."

"That startled me, too, when Carol and I first worked on projects together."

"And from the stories you'd told me, I'd never quite pictured Carol as this vigorous river goddess." Now back on the road, Carol pirouetted, revealing her taut stomach, her scant top scooping her breasts high. Her long blond-brown hair swirled, luminous in the angled canyon light.

Carol had already reached a Park Service pickup parked in a turnout. Jenny wondered if it belonged to the ranger who would be joining the volunteers this afternoon. According to her paperwork, the ranger would be finishing up a project removing invasive trees before embarking with the Wildlands Society volunteers on their three-week mud study.

Jenny found it easy to scout the ranger's progress. Young saplings had been tossed upward from the river's steep banks as if rejected by some celestial gardener. "Hey, can we help you out?" Jenny called into the thick brush.

"Thanks," he called back, unseen, "but I'm hoping this one's the last weed tree in the entire watershed. We got it, I think."

"Not quite," yelled a high-pitched voice closer to the river.

Another girl's voice joined in unison: "Timmm-ber!"

The gray-green crown of a young Russian olive slid, as if in slow motion, above the coyote willow tops. After a soft, slapping whack, it disappeared from Jenny's field of view. She could see more of the river winking through fingery leaves but couldn't spot a trace of the girls—her crew's youngest volunteers, supposedly off on a short hike—or the ranger.

The ranger emerged from the underbrush, still in one-armed battle against a pile of Russian olive debris. His empty left sleeve dangled from his stiff, filthy shirt with each assault. He held his machete straight out, circling the stack as if it were full of potential enemies.

"See," the ranger said, nodding toward the river and the unseen girls with his slight, shy smile. "I had lots of help."

"So, Annette and Tess have been working down here all this time?" Jenny peered through the dense brush. She clenched her jaw, concerned about her student volunteers. "They told me they were taking a short walk up the riverbank."

"We meant to, Jenny." Annette's disembodied voice echoed up, a bit timid.

"But we decided to help Duke out," Tess added from farther off.

"The girls have been great," Duke said. "I would've never finished hacking these evil Russian intruders without them."

"And we are almost done!" Annette cried.

The ranger set his machete down and extended his hand to Jenny. "So, *you're* the official volunteer leader."

"Yep," Jenny said, trying to match his vigorous handshake. "And you're our official project ranger." She hastened to introduce Carol and Ray.

Ray stumbled forward, shaking Duke's hand. Why was Ray's face reddening? It made him look so young, like a little kid caught doing something naughty. "Howdy, ranger," he managed to stammer to Duke. "I'm the last-minute, know-nothing, wait-listed, unauthorized crew member."

"You are not unauthorized, Ray," Jenny said, slapping his arm, wondering if his shaky volunteer status was what embarrassed him. "You may know nothing, but I do the authorizing around here, and I hereby authorize you."

Duke seemed to scrutinize Ray for a moment, smiling, then pointed back to the willow thicket. "Hey, you folks have got to see what we found hidden for who knows how long behind a grove of Russian olives. A little vestige of the nineteenth century the girls and I just uncovered on national park land." Duke pressed back the branches with his arm, letting Jenny and Carol pass. "You too, Ray. Check this out."

Fenced by collapsing pickets, four small pioneer tombstones leaned in a barren clearing. Ray could detect crude numbers scratched into wooden slabs.

"Ah," Carol sighed. "Look at their life spans."

"Two, three, five," Duke said, "and six years old. They all died the same year. Diphtheria, most likely."

"Imagine the poor mother," Carol said.

Jenny crouched to inspect the slab gravestones. "No last names. They're probably John Doyle Lee's kids, or one set of them. He had nineteen wives." Jenny turned to Carol and Ray. "Lee got exiled here by the Mormon church in the 1870s after he led a massacre on non-Mormon pioneers. Just killed 'em all in cold blood."

"Hear that, Ray?" Carol asked. "What did I tell you about the human race?"

"Lee was less than human," Duke said. "He even tried to goad the Indians to murder the non-Mormons' children."

"It's a disgrace we still call this place Lee's Ferry." Carol stared at the graves, her head lowered, her strong mouth crumpling.

"Think how rushed these children's funerals were, one after the other," Duke said, shaking his head. "Lee probably became very proficient at grave-digging. Like I did." He removed his cap, then held it over his chest. "Back when I was stationed in ex-Yugoslavia, I got familiar with religious massacres." Quiet for a moment, Duke breathed slowly. He stepped a little closer to Carol, who was crying softly. Jenny marveled. So, Carol the no-nonsense super-volunteer, the tough-minded Texas nurse, weeps over nineteenth century children's deaths?

Duke put his arm around Carol, who swiped at her tears and leaned into his embrace. "This reminds me of the makeshift children's cemetery in the Sarajevo stadium. Muslim parents had to plant them in the ground fast, before the Christian snipers shot up the funerals."

A scream ruptured Duke's words. Intense and high pitched, it ricocheted across the river and up canyon walls, then shrieked back to the graveyard.

Duke hustled through the thicket with such speed and force that the brushy branches slapped Jenny full in the face as Ray and Carol pressed behind her. Ahead, Duke slid down the embankment, crying out, "Tess? Tess!"

Carol raced ahead of Ray after he slipped in slick mud. When Jenny grabbed his T-shirt, Ray brought her down, too. Between the brush and the road, the two landed hard on their rears. Unseen from the thicket, Annette cried out, "Holy God!"

Jenny turned to see Duke holding Tess aloft on his shoulder, rising from the thicket like a virgin prepared for sacrifice. Eyes closed, the girl lay limp above his arm, Carol and Annette supporting her bloody ankles.

❖

RAY told Tess, back at the volunteers' campsite, "I thought your scream was a broken car alarm mating with a test of the Emergency Broadcast System."

"I know it's terrible," Tess Saarinen admitted, lowering

her pale blue eyes. She sat at the camp table sipping a soda. "It's been that way since I was a little kid. I'd squeal over a scraped knee in the playground, get over it, then look up to find the whole place in a panic around me."

It had been more than a scraped knee, though. Down at the work site, Tess's boot had gotten stuck in the mud just as she hacked at the last pile of Russian olive debris. She'd stumbled backward, her lower calf spiked by a huge thorn in a fallen branch. When she'd tried to pull her leg free, she ripped the skin. As blood cascaded into the sandy muck, Tess let loose her notorious screech.

Carol Carne leaned in to apply a new bandage. "It's not deep, honey. It's just a long tear. I'm sure it hurts like hell, but it's not fixin' to bleed anymore."

Ray liked how Carol, a pediatric nurse in Amarillo, seasoned her professional efficiency with maternal kindness. "Oh, girl, you've got such supple, golden skin!" she went on. "What I wouldn't give. As strong and young as you are, Tess, this is going to heal like magic."

"Good," Jenny said, coming from the camp kitchen to hover closer to Tess and Carol. "We could use some magic around here. Let's hope it's the first and last of bandages and broken skin."

Having missed yesterday's volunteer introductions, Ray was still struggling to match up faces to names and relationships. He knew Carol Carne, a longtime Wildlands Society activist, had come solo on Jenny's other volunteer projects. The contrast between Carol and her husband Jack kept jolting Ray. Jack Carne was neither a Society member nor much of an outdoorsman, and even though they were both past forty, Carol could have been mistaken for Jack's daughter. Despite suffering from acute negativity about humanity, Carol was youthful, athletic, and adventurous.

Her husband was a different story. According to Carol, she'd found Jack blacked-out, beer-dazed, and dozing when she'd brought Tess back to the camp. Now, Jack lay resting in the Carnes' tent with a queasy stomach.

"And the last of the nausea, for the whole trip, okay?" Jenny called to Jack Carne, teasing. "There's no hospital anywhere in the canyon, so according to old river tradition, we have to throw all injured crew members overboard."

"Well, before you cast us both off," Jack called, steadying himself as he crawled from the tent, "let me see how our girl Tess is doing, too."

Tess recoiled as Jack approached, just as Carol smoothed down the tape over the gauze patch. "Now look what you did, scaring the poor kid," Carol said. With the back of her hand, she rapped the base of Jack's receding hairline.

"Ow! I was just going to help you, Carol," Jack said. "Tess, anything I can do for you?"

"No." Tess crouched to press the tape herself. "No thanks, mister."

The big guy laughed, fingering his broad belly. "Hey, I'm not *mister*, Tess. I'm just ol' Jack. I already told you that."

Ray, who'd been avoiding kitchen duty, circled nearer Jack. "You're looking pretty well now. You gonna be okay?"

Carol intercepted the question. "He'll be okay if he stays away from junk food, chain smoking, too much beer, and too much sun. And it's no wonder he's tuckered out, given we're almost four thousand feet above sea level."

Jenny tried to smile at Jack. "I just hope you realize we'll need to maintain strong stomachs tomorrow. We start one of the planet's greatest adventures. We'll be screaming down some of the continent's biggest rapids in wooden skiffs."

"Hear that, Jack?" Carol called. "Be cautious, honey, or I might collect on our Texas Life premium after all."

"Why should I be cautious? I'm not doing any navigating. I'm just along for the ride." Jack slapped on his red cap, tipped it only to Jenny and Tess, and started toward the neighboring campsite. "Let me know if you need me. I want to see if that poker game is still going next door."

As Ray eased beside Jenny to chop garlic, he kept an eye out for Jack. He'd learned that the neighboring group was en route to a "personal weaponry conference" in Las Vegas—some big-ass gun show, the kind his stepfather liked to attend for lost weekend benders.

"With the Colorado River off-limits to the public," Jenny said, her voice low, "I figured we'd have this campground all to ourselves." Stirring the spaghetti sauce, Jenny shook her head in the neighboring campsite's direction. Jack's barking laugh echoed back. "A miraculous recovery, wouldn't you say?"

"It was just sunstroke, most likely," Ray said. "Jack's probably used to working indoors all day in an air-conditioned office."

"Great. He'll be working in full sun for weeks to come. When I invited Carol to bring her husband, I didn't quite picture a dolt with a beer belly. It's like having Homer Simpson along on a wilderness adventure."

Ray shrugged. "Maybe beer and donuts will keep him going just fine."

"Would you mind checking on him over there, Ray?" Jenny lowered her voice even more, sprinkling diced garlic into the sauce. "Let him know we're going to be in excellent hands on the river."

"Yep, ma'am." Ray set down the knife. "You're the boss."

He bounded toward the next camp, where a hulking motor home's only intact headlight peered over a high clump of rabbit brush. He could hear one of the neighbors saying, "I wouldn't mind dragging those granola babes to my sleeping bag." With only a touch of self-reproach, Ray halted behind the brush to hear more.

"Maybe that sounds good," Jack Carne said, "but it all comes with sermons on organic food and littering and smoking." Jack took a swig of canned beer. "My wife's like that. Believe me, I been puttin' up with it for years."

"I could stand the sermons," the hatchet-faced campground neighbor said, "for a turn with that blue-eyed nigger chick in your crew."

Ray flinched. Hatchet Face meant Tess.

"Ah, she's just a kid. Eighteen," Jack said, his Texas drawl suddenly clipped. "From Minnesota. Black mom and Finnish father. Starts college in the fall."

"Eighteen! Choice."

"Yow!" Jack lit a cigarette on the filter end, then cussed himself out.

"And here you're going to spend three more weeks roaring down the canyon with that nigger babe. All wet and squealing in those rapids. If the river wasn't closed, I'd rent a raft, trail your wake, and join the fun."

Ray fought indignation, realizing there was no point soothing Jack's apprehensions now. After all, the lucky dude was gonna be roaring down those rapids with the *blue-eyed nigger chick*. To stanch his rising urge toward confrontation—which was not what Jenny ordered—Ray ignored her request and slipped back to their camp kitchen without saying a word to Jack.

"Jack's okay," he told her. He picked up the knife and finished dicing the garlic. "He might be more Rush Limbaugh than Homer Simpson, though. Let's see how he feels in the morning."

"Thank God I've got you and Carol along," Jenny said,

touching his shoulder. "A high school teacher and a nurse! Teenage crises and emergency health care are my biggest headaches on these volunteer trips."

With Hatchet Face's good ol' boy exhortations carrying far in the dry, windless air, the emptiness of their hilltop camp spooked Ray. This bend in the Colorado River seemed evacuated. With all private and commercial river trips postponed until high season started later in June, Lee's Ferry had reverted to what it had been before the onslaught of tourism, a ghost town named for a mass murderer.

Real inviting, Ray thought. Like the invitation this wilderness delivered to those children buried in riverside graves. The desert's vastness mocked the riverbanks' narrow flumes of life. Down among the willows and birdsong on the river shore, it was too easy to forget that yards away in the bone-dry scrabble, few forms of life could survive.

Ray's lonesome heart jumped at the sight of Duke's agency pickup appearing on the final switchback into the campground. The ranger had promised to join the volunteers for dinner.

Ray felt the force of a crush coming on. Unnerved, he sought refuge in gossip. "I've got a hunch about Duke," he told Jenny. "After getting injured in the Bosnian war, he mucked around in espionage."

"You're dramatizing, Ray. You know nothing."

"So the Army issued him a new identity. He disappeared into Grand Canyon without a trace."

"Who needs a new identity when your real name is Ivan Dukarić?" Jenny asked. "And you grew up in Pleasanton, California? Poor Duke's been holed away for years in some godforsaken, unvisited sector on the canyon rim pretty much all by his lonesome. Park Service big shots must be grooming him to learn the river since he came to us pre-approved."

"I thought you just met him this afternoon, Miss Know All."

"I studied our assigned ranger's information before the trip. It included his war service but never mentioned his... arm."

"When you finally met him today, I bet you studied more than his résumé, Miss Priss. He's a hunk."

"Just keep slicing, boy, and decide for once and all whether I'm Miss Know All or Miss Priss."

Ray smiled, looking up just as Duke parked nearby and hopped out of his pickup. Bearing a bottle of wine, he was dressed in khaki shorts and a button-down, his hair slicked back with gel. The ranger wowed Ray all over again. He had a thing for clean-cut guys. And tall guys. And dark, handsome guys.

Duke crossed to the neighboring campsite to chat amiably with Jack and the Personal Weaponry guys. Ray caught snatches of conversation, mostly Jack's hearty affirmations of his renewed health and appetite.

Then, as Duke paced away, the still air carried the older man's words. "Isn't it just like the Feds? Gotta fill their quotas for hiring cripples."

"The *physically challenged*, Dad," Hatchet Face corrected before he erupted in laughter.

Jenny aimed her strong chin at the other camp, her eyes fierce until they softened, crinkling with sympathy as Duke crossed between camps.

What did they do? Ray wondered. Pretend it wasn't audible, or attack the Personal Weaponry gents with whatever personal projectiles—knives, corkscrews, cheese graters—were handy? As Duke approached, Ray told him, "Hey, you're looking pretty spiffy, ranger."

"I'll say," Jenny said. "You're killer gorgeous, Duke. And

you brought wine. We didn't dress for the occasion, as you can see, but I'll be proud to sit at the table and bat my eyes in your direction."

Duke attempted a smile, but it failed to banish the pain in his expression. "Well, you're going to have to take a good look now, Jenny. I can't stay for dinner after all. I thought I'd drop off some wine for you guys and see how Jack and Tess were doing. See if you needed anything from the clinic or pharmacy before I went into town. But it looks like all's well, huh?"

"Oh, Duke," Jenny said, reaching to clasp his arm. "Can't you please join us?"

Duke eluded her by placing the wine in her hand. "Enjoy. With all my last-minute errands, I better get going." He hurried off to his pickup, avoiding the other camp with a wide, unnecessary arc around the parking space. "See you in the morning. At the launch!"

The men in the adjacent camp exploded into more laughter as Duke slammed his pickup's door and sped away. "Check out the knob on the steering wheel," Ray could hear Hatchet Face say. "And automatic transmission, I'll betcha," before another burst of hyena howls.

Ray glared in the other campers' direction, waving the knife. "If I had a rocket launcher…"

"They're pretty messy, especially at close range," Jenny said. "You'd probably kill Jack, too."

"Goodness gracious," Ray said, stabbing into onion flesh. "How could I ever bear the loss?"

CHAPTER 2

Mile Zero

JENNY hoped to calm the lead river guide, Glen Hayes, during their first dinner as a crew. With the volunteers meeting the guides for the first time, she wanted harmony around the camp table.

Instead, Glen detonated one of his legendary rants after Jack Carne expressed alarm at the idea of obliterating Glen Canyon Dam.

"Yep. Bomb it to smithereens! Until every drop of water in Lake Powell runs free again." Glen waved just upstream, using his fork as a pointer, to where the dam held back the massive reservoir. "Then Glen Canyon can get back to its real business. Eroding in the desert sun."

"Speaking of business," Jack said, "if you emptied out Lake Powell, wouldn't that completely destroy all the Jet Ski and houseboat rentals?"

"Let 'em dry up and flake away for all I care," Glen said, dousing his spaghetti with sauce. "What kind of Wildlands Society volunteer are you, Jack Carne?"

As twilight deepened around the clatter of the camp dinner, Glen and Jack faced off like dueling family patriarchs at each end of the table. Jenny thought Glen Hayes had the advantage, with his elder-but-ageless look of many men with full, graying beards. His face was deeply lined, more by weather than age, but his pale eyes had a boyish way of including everybody in their mischief.

"Well, I care. I'm a small businessman myself," Jack said. "Besides that, Powell's a damn pretty lake. I'd hate to see it destroyed by terrorists."

This inspired a cackling laugh from Tycho Bracken, almost the first sound he'd produced since he'd arrived from Flagstaff with Glen, just in time for dinner. "The terror's already been done, man," Tycho said, each word a burst. "That damn dam was terrorism in the first place. And no matter what Glen might have done or might still do, he's a hero, man. Not a terrorist."

Great, Jenny thought, now Tycho's going to scare Jack into thinking he's headed downriver with two gleeful ecoterrorists. She'd forgotten how disarming Tycho's laugh was, his head bobbing while his shoulders hunched, his long red-blond hair a mass of quaking curls. Those shoulders had broadened in the few summers since Jenny had seen him last. Now a twenty-year-old college freshman, already an oarsman on several river trips, Tycho would be in for more training. Under Glen's guidance, Tycho was to pay his Grand Canyon dues as swamper for the party's rubber raft, loaded with kitchen supplies and, eventually, all their waste and garbage.

Jack watched in silence as Tycho's laughter calmed, and he fell back to hunched silence over his plate. "Well, if y'all will excuse me," Jack said, rising, "I'll wander off and have a cigarette."

"Don't forget, you're on dish duty tonight," Carol Carne called after him. "Dear."

"Ah," Glen said, in Jack's absence, "so that's it. Jack married into the Society. Boy, am I glad, for once, I kept my damn mouth shut."

"You call *that* keeping your mouth shut?" Jenny asked.

"It's okay, Glen," Carol said. "I loved everything you said about Glen Canyon Dam. My husband needs to hear it from someone besides me."

"There's gonna be a holy war," Glen said, toasting Carol, "and it won't be won until the Colorado River flows free again. Whether through politics or dynamite."

Tycho shuddered with more laughter, raising his plastic cup. "To anarchy!"

Carol raised hers. "Hell yes!"

Great, Jenny thought, now we have three faux ecoterrorists to scare the bejesus out of Jack, one of whom he was bound to in marriage. Jenny turned to Carol, forcing a deliberate, matter-of-fact transition. "Glen's father named him after the canyon. And just before the dam was finished, Glen was among the last to raft the Colorado River through Glen Canyon."

"Yep, when I was just a kid," Glen said, "with my father and Tycho's dad." When Glen touched Tycho's shoulder, he flinched a bit before he allowed Glen's hand to remain. "Along with Andrew Pinch Senior. Jenny's future father-in-law."

"Future *ex*-father-in-law," Jenny corrected.

"Sorry. Ex. We four rafted the free river's final days. Before it was drowned, Glen Canyon was even grander than Grand Canyon." Glen paused, turning as headlights scanned the darkening campsite and halted near the camp table. "Lake Powell. What we sacrificed for that Jet Ski sewer!"

"*Jet Ski sewer!*" mocked a high, thin voice. It was Faith Brattle, the other senior river guide, emerging from her car as soon as she parked beside Jenny's truck. "Glen Hayes! Are you still ranting about Lake Powell? It's like a conversation that goes on forever, and I just happen to step into it every couple of years." The rail-thin blonde sprinted into Glen's embrace as he stood to meet her. "Just like this crazy river."

"And never quite the same, no matter how many times you encounter it," Glen said, smiling and taking a step back to regard her. "Just like you, Faith. You get more damn beautiful as the years go by."

"Glen Hayes, you're not bad for a male, you know that?" Faith perched on her toes to kiss him, then she embraced Jenny, Ray, and Tycho.

Jenny had already noticed Faith's passenger, who stood beside the hatchback muttering and reshuffling baggage, but decided to let her ex-mother-in-law greet everyone in her own sweet time. After driving down from the Montana college where she directed the Women's Studies program, Dr. Faith Brattle had picked up Hannah Pinch in Denver.

"Okay, everybody," Faith announced on her way to the table, "since I'm guiding the other boat, just remember you have to like me. Or pretend like you do."

"But nobody has to like me." Hannah's deep, gravelly monotone contrasting with Faith's excited soprano, she appeared among them as if materializing from the surrounding dark. Nearing seventy, Hannah Pinch was as thick and solid as Faith was weightless and wraithlike. Her gray hair hung lifeless, bowl cut just below her ears. "I'm the cook, so it doesn't matter a damn what you think of me as long I keep you well fed. Hello, Ray. You're looking as pretty as ever. Jenny, did you save any leftovers for your mother-in-law?"

"Of course, Hannah." Jenny approached with her tightest smile and a quick, businesslike hug. "We knew you were going to be a bit late, so we saved plenty."

"Ah, spaghetti. I told Faith it was gonna be hot dogs, burgers, or spaghetti. Nice to know some things never change," Hannah said, accepting her plateful with a nod. "Amazing that my granddaughter turned out so well after all those years of hot dogs, burgers, or spaghetti."

"Come on, Hannah," Jenny said, "other meals were in the rotation. When Amelia was younger, we had Angelo's Pizza on speed dial."

"Now, Mother Pinch, give Jenny a break." Glen stood, offering his seat to Hannah and standing behind her. He placed his hands on her shoulders. "Not only is her spaghetti excellent, but we all need to thank her for making this trip possible."

Faith nodded. "Yeah, Jenny! How exactly did you bring this off?"

"Isn't it amazing?" Standing beside the table, Jenny hugged herself with childlike self-delight. "And all I did was contact a few friends in high places who owed me favors. I convinced the Park Service we'd be the perfect mix, all ages and all of us research volunteers. I'm sure it's great publicity for them. You know, Just Ordinary Americans witnessing the effects of the Biggest Ever Canyon Flood Release. All by our lonesome between two other research crews."

"The Park Service crew started downriver this morning?" Faith asked.

"Yes, they're studying beach restoration. The Canadian hydraulics crew will start a day behind us."

"So, we really are putting in first thing tomorrow," Faith said. "Just us! In dories!"

"Yeah!" Glen said. "I didn't have my heart set on them. I figured some Park Service lackey would give you guff about the extra risk."

"Hear that, Carol?" Jack called from the darkness, his cigarette aglow. "I figured those damn little dinghies were dangerous."

"But they're not, Jack." Jenny raised her voice, turning to the darkness. "Rafts are a little easier to navigate, but—"

"But that was my doing," Hannah said. "I had to take what my son was willing to spare from the company's summer rafting inventory, so we've got dories." She studied the spaghetti with a scowl. "Jenny, just in case you're wondering, Amelia—you remember your daughter?—missed you at her graduation."

"You don't say, Hannah?" Jenny strained for a light-hearted tone despite the rising boil in her blood. But she had to make a stand in front of the crew and volunteers. "I spent last weekend with Amelia—you recall your granddaughter?—before I hit the road for the ceremony on the dam."

"I can't help but wonder which ceremony Amelia felt was more important to you. Whether it was the canyon flood release, you know, or her own graduation from high school."

"I *do* know, Hannah. Because I told her I'd turn down the invitation from the Secretary of the Interior and the governor of Arizona. Gladly. But Amelia told me if I didn't accept it, she'd ditch her own graduation and attend the flood release ceremony herself."

Hannah shrugged, idly pushing her fork as if to create a spaghetti barricade. "I can't help but wonder where on earth Amelia gets her headstrong, impulsive streak."

Carol stood with Jenny and Ray, clearing plates. "You're a saint, Jenny," she whispered with a nudge. "I would have added a little of the ranger's olive-stump herbicide to your mother-in-law's pasta sauce."

Jenny tried not to laugh, whispering back. "You mean *ex-*mother-in-law."

❖

JENNY took her wine down to the river after dinner and sat alone on the edge of the boat launch. Glen, Hannah, and Faith had turned in for the night. Tess, Annette, and Tycho had invited her to join their stargazing session just up the riverbank, but

Jenny felt too restless and self-excluded. Too young for the sleepers and too old for the stargazers.

The river's urgent plash grew louder now, its artificial tide suddenly rising, controlled by the ebb and flow of energy demands in cities downriver. Jenny imagined millions of Southwestern households switching on power—Phoenix commuters getting home in the hot evening, turning up the air conditioning, pressing ice levers for cocktails, and Los Angelenos running automated sweeps in their pools. For the first time ever in the canyon, Jenny yearned for that distant domesticity, those serene and unacknowledged comforts of city families, so dependent on this river.

She had never before visualized the river's tethered tumble, the engineered interference of dams and diversions as anything other than an ecological disaster, a titanic technological mistake. Yet tonight Jenny was willing to see even the power lines as spinning a friendly familial web, a connected human cocoon spun across the wired desert skies. A cocoon from which she had expelled herself.

She dared to imagine the impossible scenario of an alternative life: a Jenny *née* Bridger ex-Pinch with big sticky hair and an even stickier heart, content in some suburban four bedroom, surrounded by 2.7 kids and any faceless, semi-tolerable husband who'd accept the position. The Normal American Mom who possessed Normal American sentiments. The good mother who wasn't dispensing wonky river restoration news bites atop Glen Canyon Dam for a cub reporter from the *Tuba City Weekly Clarion* the moment her only child crossed the stage at Denver's East High School, bearing an honors diploma.

Jenny heard faint male voices getting louder over the river's surging. Ray's words had a schoolteacherish, reprimanding tone, echoing down the dark slope to the ramp.

"Before we start rafting downriver, Jack," he was saying, "I hope you realize you shouldn't talk about Tess that way."

Jenny stood, intercepting the two as they headed down the riverside trail. She slipped quietly into step beside irrepressible Ray.

Jack tried to defend himself. "But I didn't say anything!"

"Don't you have kids?"

"No…" Jack sounded like he had to think about it. "Uh, no."

"I didn't think so," Ray said. "I saw you in the other camp, belching happily while your poker buddy called Tess a nigger and leer about having sex with her. She's just a kid!"

Concerned as she was about Jack's misfit status among this crunchy crowd, Jenny smiled at Ray's passion. He was barely five years older than Tess, a kid himself, but he felt called upon to be the Grand Poobah of adolescent womanhood.

"I've got to tell you, man," Ray said, "Jenny's wondering if you're fit for this trip."

"I didn't say that, Jack," Jenny said, leaning around Ray's lanky form. "Ray's riding this high horse completely on his own."

"Ray," Jack said, "you gotta realize what I think of Tess. She's a very special girl. As far as I'm concerned, she's an angel from heaven. I didn't like that kind of talk any more than you did."

"Then you should've made a stand, not to mention how you and your poker buddies taunted Duke. That was unforgivable."

"What the hell did *I* say?"

"You guys hurt his feelings so bad he decided not to join us for dinner."

"Ray, I did not say one damn thing about Duke."

"I've got to judge you by the company you tolerate. Man, this isn't about political correctness. It's about survival, Jack. We've got to depend on each other. Us, alone together, through three hundred miles of whitewater and wilderness."

"I'm an insurance salesman, Ray. My livelihood depends on my getting along with everybody. Jesus, I don't have a damn thing against ol' Duke. Hell, I think he's a war hero. A peacekeeper in Bosnia, right?"

"Yes," Jenny said. "He lost his arm when a land mine exploded."

"I just don't get why he doesn't have a prosthetic," Jack said. "It'd sure make his job a lot easier."

"The explosion must've taken a portion of his left shoulder," Ray said, recalling his glimpse of Duke's naked physique at the swimming hole. "So he has nothing to attach a prosthesis to."

Finally, the two men fell silent. Ray could be so impetuous, Jenny thought, so righteous once he felt called to defend the vulnerable. He'd had to learn to fight for his dignity from his stepfather's random attacks and torments, and had been vigilant against all attackers and tormenters ever since.

Ahead, where the trail joined the dirt road, Tess let loose a one-note version of her bloody murder scream, followed by giggles, then Tycho's boundless, near-hysterical laughter.

Jack walked ahead, lighting a cigarette. "I love those kids," he said. "You got me all wrong, Ray. Well, Tycho might be a little on the queer side for me, but hey, live and let live, right?"

"What do you mean," Ray asked, "by *queer*?"

"Odd, you know. Kind of a free spirit."

"You're so full of it."

"Hey, Jack," Jenny said. "Are you feeling better? How's your stomach doing?"

"Never better, Jenny. Your pasta sauce was perfect, by the way. I thought your mother-in-law was way out of line."

"Thanks. But wait'll you taste one of Hannah's meals. She's an artist of riverine cuisine. I didn't invite her along just for the Pinch family's dories, you know."

"Speakin' of which, are you really sure it's safe, Jenny, heading hell-bent down the Grand Canyon in those little boats? Down this empty river?"

"This empty river's a once-ever opportunity." Jenny smiled. "Otherwise, we'd be fighting the multitudes gathered here at Lee's Ferry. We get to glide the Colorado River with the Grand Canyon all to ourselves."

Jenny saw Jack's cigarette taking the lead farther ahead of them, and she regretted his unease. She knew it was her worst tendency as a leader to personalize the volunteers' reactions, to calibrate the degrees of their enjoyment. This trip would generate vital scientific data, that's what mattered. She had to stop worrying that Jack Carne suffered a river virgin's cold feet about rapids and wilderness isolation.

With Jack out of hearing, Jenny felt Ray's nudge. "Thanks, Jen," he said, "for leaving me alone up there. On my high horse."

"Honestly, Ray. Once you decide to defend the virtue of innocents, there's no stopping you."

"So, who's gonna stop Jack Carne from being a lech? Dogging after the girls, sniffing down their halter tops?"

"Annette and Tess have lovely young bodies. Jack's a red-blooded kind of guy."

"Yeah, being red-blooded covers a multitude of sins. Straight guys will be straight guys, right? What are you gonna do with 'em? Meanwhile, I'm just a big *queer*. What would I know?"

"Jack didn't call *you* one. And you use that word yourself, Ray."

"I have queer privileges. Jack doesn't. But I can't win this one. You straight people stick together like thieves."

She squeezed Ray's arm. "How else are we going to combat the gay menace?"

Jenny was glad Ray laughed at this, but as much as she loved to torment him, she already regretted her too-ardent defense of Jack. Before Ray's arrival, when the volunteers had gathered at Lake Powell the day of the dam ceremony, she had witnessed a curious scene when they'd all cooled off at the marina. Tess had done a jackknife off the dock and almost lost her top just as a Jet Skier cut way too close. Jack ran down to the dock and made a spectacle of himself, putting on a big show, cussing a purple streak and shaking his fist at the skier. Then he made a huge fuss over Tess. The poor girl was embarrassed, trying to tie on her top underwater while Jack strained to fish her out of the lake.

Still, something told her Jack wasn't just leching. He was more like a big dumb retriever, wagging his tail, acting the hero, and making everything worse.

Jenny still felt Ray deserved a comeuppance. She thought of his Miss Priss comment while they cooked, when *he* was the damn priss. Maybe teaching high school was turning Ray into a prude. "I wish I were as pure as you, little buddy," she told him. "Are you going to condemn me tomorrow, if I take a second glance when you and Duke bare your sexy chests in the desert sun?"

"Sexy?" Ray laughed again. "Don't waste a second glance on my scrawny pecs. Compared to Duke's, my chest is concave."

Up ahead, Annette was scolding Jack for dropping his

cigarette butt on the river beach. "The Grand Canyon is not your ashtray."

Before they joined the others, Jenny said, "I'm actually looking forward to what the canyon is going to teach poor Jack."

"I just hope," Ray said, "this poor canyon survives Jack."

❖

RAY paced upriver alone, leaving Jenny and Jack behind to join the stargazers. He already regretted badgering Jack Carne. He didn't want to be such a judgmental prick. Overdoing his outrage at Jack's "queer" comment could burrow like a tapeworm into his guts. And for what? It was just the way some straight guys talked, so drop it. By Jack's Texas Panhandle standards, he probably thought he was being restrained and polite.

It was so dark, Ray wasn't sure where the riverside trail would join the Jeep road until he realized he was already walking down it. A yellow light jittered down in the willow brush, moving, disembodied, under the dark thickets. Closer, he could see a figure crouching, casting the beam along the ground.

Somebody who'd lost something valuable earlier, a watch, a ring, sunglasses? Ray took a head count of everyone— Annette, Tess, Tycho, and Jack were stargazing with Jenny at the ramp, and the older river crew were bunked in their tents. That left Carol. He couldn't remember whether she'd also gone to her tent after dinner.

He didn't get Carol Carne. Why would such a smart woman marry such a dumb cluck, why would such a goddess get stuck with a pot-bellied oaf? And why her open sobbing at the old gravesite? Easing closer as the beam moved upriver, Ray scuffled down the slope into the brush. Was Carol searching for those children's tomb markers? Had she left something precious there?

Ray made a deliberate noise, snapping a branch. "Hey!" he called. "Everything okay?"

The beam itself answered, shining in his eyes. "That you, Ray?" It was Duke.

Blinded by the flashlight, Ray staggered closer into the opening where Duke crouched among Russian olive stumps. "You've been here all this time?"

"No, I went up to the junction store and got some grub. Then I decided to come back and see if the herbicide had done the trick on these stumps. I won't have a chance to check them in the morning. We'll hit the river first thing."

"Grub at the junction? You should've joined us for dinner."

"Check this out, Ray." Still in his button-down and pressed khaki shorts, Duke seemed overdressed, out of place in this muddy clearing, shining the flashlight beam on a bunch of freshly hacked stumps. "The weedy olive stump rings are so porous, they've already gulped down all the herbicide. Good. Kill 'em!"

"Your wine was great," Ray said, crouching nearer Duke to inspect a stump. "But there was an empty place at the camp table."

"Okay." Duke sighed, rising. "I'm kind of thin-skinned. I get itchy around guys like those gun show fools. That kind of intolerance, that taunting. Seeing how it tore up Bosnia, sometimes I just can't hack hearing it back in the States. I was afraid of what I might do, so I decided to bolt."

Ray wanted to repeat "Oh, Duke," exactly as Jenny had, to soothe the wound crude minds inflicted on good people, and pull the ranger into an embrace. But, manly man that he meant to be, Ray straightened up and stood, hands stuffed in his pockets. "I'm kinda thin-skinned about fascists myself."

"I figured you would be."

Ray felt swept away, alone face-to-face with Duke. "You're not driving all the way back to your ranger station tonight, are you?"

"No way. I've got a dory to catch here right after sunrise." Duke cast the beam up to the road, lighting up his pickup. "Being a freelance lone wolf ranger roaming these parts, I usually sleep in my camper shell, anyway."

"Among all those axes and loppers and herbicide canisters?"

"That's my life." He aimed the flashlight to show the way out of the thicket, leading Ray up to the road. "Well, we'd both better get some shut-eye."

"I reckon," Ray drawled, laughing at their cowpoke improvisation. "But you're welcome to join the rest of us up yonder in camp. You know."

"I do know, Ray," Duke said. He let the phrase linger. Beside his pickup, he shut off the flashlight and leaned against the cab door.

"There's room in my tent," Ray said. Great. Now he was trying out a casting call for *Brokeback Mountain.* "It's a two-man."

"Thanks. But I better, you know, sleep here tonight. I've got to stand guard."

"Over what?"

"For starters, myself."

Chapter 3

Mile Zero to Mile 17

RAY absorbed the thrill of their journey's silky start, his stomach still weightless from the first slide into the Colorado River's current.

"Say goodbye to Mile Zero," Glen said as he rowed *Last Chance* from the Lee's Ferry put-in. "From now on, boys and girls, you'll date your life B.C. and A.C. Before Canyon and After Canyon."

Ray enjoyed the golden flecks sparkling on the river's dark surface as the morning light slanted into the canyon walls. From the launch, Tycho shattered the serenity, whooping as he guided the supply raft into the river, just before Faith did the same in her dory, *Dirty Devil*.

"This Kaibab sandstone we're passing through is kid stuff, only a couple hundred million years old." Glen pointed to the sudden appearance of the new layer. As the dory glided downstream, the color and textures of the canyon walls changed so quickly, it seemed to Ray like a special effect in some tricked-out nature show. "The river's gonna drop us nine layers and a billion years until we hit the basement of biology itself."

"Spooky!" Annette said, hunching her shoulders. Peering

over the bow hatch from the front seats, she and Tess rubbed sunscreen on every exposed inch of skin.

"Spooky as hell," Glen said. "We'll rock and roll deeper and deeper over steeper and steeper rapids. Then we pay a visit to the birth of Earth."

"Cool," Tess said, turning around to flash Glen a smile of pure gleeful anticipation. After weeks in the sun, when the crew finally reached the canyon's end at Lake Mead, Ray wondered if all the white folks' skin would alchemize into one tribal tone, matching Tess's burnished golden brown.

Pulling the long, tapered ash oars from his boatman's seat, Glen seemed to exult in Tess's approving smile. He settled into his raised plank and lifted his face to the still-merciful sun. "You all see the bridge ahead? That's the only road crossing the Colorado River for hundreds of miles. Consider the Navajo Bridge your goodbye to civilization." He signaled to travelers waving from the bridge. "Bye, folks! Goodbye to traffic and email and phones and media static and serial-killer-of-the-week. From here, it'll be like one of those pioneering river trips. Like Bert Loper's in 1907."

"Or even John Wesley Powell's in 1869," Faith called out, maneuvering red-trimmed *Dirty Devil* closer to turquoise *Last Chance*. Ray marveled at how flimsy each dory looked afloat in wide water. As if to stress their fragility, each was named after a side canyon drowned under Lake Powell.

"Major Powell!" Duke said, beside Ray in the snug stern, smiling and tipping his cap to Faith. "A legend among one-armed men."

"A legend to us all!" Faith cried. "The canyon's first known river explorer. What he did was miraculous for someone with twenty arms." Her smile expired when she glanced toward *Dirty Devil*'s bow. "Jack, I need for you to snap your life jacket completely shut."

Jack looked down. "Jesus!" His belly, as white-gray as the underside of a bottomfish, sagged through the open life jacket. He looked seasick. "It's so tight, I guess I loosened it without thinking."

"Please think! Always, always, when we're on the water. We'll adjust it at lunch."

"Geez, I got the message, okay?" Jack occupied the bow seat alone, Jenny and Carol balancing out *Dirty Devil* in the stern seats behind Faith.

Ray smiled at the spectacle of big ol' Jack Carne, slumped and ornery under sunglasses and a Texas Life cap, taking orders from reedlike, hard-rowing Faith. Her slender arms must have steel instead of marrow.

"Let's just hope we don't suffer Powell's fate as far as provisions," Glen said. He pointed back to Tycho's rubber supply raft, bearing Hannah Pinch and their kitchen, food supplies, and groover—the latrine—along with the satellite phone. "Powell lost his supply boat early on."

"And gave up another boat and three men who chickened out," Jenny said. "It's just so amazing he ran rapids in those awkward oak boats."

"Our little dory boats are direct descendants." Glen raised his voice to be heard on *Dirty Devil.* "More river-worthy and pleasing to the eye, but we're essentially doing it Powell's way."

Jack pulled his cap down his forehead. "So what are we gonna lose? Our lives?"

"Only those of us who don't snap our life jackets properly," Glen said, mock-schoolmarmish, then laughed. "Powell survived very well, Jack. Even laid the blueprints for his namesake lake. Your Jet Ski sewer."

"Not that sermon again!" Faith cried, digging in with her oars to splash Glen.

But she missed, so Tess ended up taking most of the soaking. "Hey! I didn't say anything," Tess called, reaching into the river to slap water in Faith's direction. She splattered Carol instead, and a true water skirmish engaged, with Jack roused to his wife's defense. Finding a bailing bucket under the bow hatch, Jack attempted to answer new water-fire from Ray and Tess just as Annette discovered the bailing bucket at her own feet. While Tycho, grunting in glee, rowed the supply raft ever closer, Tess screamed at the twin catastrophes of Jack's water bucket volley and Tycho's oar-slapping rear assault.

Startled by Tess's high-pitched caterwauling, as bloodcurdling as yesterday's, Ray raised himself to make sure she was still playing, and so missed the huge splash that had Faith shouting above the chaos of the water war, "A swimmer! Hey, Glen, I've got a *swimmer!*"

At some point, Jack had been tossed over *Dirty Devil's* bow. As the three craft drifted downstream, their battle halted in a dead silence. Jack blubbered, arms flailing, face-down, attempting a freestyle crawl almost impossible in a life jacket.

Frantic, Faith rowed upstream while Glen and Tycho lined up their boats to form a floating barricade. Carol buried her face in her hands, then peeked between her fingers. As Faith called out instructions, holding out the ten-foot oar to the still-flailing Jack, Annette turned away in disgust. "He's doing everything the opposite of what you and Faith instructed at the launch," she told Glen. "He's still face-down, rather than lying back. He's not helping in his own rescue. He's not even moving toward Faith's boat."

Glen sighed. "I guess he wasn't listening."

"There goes his cap," Duke said. "That's the last of Texas Life."

"He can't stay in that water for long, you know." Glen

shivered with concern. "It shoots from under the dam at forty degrees. Instant hypothermia."

Breathing hard, still preoccupied with the last volley in the water war, Ray didn't fully register the danger until Glen reacted, his face tightened and alert. Should he jump in and help steer Jack back to the dory? What exactly had Jenny and Faith preached at the launch about joining in water rescues?

"Okay, there he goes, over on his back, finally," Duke said. Good. "He's grabbing for the oar. All right, Faith's got him in."

As the two dories rocked side by side, Duke helped Jack flop back into *Dirty Devil*. Without sunglasses and cap, Jack's wide, bare face now matched his belly's sick fish color as he sank hard into the bow.

"Jack," Carol called from her seat in the stern, "why didn't you have your cap leashed to your T-shirt? And what happened to your sunglasses straps?"

"Look, whaddaya want?" Jack scowled. "I lathered myself in sunscreen, then got called to the boat. Who had time to think before we went our goddamn merry way?"

"We'll see if we can find spare shades," Faith said. "We sure don't want you getting your eyes sunburned."

"You steer the boat, okay, lady?" Jack leaned back, eyes closed, pale, pudgy face raised to the sun. "And I'll take care of myself."

Ray looked sidelong at Duke. His long-lashed dark eyes seemed half bemused and half disgusted by Jack's petulance. Shy about staring, he couldn't disguise his admiration for the olive cast to the ranger's deep tan, or his long, handsome Mediterranean profile. Duke didn't wear a shirt under his life jacket, and Ray liked how Duke wasn't inhibited about showing his amputated wound—smooth and concave, except a slightly jagged remnant of his shoulder.

"You're lost in thought," Duke said, out of the clear green-blue. "What about, Ray?"

Trying to hide his attraction and thinking quick, Ray searched the canyon rim above. "When I was a senior in college, I spent spring break up on the South Rim. I hiked down to the first overlook where I could see rafts running the Colorado River, a thousand feet below. I vowed I would do that myself someday. And here I am, waving to myself, back up there."

"That's cool," Duke said, looking less ranger-like in his Global Fund For Women cap and quick-dry shorts. "When I was stationed in Bosnia, we camped along a muddy stretch of the Sava River all winter. This medic in our unit kept talking about his raft trip through Grand Canyon like it was the only dry piece of warmth and sunshine his sanity had left to cling to."

"So, you were in the Army overseas before you became a ranger?" Glen asked.

"Yeah, as an extra-dumb eighteen-year-old. Got stationed all over the Balkans. The cleanup operations after the civil wars. Bosnia, Kosovo."

Annette asked, "Isn't your real name something Slavic, like, Duj…Duku…"

"Dukarić? Yeah, that's how I got my nickname as a kid. Nobody could pronounce the damn thing any better than you just did. It's Yugoslavian. Ex-Yugoslavian. Well, Croatian."

The whitewater ahead seemed to growl. It amplified as they drifted into an eddy, the two dories still side by side. Tycho paddled the raft into the gentle whirlpool to join them, becalmed just beside Badger Rapid's churning top.

"Please be ready to bail soon as I call out," Faith announced. "And everybody remember what Glen and I told you about high-siding. When a big wave tips one side of the dory and shoves it upward, throw your whole body upright against that side."

"That goes double for my crew!" Glen cried. Ray noticed sudden changes in each boatman's demeanor. Even Tycho's churning mania quieted. Faith and Glen traded technical comments about which side of the rapid looked best to run. "Of course," Glen said, "our past experience isn't going to count for much since the release. Kinda fun, huh?"

"Yeah!" Tycho cried with forced merriment. "Big fun."

"That's reassuring," Jack deadpanned, slouching even more.

Surprising himself, Ray felt sorry for Jack and even empathized. He'd never run a danger-rated rapid in a wooden craft and knew Jack had never run whitewater at all.

Glen took the rapid first, angling to avoid exposed rocks. Despite his jumping stomach, Ray loved the way the rapid's tongue lured the boat on a seduction of fast, glassy water, then whipped them onward. Instantly, the seducer transformed into bully, whitewater snapping to cast them helter-skelter over the surging water.

Ray caught his breath as Tess and Annette disappeared down a deep wave crest, then reappeared immediately, airborne over the next. They bucked as the prow slapped a V-shaped wave funnel. Even amid the blind, roaring gush that saturated everything, Glen leaned back, digging in the oars. *Last Chance* traversed the rapid's heart with such definite zigs and zags that the prow seemed to ride a track through the spewing white chaos. Then a surging wall of angry water smacked the dory starboard.

"Okay, *high side!*" Glen called. Before Ray had time to react, Duke had shoved himself upright into the rising gunwale, over and against Ray, gripping the edge with his one hand while digging his armless shoulder into Ray's back.

As suddenly as that churning had overwhelmed *Last Chance*, Duke resettled into his own side of the stern seat and Glen cried, "Bail! Bail the son of a bitch!" Then they were cast free on roiling but calmer, greener water. All hands emptied inches of water from the bow and stern with leashed plastic scoops. Ray glanced back at the Colorado River's tantrum as it squeezed through a cascade of rocks.

Ray and Duke bailed the stern while Tess and Annette still scrambled in the bow, laughing as they raced to drain the last of the water in the bottom. Ray watched Tycho yelping though his mad slide in the yellow supply raft, following the same course but taking the rapid headlong, his rubber craft bouncing and slipping instead of a dory's technical, traversing turns.

In the raft's bow, unruffled, smiling under her big red, strapped hat, Hannah waved at the awaiting dories. "This kid's a helluva boatman!"

"Yeee-ow!" Tycho cried, slapping his oar against the water. "*Eeeeee-ooooo—eeee! Big fun!*"

That was that. With suddenness as dazzling as the rapid's fury, the raft eddied in flat water. Ray glanced back to watch Faith dip *Dirty Devil* into the rapid's tongue above. Only a sudden lurch and her hasty dig of one oar clued Ray that something had gone badly wrong for Faith's dory.

It must have been Carol who screamed just as Jenny arched the entire length of her body, high-siding over Carol to grab the gunwale. With Jack collapsing into the bow, *Dirty Devil* dribbled sideways down a chewy breaker as if spat from the sky.

❖

RAY nervously ripped his sandwich into strands.

"Did you all notice the change?" Glen said on the beach at Salt Water Wash, gesturing toward the tan-pink canyon walls. "The canyon's deeper here. We'll see fossilized mud cracks, prehistoric plants, and reptiles. We're in the Supai now."

"And we're in the soup," Jack said, devouring the last bite of a sandwich. "Since that crazy woman driver almost pissed our lives away."

"I heard that, Jack," Faith said, approaching with a sandwich of her own from Hannah's lunch board. Faith sat beside Glen in the sandy tamarisk shade. "If you're going to keep dishing this abuse, I'll let *you* guide us down the next big rapid."

"Great," Jack said. "I guess I should keep my mouth shut. Pretty damn stupid of an insurance man not to have checked the risk before I agreed to this."

"*Agreed?*" Carol glared down, sitting on a rock above while Jack sprawled in its shade. "You make it sound like you've done us a favor by coming along, when you should be thankin' your lucky stars for this privilege."

"*Privilege?*" Jack snorted. "You didn't tell me a thing about the size or the scale of these goddamn rapids. You didn't tell me this was going to be some white-knuckle, life-threatening crisis. I thought we'd be in the hands of professionals."

"We are." Ray stood, his half-finished, torn sandwich unwanted in his hand. Acrimony always robbed him of his appetite. He'd heard too much mealtime hostility as a kid. This sniping hadn't let up since they'd stopped for lunch.

"Please, Jack," Jenny said. "River guides don't come any better than Glen and Faith. That's why they got clearance for this trip. What happened to Faith happens to all boatmen under the best of circumstances."

"I misjudged the power of that hole to the left, and that's why I had to overcorrect," Faith said. "But we all stayed in the boat, and the dory is unscratched."

Cross-legged next to Faith, Glen said, "That rapid's whole structure has changed since the release."

Tycho approached the group with his second sandwich. He pointed it toward Jack, who still lolled in the rock's shadow. "But this dude didn't even get off his ass to high side. He just sat there clinging to the hand grip while Jenny and Carol were up and at 'em. That makes it real tough on Faith, man, when the only guy in the bow is just dead weight."

"The key word being *dead*," Jack said, sitting up, squinting into the sun. "I'm not into daredevil shit. I don't get off on threatening my own life or the lives of others. My life's about reducing risk, okay, boy?"

"That's bullshit." Tycho turned away, then spun back. "That rapid was a hell of a ride. You're lucky to have shot it with Faith, and even luckier to have made it so nice and safe and dry. You're the one pissing in our soup."

Duke appeared from downriver, where he'd been testing the satellite phone on the supply raft. "I got it up and crackling," he said, his tone mild and shy in the heavy silence following Tycho's outburst. "I told them I hope they don't hear from us from here on out. No news is good news, right? As long as we're one big happy family. Oh, and Jack," he went on, holding out a cap, "I had an extra. A freebie I got from my donation to Greenpeace. And I had a spare pair of sunglasses, too. Here."

As Jack accepted the cap and glasses with open-mouthed astonishment, Ray moved aside to let Tycho skulk past, his sandwich raised like a weapon as he hacked through the screen of tamarisk branches and disappeared upriver.

❖

RAY assumed Jack was napping, beer zapped, as the group gathered in a circle for dinner on the sandy beach above House Rock Rapid. His face was hidden under the beak of Duke's Greenpeace cap.

"That's about three hundred million years old," Glen said, pointing toward a formation across the river. "A middle-aged fissured dike."

Jack suddenly laughed, low and contemptuous. "I won't say who that reminds me of," he said without glancing up.

Faith stabbed into the last of her meal, a broccoli spear. "Then I won't ask."

Ray tried to ignore this after-dinner rerun of lunchtime sniping. While everyone else fussed over the apple cobbler, he paced across the beach to study the fissured dike. Above it, he found a solitary star blazing in indigo twilight above the canyon rim. The only wish he could muster was to recapture the morning's first, fleeting thrill, that buoyant glide onto the water, now doused in the day's bitterness between Jack and Faith and Jack and Tycho.

After assisting Jenny by notetaking during her investigation of the mud line and botanical impacts at Salt Wash, Ray had taken the oars to give Glen a break. On a long stretch of serene water, he'd learned to maneuver the dory over a minor rapid, a diversion from the day's contentiousness. Now, as star after star punctured the dark blue between the narrow canyon walls, he looked forward to a calm, sleepy campout on this beach.

No such luck. In response to some provocation in the line for dessert, Faith bore a new argument along with her cobbler.

"Try to imagine any historical tragedy, any war, any genocide, if women had been in charge. And I'm not just talking to Jack, but to all you miserable penis people." Cradling her dish, Faith sank cross-legged among the miserable penis people—Glen, Duke, Jack, and Tycho. Ray kept his place, cobbler-less, on the group's edge, as Faith continued. "War is a male project. Women are usually supine, being raped by former neighbors, former students, their own nephews and brothers-in-law, like in Bosnia. In my research on the Serbian rape squads—"

"Excuse me," Duke interrupted, still calm but with an undercurrent of irritation. "Let's not get bogged down in Bosnia. Anyway, this argument always seems peculiar to me. The point isn't male versus female. It's all of us, regardless of our gender, versus the same male bullies you describe."

"Duke, I'm not talking about schoolyard antics."

"I'm not either. Bullies, then thugs, then full-grown predators. That's how killers evolve from a tiny percentage of the male population. In any war, the average guy is a reluctant soldier. The average guy hates the bloodshed deep in his guts. So maleness is almost incidental."

"Duke's right," Glen said. "Otherwise, why are the huge majority of men mostly nonviolent?"

"Are they?" Tycho said, lighting a cigarette. "I think the *average guy* would kill you as soon as look as you. Especially if you're related by blood."

The circle fell silent at the quick flare of Tycho's contempt as abrupt as his lighter's flame in the twilight. House Rock Rapid, just downriver from their camp, gushed and surged as if a half-deaf river god had punched up its volume.

"That damn rapid," Jack finally drawled. "That's what sounds hungry for blood."

Carol stood beside him, forking the cobbler on her plate. "I think Duke's got a point, and Tycho does, too. But there's violence in all of us, and it takes different forms in every heart. It doesn't matter if whoever's responsible has a penis or not. Out near our hometown in Texas, a farming conglomerate let field workers, including children, be exposed to toxic pesticides. And that decision was made by a female executive. Who had children of her own."

"A boy," Jack added, suddenly wistful, "and a little girl."

"Yeah, it's indirect, but violence just the same," Duke said. "Which includes those who sit by when others are abused." He rubbed the stub of his left shoulder while he glared at Jack. "I wasn't such a big kid, didn't get my growth until high school. You should've seen the little monsters in the grade school I attended when my folks first moved to the States. A working-class neighborhood in Oakland. Mean guys who would hurt you as soon as look at you. Hungry for provocation and ready to see blood squirt from anyone smaller and weaker. Or any off-the-boat loser with a funny accent." Duke spiced his own perfect Californian inflections to pronounce it *weeth a fonny ahccent.* "I was terrified, practically speechless, for several months. But my silent classmates, my little 'friends' who said and did nothing, were almost worse than the bullies."

"Amen," Ray said, finally moved to join in. He shuffled closer to the circle in the sand. "But even bullies don't always behave according to individual will. The prisons are full of violent offenders, almost exclusively male, who haven't got a clue what led them to strike again and again. It's not like they reasoned out their acts or made active choices. They might even feel detached from their own action, as if done by a shadow self. And these repeat offenders have almost always been victimized as kids, sometimes since birth. In every case I've studied for the documentary play we're working on, the criminal research subjects are scarred for life with multiple internal injuries."

"My heart just breaks, Ray." Even in the deepening dark, Ray could plainly catch Jack's violin gesture. "Is your play gonna use the excuse of every scum in a prison cell? That his daddy once spanked him?"

Tycho made a snorting noise, then squashed his cigarette in the sand. He pinched the butt, slipped it in his shorts pocket, and scrambled down the beach alone.

Ray turned back to face Jack. "Yeah, and after the spanking, then his daddy bashed his skull with the blunt end of an ax. And knocked him down the second-floor steps. And kicked him down the basement stairs. And locked him in a closet with no light, water, food, or toilet for five days. Our documents are full of those *excuses*, Jack, but not from the prisoners. The researchers have to dig through testimony because the prisoners won't disclose any of it."

"If we could raise an entire generation that never experienced violence," Carol asked, "do you think there would be any violence in later generations?"

"I suspect there could be," Faith said. "And I go back to my original point, which Ray helped clarify when he said virtually all your repeat offenders were men. Couldn't the violence grow out of maleness itself, out of testosterone? Why aren't there any such women to do your research on? Why aren't women predators?"

"Enough about penises and predators!" Hannah cried from the camp kitchen. "While you intellectuals have blathered on, these young ladies have been slaving over the pots and pans."

"Yeah!" Tess and Annette hollered, side by side behind steaming pans of dishwater set on a portable tabletop.

"Now, everybody get over here with your dessert plates, and I'll show you a system where every man and woman does his or her own damn dishes."

As Ray approached, Tess smiled, dried her hands on her T-shirt, and slipped away upriver into the darkness that had swallowed Tycho.

After Hannah rebuffed Ray's attempt to wrest the remaining pots and pans—"Let's say it's your turn tomorrow night, Mr. Criminal Sympathy"—he decided to stroll upriver in hopes of winding down for a good night's sleep. He concentrated on the river's slow rush, a kind of hard swallow before the big growl a few hundred yards downriver.

When Ray bashed through a willow thicket, he halted at the sight of Tycho and Tess, silhouetted against the river. The two sat on the sand side by side, arms hugging knees until Tycho pointed to the stars. "The summer triangle, see it? Three bright stars, Deneb, Altair, and Vega."

Tess giggled. "They sound like old cars."

Behind a thin screen of brush, Ray cleared his throat, but the river's roar made it inaudible, so he went on eavesdropping while Tess and Tycho went on chatting.

"You know so much about the stars," Tess said. "Are you into astrology?"

"Who needs a bunch of fake mystic bullshit leftover from the Dark Ages? Not when there's all this astronomy!"

"Wow! I love the way you put that. I'm getting more and more interested in science. Maybe majoring in biology. Are you studying astronomy, Tycho?"

"God, no. My real father was an astronomer. I don't want anything to do with that, not in school. But for fun, yeah. Over the winter semester, cooped up in Glen's converted garage, man, I almost forgot how much I love being out here under this whole symbiosis of canyon and river and stars, the whole outrageous arc of nature."

"How come none of you granola nuts ever mentions the

outrages of nature?" Jack's voice startled Ray, who hadn't seen Jack's standing silhouette until he paced closer, zipping his fly. Ray watched as Tycho sighed heavily, rubbing his head with both hands. Jack went on. "Most of the pain I see in the world is the direct result of Mother Nature."

"Why don't you go back to pissing in the river?"

"I'm serious. I just finished mopping up tornado claims in the Texas Panhandle. This goddamn road sign, metal pole and all, ended up pulverizing an old lady's bedroom and then slicing right through her lower leg. Which had to be amputated. But you know what the real scary part was, nature lovers? There in Scots Spring, Texas? That road sign read Oklahoma State Route 47."

Tess huddled closer to Tycho. "That must have been hard to witness firsthand."

"That it was, sweetheart. Very hard. So forgive me if I'm not too keen on the *outrageous arc of nature*." Jack stretched out his hand. "Anybody want a cigarette?"

Tycho picked one from the pack, thanking him while he offered Jack a light. In their first silent, smoky drags, the rapid seemed to gurgle on a fresh slurp of agitated whitewater. "Man, that's one mighty rapid," Tycho said. "I can't wait. And first thing in the morning, too!"

"You really are nuts, kid. It's probably gonna spit us out."

"Ah, you gotta relax, man! Hell, I'll take you down on the supply raft with me if you want. That thing slips and slides. All slippery like a goddamn orgasmic ejaculation!"

Jack laughed. "Sounds too damn queer for me." He turned in the direction of camp. "Enjoy the stars, kids."

"Oh man," Tycho said, lowering his voice, "would I love to give that loser the short, happy ride of his life!"

"Jack gives me the creeps, you know?" Tess hugged her

knees. "The way he stares at me, like there aren't any limits for him. I do feel sorry for him, because he's so out of place on this trip, but he still scares me."

"Do I?"

"No, no, Tycho. Not a bit."

Tycho set his cigarette filter-down in the sand and stretched his arm toward Tess, his hand on her neck. "How do you know you can trust me? I'm a pretty strong guy. Look." He clasped her neck with his other hand. Tess tossed her head back instinctively, then let out a strangled-sounding squeal. A laugh? Or an outcry? "Your neck's so delicate, Tess. It'd be so easy to snap." He leaned closer.

So did Tess, pressing his surrounding hands with hers.

Ray, who'd been ready to pounce on Tycho, now became the incarnation of privacy and discretion. He withdrew quietly just after he caught sight of their lips touching, Tycho's hands still cupped as if seizing Tess's neck.

❖

RAY continued down the beach, scouting a secluded place to raise his tent as far as possible from any further Jack-Faith-Tycho acrimony. But on a flat, dry dune ahead, a dark shape already claimed the perfect spot, the figure's headlamp spotlighting a sagging dry bag, pad, and sleeping bag. It was Duke, inflating a vinyl pillow.

"Hey, varmint," Ray called. "I was gonna pitch my tent here."

"I reckon there's plenty of room for you." Duke continued blowing into the valve, then capped it. "But you don't really need a tent, buddy."

"Really?" Ray dropped into the sand beside Duke's pad.

"You're planning to sleep with nothing between you and the bugs and the thunderstorms?"

"Nothing, and naked as the day I was born. The bugs aren't too bad. I heard there's almost no chance of rain for the next few weeks."

Ray couldn't concentrate, stuck on that forecast of nakedness. "Okay, then I'll give it a try."

"What?"

"Sleeping without a tent."

"Yeah. You're going to like it. I'll even share my exclusive stretch of sand." Duke laughed. "But I'll bet we're not the only two looking for some seclusion tonight."

"Yeah?" *So, you're looking for seclusion, too?* Ray liked the direction this was going, but it seemed to be heading there too fast. What if it wasn't the direction he thought it was, and he had to deal with the embarrassment of making a failed pass for the next hundreds of river miles? His throat felt tight and airless. "Who else?"

"Those two kids, Tess and Tycho." Duke aimed his headlamp in the direction of the willow clump upriver. "I saw 'em smooching on my way down here."

"I did, too." Ray tried to catch a full breath. "Already, romance on our first night on the river."

"What about you, Ray? Did you leave a sweetheart behind in Denver?"

"No." He smiled at the old-fashioned, gender neutral *sweetheart*. "A few months ago, I started going out with this…" He paused, searching for more gender ambiguity, still not sure how much he should reveal. "This kind of socialite."

"A socialite, huh?" Duke set down his pillow and sat on the pad next to Ray. "Wow."

"No wow. I possess no *wow* whatsoever. I don't know where I stand now, probably nowhere. When it comes to attending galas and fund-raisers, man, I just can't muster the glamour."

Duke's headlamp scanned Ray, toe to head. "I'm sure you're a lot more glamorous than I am. Even in your river grunge." He laughed. "Sometimes, alone in the wilds for such long stretches, I lose my whole grip on being civilized—on all that society expects, like looking decent and acting polite and seeking human company. I can't remember the last time I went out with anybody. So I envy those two lovebirds in the brush, finding each other's lips like that." His headlamp scanned the brush and the beach, turned back to Ray's face, then went off. "It's so natural."

Ray sat frozen in the dark, all traces of twilight obliterated. He couldn't see Duke's face, only the outline of his head, that classic profile faint against the stars. "Nothing's more natural, seeking human company."

"Yeah," Duke whispered. "I've got to relearn that." Shuffling, he seemed to lean closer.

Ray leaned closer, too, remembering to breathe, airing out his heart for whatever came next.

What came next was a soft clatter in the sandy, surrounding dark. A disembodied headlamp approached.

Duke's headlamp scanned the intruder. It was Faith. She waved at Ray, then reached out to touch Duke's arm. "I just wanted to apologize, Duke. I didn't mean to get all women's studies professorial on you back there. Not here on the river."

"You don't need to apologize, Faith. I thought it was an interesting argument."

"I just noticed how your face changed when I mentioned the Serbian rape trials. I didn't mean to be glib about your experiences during the war. It's not my place. I know I can get overbearing about violence against women. I didn't mean to put you on the spot."

"You didn't. Really." He reached his arm around her, pulling Faith close. "I'm kind of against violence against women myself."

To Ray's surprise, Faith got on tiptoes to kiss Duke's cheek. "Okay, now I'm going back to my sleeping bag, before I get any ideas. Good night, gentlemen."

Taking off his headlamp, Duke lay back against the pillow. "Anyway, back to my plan to return to civilization. Right after this trip, I'm gearing up to spend my summer vacation back in California. I know my folks are worried about me being alone for such long stretches in this godforsaken desert. My mom's so old school, so old country, forever trying to fix me up with a nice Catholic girl from the parish in Pleasanton. Trouble is, I'm pushing forty, and her supply of eligible women keeps shrinking."

Forty? The ancient number jolted Ray, who'd been guessing Duke was ten years younger. He studied the way the ranger sprawled before him, barely illuminated under a night sky crazy with stars, and he didn't really want to talk about families, least of all expectations of heterosexual matrimony. "I guess I'm lucky. One good thing about not having a family is there's no pressure."

"How can you not have a family?"

"Okay, I do have a brother. And a stepfather I never see. Plus Jenny and her family in Denver. They kind of adopted me when I was a teenager." Listening to the river's plashing, he imagined the strong current rushing, seduced, helpless as the next rapid lured it into its jaw. "You know, I was born not too far from the Colorado's source. My little brother and I always skylarked around the marshes." Ray felt like he was babbling, saying anything to keep the connection with Duke ignited. "The Colorado River's hardly more than a creek up there, and when I was a kid I could never understand how that little seep could ever carve canyons through solid rock a thousand miles downstream."

"It must've been a great place to grow up."

"It was, when we were little. Back when my stepfather was still sober, he'd take us on what he called moose hunting expeditions."

"Moose! What kind of caliber did you use?"

"Just one pair of binoculars. We'd pass them hand to hand, freaking out when we spotted one of those giants grazing in the willow thickets. Moose were more rare in Colorado back then. We'd be totally jazzed."

"You were lucky, man." Duke sat up again, shuffling closer, face-to-face with Ray. "When I was little, we sure didn't see wildlife on the streets of Oakland. Not when we moved out to Pleasanton, either. A squirrel, maybe. Once in a while."

"Becoming a ranger's gotta be pretty cool for a city kid, then." Ray searched Duke's face as best he could in the darkness. He was within easy kissing range.

"It's what I always wanted, yeah, getting intimate," Duke said, lowering his voice, "with wide-open spaces."

Was this really going to happen, the first night on the river? Ray tried to calm his jittering nerves for whatever came next.

Which happened to be another headlamp glaring at his face. Duke shuffled away, back to his sleeping pad.

"Ray? Ray! That you?" It was Jenny, tromping closer through the sand, dragging two drybags, his and hers. She dropped their camp gear in the sand without waiting for an answer. "You ready to set up our camp for the night? Hey, Duke! Didn't see you there. You boys mind if I bed down with you both, right here?"

CHAPTER 4

Mile 17 to Mile 33

JENNY told Jack, "The river is constantly changing, sure." They had just broken camp, loaded the boats, and climbed into Glen's dory. With only a few hundred yards before they braved House Rock Rapid, she was already calming and humoring Jack Carne as if she were his floating den mother.

As Glen guided *Last Chance* into an eddy above the rapid, Jack squinted downriver. "So since the flood release, you don't know how dangerous these rapids really are? Not one of the hundred sixty of 'em? They could all be worse?"

"Possible, but not likely," Jenny said, settling beside Jack in the stern seat.

The rapid snarled ahead, a seething, jagged white river horizon. "That's what the Canadian team is studying, a day behind us." Glen leaned back, rowing the dory into the eddy's stable center. "The big release had to alter the rapids' structure, but there probably wasn't enough volume for huge changes."

"As far as this rapid, I could barely sleep, listening to it spit up the river all night," Jack said, yanking down the brim of the Greenpeace cap. He stared toward Faith as she guided red *Dirty Devil* closer to blue *Last Chance*. "I hope you oarspeople know what you're doing."

"Oh, we do!" Faith called over, her voice laughing,

resolutely cheerful. "The river is never exactly the same, even in the stable conditions for all the decades since Glen Canyon Dam."

"Change is always part of the adventure," Glen said. "This time, we'll get a bigger adventure than most."

"And bigger fun!" said Duke, alone in the bow. He turned to Jack. "Enjoy it!"

"Like the big fun you got when you ran off to Bosnia, or Albania," Jack yelled to Duke, leaning around Glen, "or wherever the hell you were?"

Duke's smile died. "I didn't run off to Bosnia for fun, big guy." He turned away, facing forward, bracing himself with his hand on the gunwale. "I was assigned."

Jenny glared sidelong at Jack, steadying her nerves. Why did she feel so responsible for Jack Carne's comfort? If he wanted to cower and pout, let him. After the attempt to cajole, soothe, and jolly Jack into a more relaxed state of mind all morning, her patience had unraveled to its final frazzle. Now the beer-bellied, chicken-livered claims adjuster had managed to turn a young soldier's sacrifice into an insult.

Faith's dory was close enough that Carol, in the stern seat with Ray, was able to reach over and touch the back of Jack's neck. Jenny was surprised by the sudden, apparent affection of the gesture until she realized Carol was simply fussing with the straps to Jack's sunglasses and cap. "Let's make sure you're good to go," Carol said, laughing, as she leaned back into her place beside Ray. "Especially since Duke was nice enough to loan these."

"Ah, they're yours now," Duke said without looking back. "Hope they help."

Jenny wanted to hug Duke for his refusal to nurse a grievance. She wished the ranger were beside her in the stern, not the whiny Texan.

She raised her face to the sun. So much serendipity had coalesced to make this trip happen, including the availability of the guides and the willingness of the Pinch family's Grand River Adventures to supply the dories and the raft, even if Hannah was part of the package deal. Funny how, after all that, she'd supposed the only rocky part would be dealing with Hannah for two weeks. Who knew Carol Todd Carne, famous for her wit, grit, and down-home amiability on past service trips, would be married to this world-class jerk?

Jenny had seen too many variations on Jack's type in her ex-life with Andrew Pinch Junior, jocks who'd long lost their looks and physiques but not the certainty women would always desire them. Now they were past forty, blundering around in ill-fitting boys' clothes, flaunting their fat paunches and thinning hair. Once witty and cool with the girls, they merely grunted now, unsmiling, barking out bigotry and complaint rather than buoying up a conversation. Without the crucial adaptation of self-reflection, let alone sensitivity or even curiosity toward others, they were doomed to extinction, dazed, overmedicated, and unbearable.

But not unbearable to the many women who embraced the creatures in midlife, seeking financial and emotional security. Other women's blithe acceptance of this arrangement pissed Jenny off, and Carol's entry into their cohort had her flummoxed. At least Carol had the excuse that she'd married Jack when he was still a young, studly athlete. Maybe she wasn't yet doomed. Maybe she was quietly planning to become Jack's first ex-wife.

Of course, Jenny's critique of Carol's marriage quaked along her own fault lines. Jenny had been herself the object of scorn for insisting on divorce from the "perfect man." Andrew Pinch Jr. was still respected as a successful charmer no matter how his waistline expanded. But her ex was just as insufferable a jerk as Jack. Once he'd reigned over and reined in his pregnant twenty-year-old bride, Andrew undermined Jenny's independence and cultivated her dependency like a prize rose. He evolved into a perfect manipulator. Perfect in pruning their marriage into an ornament for advancing his business. Perfect in his emotional unavailability to Jenny and their daughter. Perfect in his periodic, tactical withdrawal of love and approval.

Stuck beside Jack now in *Last Chance*'s stern, Jenny could smell his fear. You're yella, Carne, Jenny thought, casting herself as an old-school movie moll and allowing herself a small smile before Glen stood to row slightly forward, calling Tycho over to scout the rapid.

Tycho, who'd held back, eddying near shore as he and Hannah battened down a few stray supplies, rowed the supply raft forward with a whoop, high-pitched and, as always, issuing from vocal organs alien to other humans—except Tess's. He grazed *Last Chance*'s transom with a devious, melodramatic howl, knocking all four passengers a little forward, inspiring Jack to bark, "Hey, kid, watch it!"

"You change your mind, Jack?" Tycho asked, belligerent and mischievous. "Why don't you join me? There's plenty of room in the bow with Hannah. Remember what I told you?" He closed his eyes, tossed back his head, and whooped in short, heaving blasts, his hips thrusting, his loose life vest jangling against his broad chest. "There's nothing like the silky slip of this rubber down that sweet chute."

"Like I said, kid, no thanks," Jack said, crossing his arms over his own, tightly fastened, protruding vest. Barely audible, he muttered, "Pervert."

"Tycho's psyched!" Annette cried from her place in *Dirty Devil*'s bow. "And so am I! Let's do it!"

"Look at that glassy water, man," Tycho said, "where the tongue slips into the heart of the rapid." He pointed forward with a big, toothy smile for Annette.

"I'll go with you guys," Tess said, sitting up on the bow hatch to face Tycho and Hannah. "That okay? Annette, can you bail by yourself?"

"You bet, girl," Annette cried, laughing. "Go for it!"

Before Jenny had time to caution her, Tess was standing as Tycho scooped her up from *Dirty Devil*. "Tess," Jenny said, trying to strain the parental tone from her voice, "are you sure?"

"This rapid has a high rating, Tess," Glen said, with the same forced, unconvincing attempt at reasoned calm Jenny heard in her own voice. "I'd be happier if you stayed in the dory."

"Come on, you guys," Tess said, atop the square metal box Tycho arranged as her seat. "I've got my life jacket. If worse comes to worst, I'll just surge to shore. I'm a strong swimmer. And besides, nothing's going to happen."

Faith eased into the rapid first, with Glen to follow and Tycho to bring up the rear. "I'll be damned if Tycho isn't right about that silky tongue," Glen cried out as *Last Chance* was lulled, then yanked into the hungry current. "Jeez, will you look at that glassy 'v,'" Glen said. "It's even more beautiful than sex. Jack, look back? That gorgeous sucking invitation to the rapid's own heart? It's the very meaning of life."

Smiling into the purple heart of Glen's poetry, Jenny glanced up to observe Faith's progress. She cried a barely audible "yahoo" as she negotiated the rapid's base with angled ease. In front, Annette was already bailing while Carol and Ray high-fived in back. Then *Dirty Devil* rocked out of sight behind a curling chop of white chaos.

Jenny forced herself to concentrate on the thrill of the ride while being tossed, rocking, into all that frothy, ambiguous water. But as the swells slapped from impossible directions, splashing her sandals at the same time as the back of her head, they'd already reached the rapid's bottom in defiance of all her attempts to focus. She bailed the bilge as Glen eddied out, river right.

Scooping three scoops to every one of Jack's, Jenny noticed Jack's cap had come off his head and dangled on its leash down his nape. She was about to secure it when Glen cried, "Holy Virgin Mother of God!" He was standing now, screaming to Tycho. "*Go left!*"

Faith, eddied out just downriver, added her soprano cries to Glen's baritone shouts. Tycho was slipping down the rapid into the whirlpool's vortex. The supply raft careened at an impossibly upright angle, perpendicular to the declining angle of the rapid itself. Jenny saw it all in slow motion, the yellow raft riding the whitewater on its bow tube. Shoved forward, Hannah and Tess almost dangled head-first into the waves while the raft tottered along its lunatic tightrope. Rushing to reach Tess's hand as she lurched forward, Tycho frantically unleashed, then tossed a metal box blocking his way. The box struck the rock that jutted from the whirlpool and flipped open. The satellite phone leapt out as if suicidal, heaving itself against the massive boulder.

Before the raft went horizontal again at the rapid's base and disappeared behind a surge of foam, the last thing Jenny saw was Tycho letting go of Tess's outstretched hand to retake the oars.

"Just think," Jack said, open-mouthed. "That box smashing against the rock? That could have been my brains."

❖

JENNY lied to Carol. "It's too bad Jack had to turn back."

Taking an after-lunch hike to North Canyon's upper pools, Jenny felt compelled again to disgorge this bullshit—play the diplomat and appease the customers—as if leading some cheeseball tour instead of environmental science volunteers. In truth, Jenny was relieved Jack had found the trail too tiring and turned back for camp after only a third of the way. Glad to hike with Carol, she might be able to renew their friendship unburdened by Jack's static.

"I do wish Jack could've seen this," Carol said. Her voice echoed strong and clear in the topmost pool's encircling walls of Supai sandstone. "Maybe it would finally penetrate his thick skull that we're in paradise, and he's just pouting it all away." Ever cool, Carol seemed unfazed by her husband's recalcitrance. After Tycho's catastrophe at House Rock Rapid, Jack had acted like a stubborn child, his arms crossed and his head down all the way to North Canyon.

Tess stayed in the supply raft for those four flat, slow river miles, but she agreed when Jenny insisted she ride with Faith again in the series of rapids they'd encounter next, the Roaring Twenties. "Tycho's chance to get more practice," Glen had said. Despite the loss of their satellite phone, another crisis was behind them.

Jack, though, was likely to remain a problem for the next two hundred fifty river miles. The steep, seductive canyon walls ahead, which should have felt like welcoming arms to Jenny, now seemed folded in indifference. Even for the relatively simple tasks they had set for their research around North Canyon before lunch, with half the team helping collect data on mud flows and the other half fanning out to check seed scatter around riparian plants, Jack had only lasted fifteen minutes before he dropped into the shade of coyote willows, citing "heat stroke" and taking a nap until Hannah called everyone to the sandwich board.

Now, as the stragglers arrived up the last ledge of the rocky trail, crying out, "Oh my God!" and "Wow! Awesome!" Jenny closed her eyes, enjoying Annette, Tess, and Tycho's exultant first reactions to the upper pools. This is what it was all meant to be—riding the river, wild or placid, then purposeful work on shore followed by short, steep hikes to heaven. Under the turquoise teardrop that fed the pools, Ray and Duke competed in vain to find appropriate adjectives: "surreal," "painterly," "sculpted," and even "semi-erotic dervish swirling."

To Jenny, the red and yellow rock walls were somehow smooth and tortured at once, like molded clay that had been overworked in nature's hands, all of it mirrored, flawless, in the pool. While Tess and Annette shot photos and Tycho invented antic poses, Jenny sat beside Carol in a shady alcove opposite the turquoise teardrop. "Isn't this perfect? After we've hurried through all those geologic layers in just two days, it feels right to pause here and absorb the slower pace of nature."

Carol smiled, scooping up a soft, oval rock in her hand. "It is serene." With an unexpected burst of strength, she pulverized it in her palm. "Yet it's the result of incredible violence at the same time. Like these two hulking walls that look like they collided and then fell back, exhausted, to form that crack and create all these tormented swirls. It puts me in mind of fault lines, Jenny. Tectonic plates in mortal conflict."

"But a conflict that's settled?" Jenny looked toward the volunteers. Their laughter echoed, as doubled as their images in the pool. "We can bask here, completely at peace, even with the evidence of catastrophe all around us. That's what I love about geology. The evidence of past conflict is as real and sure as rock itself, but the observer's unbothered and free."

"Just like we are now," Carol said, smiling. "Don't you

love the stillness, the stop-action look of all this jumbled rock? But really, the catastrophe is still going on, isn't it? The plates go on shifting, the rocks eroding, and the walls closing in. It's just not perceptible to human time." Carol looked up at the poolside group lending a hand to Glen as he scrambled to join them, watching as the whole bunch disappeared through a narrow chasm beyond. "Anyway, I'm just sorry that Jack is bein' such a pain, Jenny. He's much worse than I expected, or I would never have suggested he come along. I figured this would inspire him more, get him out of himself for a spell." She parodied her own Texas dialect. "But uh done gone an' figgured wrong, didn't uh?"

"Is Jack going through something, then? I mean, something more than his dislike of whitewater?"

"It's not the damn rapids. It's nature herself he's got a grudge against. Just a month ago, he had to investigate tornado claims in a little Panhandle town, Scots Spring. It was pretty bad, Jenny. Not only death and dislocation, but the soul ripped out of the whole place. Nineteenth-century houses whipped off their foundations. Old Fort Scots chewed to a pile of planks. There's really nothin' left to rebuild."

Jenny vaguely recalled the dramatic coverage now: *Twister Demolishes Historic Texas Town.* She sensed Carol had something more to disclose but was reluctant. Something had happened that knocked even Carol's bluntness out of whack and left a tender, protected bruise in the midst of her brashness. "His first tornado?"

"Oh no. You can't be a West Texas insurance claims adjuster and not see more than your share of twisters. No, Scots Spring was our hometown."

"Oh! Carol, I'm so sorry! Why didn't you tell me? You must both still be grieving."

"We've got to move on. We've lived in Amarillo for most

of our adult lives. But Scots Spring was where we started kindergarten and Bible school. We both finished high school there."

"That's right. You two were high school sweethearts. The classic Texas couple. The quarterback and the lead cheerleader."

"Yep. Although I prefer, honey, to think of myself as the lead cheerbag. Ain't that stupid? But I loved that old town. Tumbleweeds would howl right down Main Street, but they always got caught in this gorgeous grove of oaks. Main Street had to kind of jimmy around 'em, in two one-way detours lined by these bronze statues commemorating the Panhandle Plains Trail. Jack hoisted me up on the Cattle Drive statue to share a six-pack the night we graduated high school and he put the question to me.

"But it's gone now, Jenny—the oaks, the statues, the historic sites, and ninety percent of Main Street. Barren and hideous as the rest of the county now. Like God decided Scots Spring was an abomination in his eyes. Like He wanted to take away the very last thing that connected Jack and me to our old life." Carol crushed the small shards of red sandstone into tiny, sharp fragments, then spilled them on the cracked mud under her knees.

"How horrible." Jenny clasped Carol's emptied hand. "Now I understand why you wanted Jack to join you on this project."

Carol squeezed Jenny's fingers then stood just as the group's voices echoed in the upper chasm. As he bounded from the chasm and down the wrinkled rock footholds just ahead of Tycho and Glen, Duke shouted, "A dead end!"

"Like so much of life," Glen said, skirting the pool with a few clumsy splashes. "But that's for the best, since we need to get through the Roaring Twenties before it gets too late. Don't we, Jen?"

"Yes sir," Jenny said, standing to hand-whisk the mucky sand off her shorts. "I was counting on you to make sure we have time for Redwall Cave."

"Well, then, onward!" Glen called out, extending his arm to Carol as the two approached the point where the trail led back down to the river. "My lady?"

"My good sir!" Carol laughed as she locked arms with Glen. The two fell into step down the trail behind Duke and Tycho.

When Annette and Tess scrambled down from the chasm, Jenny shooed them toward the trail, taking up the rear beside Ray. She overheard a fraction of Annette's remarks to Tess. "But he has a criminal record!"

"When he was sixteen," Tess said. "That was a long time ago. And it was mostly guilt by association. He was involved with older guys."

"Association? Tycho himself said he attacked that guy with a crowbar."

"In self-defense, though. No charges were ever filed. Anyway, that's why he went to live at Glen's in Flagstaff. And look at him now. Starting college, doing his best."

"Why does this feel like such a textbook case," Annette said, brushing a smudge off Tess's bare shoulder, "of the golden girl and the juvenile delinquent?"

Tess turned around, playfully slapping Annette's hand away. "*Ex*-delinquent to you, Miss Junior Princess of Greater Boston."

Their banter transformed itself into a race, Annette and Tess jostling each other for first place down the side canyon. After glancing at the still-healing gash on Tess's lower leg,

Jenny resisted the impulse to cry out caution. She told Ray, "Terrible to reach the stage where you feel like mothering college-age women."

"Sounds like we've got more worries with our college-age man."

"Yeah. I'm still freaked about Tycho almost wiping out at House Rock."

"Still, you can't be responsible for every mishap, Big Mama. Besides, as the most successful mother in the history of the American West, you deserve to rest on your laurels. Let your *wunderkind* collect more gold stars and scholarships while buff servants apply salve to your nubile flesh."

"Gosh, that sounds just like my new life in Flagstaff." Jenny laughed. "I'm sure that's Hannah's version of it, anyway. I left my doting husband and loving daughter to frolic with cabaña boys. It's so easy for her to guilt me about missing out on Amelia's senior year because I am guilty. But on this last visit to Denver, I just longed for Amelia's presence like a big, lonely dope. Maybe that's why I'm so tempted to fuss over Tess."

"You've always been a big dope, Jen. But lonely?"

"I hate to admit it, but it's true. I haven't been very social in Flagstaff, other than Glen and a few other Wildlands Society friends and connections. More and more it feels like exile. And the funny thing? I wasn't banished from Andrew or the whole Pinch clan. I expelled myself."

"During spring break when Amelia and I went backcountry skiing, she flat out declared how much she admired you for filing the divorce. She's cool about it."

"I'm so glad you were able to join me here, Ray. I get a big smile just hearing your voice or your laugh. Sometimes, in Flag, I almost forget what it's like to have close friends. Just now, with Carol—who would probably be my best friend if she lived nearby—I realized how much I miss having a confidant."

"Did she confide anything?"

Jenny told the story of the hometown tornado. "You know that toxic pesticide example Carol used last night during the penis-people debate? It's what made her a wildlands activist. Those migrant children, their skin welted by corrosives, their lungs infected, were brought to Carol's unit at the children's hospital. She did nothing round the clock for days but try to soothe their agony."

"Puts her cancer of the planet comment in perspective."

"Yeah, she's not exactly enamored of the human race. Except that in a way, she must be. She really loved those kids. But what's strange about Carol, she never really told me any of that herself. Glen found it out from a mutual acquaintance. Just like she never told me a thing about Jack."

"Yeah, well, it's pretty obvious their marriage is more of a habit or a business deal than a romance."

"Especially since they don't have children. I can't imagine how I'd have lasted more than a few years with Andrew if there hadn't been a child at stake." Jenny accepted Ray's helping hand down a notched rock face. "Speaking of which—romance, I mean—how are you doing?"

"You were speaking of marriage, not romance. I can't imagine what the two might have in common." Ray smiled and turned around, his arms upraised. "Here in paradise, this three-hundred-million-year-old rock sure puts my little life in perspective. I could learn to like self-obliteration."

"I don't know how much I like the sound of that, Ray. When we get into the two-billion-year-old schist, what's going to be left of you?"

"Just more of my bullschist. Maybe there won't be anything left of my ego or my psyche at all. And good riddance."

Before Jenny could conjure a response, the trail dropped them right into the assembled group, gathered around the spot where Hannah proffered her "anti-dehydrating sludge," made from orange, cranberry, and apple juice. Duke raised his glass to Jenny and Ray with a curious half-grin on his face, then turned to join the others helping Hannah put away the lunch fixings.

Jack, however, was collapsed in the shade with one beer can in his hand and another crushed at his side. Jenny called, "Jack, are you feeling all right now?"

Jack glanced over and raised himself briefly up, but only to gulp more of his beer. "Never better, thanks."

Hannah sidled over to Jenny, wiping her hands on her apron, with her back to Jack. "He was dizzy and out of breath when he staggered down from the trail. He's been under that bush the whole time, burping and gurgling and getting into the beer against my advice."

"Jeez," Jenny sighed. "What would Marge Simpson do?"

"She'd fume, then giggle," Hannah said. "But I don't approve of beer at lunch. It's against an old river rule."

"I don't approve either. It's a good rule."

"Then enforce it. I thought you were going to screen people for this trip."

Before Jenny had a chance to indulge her fantasy of lunging for her ex-mother-in-law's throat, Hannah went on. "Our end point at Lake Mead is starting to look pretty good already."

Don't Lake Mead me, lady. You connived to come on this trip, and now you're begging for it to be over before it's barely begun. Jenny decided to say aloud only the most insipid response she could muster. "Well, I'm not going to let one difficult personality make me wish my trip away. And thanks, Hannah." She raised her cup. "Your sludge is delicious."

❖

JENNY peered into Redwall Cavern to see what was wrong. Tess's high-pitched squeal echoed throughout the vast arena. But even as her eyes adjusted to the cavern's deep shade, Jenny realized she'd been tricked again. Nerve-needling as Tess's outcries were, this one just signified more late-teenage ecstasy. Tycho was scaling the back wall, finding freestyle footholds. Now, as he spidered up the ceiling, Tess had apparently tried to follow and fallen, rear end on the sand floor, laughing.

Jack hovered nearby, a beer in one hand while his other traced the smooth, intricate indentations in the cavern's red-gray limestone.

Relieved, Jenny eased back to her post-rapid powwow with Duke, Ray, and Glen. "They're just playing Spider-Man on the cave ceiling," she announced. The three sat cross-legged in the soft sand just under the rock amphitheater's archway while the volunteers explored the cavern, giddy and goofy after the long afternoon. Their descent through the Roaring Twenties had gone superbly—no people or objects expelled from either supply raft or dories—each quick, short rapid a perfect chance for Tycho to regain his confidence. "I'm so thrilled Tycho played it safe and solid, I don't care if he and Tess scream their brains out. I'm even more thrilled we didn't pull a Bert Loper at Mile 24 Rapid."

Glen laughed, nodding. He explained to Duke how the river-running canyon pioneer had been killed there, either by heart attack or a planned suicide in the whitewater. "Either way, Bert went out celebrating his eightieth birthday exactly where he wanted to be."

"I hope no Park Service folks on the rim have a heart attack when they don't get any calls from us." Jenny sighed, leaning into the sandy slope. "I don't suppose that satellite phone has any intentions of piecing itself back together and floating downstream."

"Yeah, but the Canadian team is," Glen said. "Heading downstream, that is. They're only a day behind us, and they'll be moving faster than we are."

"Yeah, they could pass us sometime tomorrow," Duke said, digging at the sand with his hand as he sat between Glen and Jenny. "We can use their phone to let the Service know that all is well."

"Is it?" Jenny asked. "I'm glad you think so, Duke, because I didn't want you to think all our volunteer trips were quite this socially challenging."

"Are you kidding?" Duke smiled. "I was in the Army, remember? I think you assembled a great group, Jenny."

It was a kind thing to say, and maybe Duke's impression was also correct, despite the wild card shuffle of Jack and Tycho and Hannah. If Jenny reflected on the whole arc of this long, busy day on the river, the volunteers had accomplished a great deal, despite their shattering start at House Rock. Midafternoon they'd gathered data at the mouth of South Canyon, where Jenny's confidence was restored by the group's strict attention to detail. They'd asked intelligent questions during her streamside talk on Great Basin ecosystems, essential to prepare them for tomorrow's entry into Sonoran Desert vestiges.

For the first time since putting in at Lee's Ferry, Jenny had felt herself fully caught in the current of pure fascination with research rather than stranded by unexpected, interpersonal side eddies. The dories, rocking side by side in the placid cove now, seemed to soothe Jenny's hopes. Turquoise and crimson in the evening's last light, plashing on their bow lines, the boats cheered her, renewing her faith in the adventures—and kick-ass data collection—awaiting around a thousand river bends.

When Tess squealed again, Jenny made a point of not glancing into the cavern. She attempted to focus on Duke's halting attempt to describe his first kaleidoscopic impressions of the river trip so far. She noticed he smiled at Ray, directing most of his words to Ray, who smiled back as he elaborated. But Duke stopped talking when Glen rose, his brow scrunched with concern.

"Oh God," Jenny said, almost unwilling to turn, "what is it now?"

When she brought up the rear behind Duke and Glen at the cavern's back wall, Jenny regretted having hesitated. It was like arriving late for the play's first act, so nothing in the scene before her made immediate sense. The kids had dropped their cave-spider antics and stood upright, feet planted in the sand. Tess hovered behind Tycho with head bowed and arms crossed. Tycho, hands on hips, demanded to know why Jack, who paced slowly backward, had been "pawing Tess's legs."

"Look, I was just trying to find those shellfish fossils Jenny was telling us about."

"They're not on Tess's legs, man."

"It's okay, Tycho," Tess said, hoarse, quieted now. "He just gave me a scare."

"I saw her fall the first time," Jack said, steadying his voice while he turned to the arriving trio as if for backup, "and Tess was so much higher up, I didn't want her to hurt herself. I was just trying to help."

"I know what you were trying, dude." Tycho stepped forward as Jack hunched, protecting his ground.

Glen checked Tycho's advance by placing his arm around his shoulders. Tycho promptly shook Glen off, but the gentle, restraining gesture had impact. Tycho turned to the cavern wall and kicked it.

Jenny hurried to Tess's side, determined to hear her version of events out of everyone's hearing, when an off-tone chorus burst from upstream. "Happy birthday to youuuu!"

Appearing around the jagged downstream edge of the cavern's sandy arena, Annette and Hannah each carried one end of a Dutch oven cake, lit with a few candles. Faith and Carol marched behind them, each bearing a single candle and joining voices to echo "Happy birthday!" throughout the entire, arching limestone amphitheater. Tess's eyes lighted. She recovered her broad smile and her laugh. "I can't believe you did this! Annette…"

"It wasn't just me," Annette said. "Hannah was the real force behind this. I suggested a cupcake, for God's sake, but Hannah said she had ingredients for upside-down pineapple cake and whipped it up with last night's dinner."

"Look," Hannah said, "it survived the Roaring Twenties just fine!"

"A perfect afternoon treat, huh?" Annette said, rushing into Tess's outstretched arms. "We decided to have it here instead of camp tonight, to totally surprise and embarrass you!"

Everyone gathered in a semicircle except Tycho, who pushed through it, breathing hard in measured breaths.

"So you're nineteen, honey?" Carol asked, as giddy as the other birthday party conspirators. "Today?"

"No, eighteen," Tess said, her eyes on Tycho, brooding near the waterline. "I guess I've been telling everyone that kind of prematurely." When everyone laughed, she smiled, shaking her head. "Before my birthdays, I start thinking I'm already the age I'm going to be. I've been doing that since I was a little girl. Plus, my dad altered my records so I could start kindergarten early. It's been a mix-up since the beginning."

"So," Carol said, "you really were born eighteen years ago? On this day?"

Jack joined the circle. "Not on school records, but for real?"

"Yeah, for real." Tess looked puzzled. "God, you two sound like you're going to report me to the Minneapolis public schools for fraud or something!"

Everyone laughed except Jack and Carol, who exchanged the same wide-eyed, quick-frozen expression on faces drained of blood.

Chapter 5

Mile 35 to Mile 42

RAY traced a fossilized shellfish etched into the limestone of Nautiloid Canyon. With this short side canyon hike an afterthought to midmorning data collection on the riverbank below, he caught a moment alone when he realized everyone else had started down the trail.

Ray was glad for the momentary solitude. For the first time, he felt the canyon's deep antiquity in his guts rather than only in his mind. Glen had described limestone as the product of a vanished sea's calcium carbonate, also the building material of seashells. He'd called the startling shapes of the large nautiloids captured in the limestone as "visible seashells swimming in ground-up seashells."

Apparently there had been a second genesis 550 million years ago, with populations of shelled critters and mollusks exploding in prehistoric oceans. This rock, if Ray understood correctly, was their graveyard, high and dry under this Arizona morning's thin, almost yellow haze.

Yet it was precisely life, not stony graves, that moved him. Of course the canyon had seemed grand, but this morning, its scale, sculpted shapes, and sheer spaciousness left him more awestricken by geology than he'd ever been, even as a child of the Continental Divide. Until this moment, he had never felt the very planet as fully alive, from its molten, spewing core to the successive, unfinished stories told here on its crust. Along with the ancient impress of this shellfish, weren't we and all creatures the nervous system of a massive, orbiting organism?

Ray half expected the nautiloid to wriggle out from his fingers, its lines were so vivid, its personality so squirtsome, the wavelike, successive half circles spilling behind its tail like sudden propulsion.

Propelling himself now, Ray rock hopped down the canyon to catch up with Duke, who scrambled alone down a steep ravine. "Hey, buddy!" the ranger called, turning around at Ray's approach. "I promised Jenny I'd be doing sweep. How'd you get behind me?"

"I got absorbed by the fossils. Didn't hear your marching orders, I guess. Sorry."

Duke let Ray pass as they climbed down the steep stretch as a tight twosome. Ray did not object in the least to Duke's keeping so close behind him. He'd decided to enjoy his crush on the ranger in the abstract, the way he adored the stars and the river, jazzed by their presence without expectations. At one point, Duke reached for Ray as he faltered on a slick rock face, an irony not lost on the two-armed klutz while he enjoyed the warm, rough touch of Duke's steadying hand.

As they approached a flatter section, Duke asked, "So what got you interested in writing about killers' messed-up brains?"

"I'm really just a glorified editor, script doctor, and co-researcher. I got on the project through connections from my college playwrights' group. But I have to admit I was fascinated by the topic. I think my half brother might have experienced some neurological damage, you know, from abuse."

"As a little kid? From your stepfather?"

"Yeah. My brother never became a violent offender, but

he's had to fight like hell to avoid trouble all his life. Kind of like Tycho, getting into trouble with older guys who actually were messing with weapons. My brother's kind of channeled it these days, working for a private contractor, mopping up after the military in scary places. Somalia, Congo, Afghanistan."

"A mercenary."

"He says he's a security officer. He's only nineteen, so I'm sure he's more of a grunt-for-hire. He's really a good guy. He'd do anything for you, but he's got this wild jones for risk and danger."

"You were the family peacemaker?"

"By default. My mom brought me to live on my stepfather's ranch when I was four or so, but my half brother was born there. My stepdad could be great when he was sober, but he had a mean streak. Unpredictable. He liked to set up conflicts, pick verbal fights. I definitely got enough of that, but escaped the nastiest abuse." Ray halted, catching his breath as he dropped on his butt to slide down a smooth rock drop. Landing clumsily, hard on one foot, he turned to watch Duke maneuver the drop with two quick, elegant hops.

As they started down an easier patch of trail, Ray went on. "When my stepfather started drinking, he could be cruel as hell, taunting and insulting, and toward the end of my high school days, he was drinking all the time. When I took off for college in Denver, my little brother was left behind, at his dad's mercy. I realized too late that it got worse. Much worse."

Duke stopped, and Ray turned around to catch his reaction. Duke's eyes narrowed, and he clenched his fist. "Physical attacks?"

"Yeah, it still slays me to realize how oblivious I was. I could've at least tried to protect him. Somehow my absence just intensified all their conflicts, and I'm afraid my brother took the brunt of it. He wouldn't admit anything about the beatings or hurled projectiles at the time. Hid his wounds and hung out with troublemakers around Grand Ditch and Granby."

Ray and Duke caught up with Glen and Hannah, taking it easy on the way back, Glen bending her ear with a story about a river trip he'd guided years before for a group of creationist church people. Their leader warned Glen they didn't want to hear any theories about the canyon's geology or its alleged prehistoric natural history because they believed the canyon, along with the Earth, had been dreamed up, "Presto!" Glen joked. "Exactly six thousand, five hundred and thirty-seven years ago, just as we see it today." Glen had been frustrated for the entire length of the canyon by being muzzled, unable to share all its rich geologic and evolutionary lore. He was not even allowed to join the evangelicals' riverside prayer circles, "despite my own Catholic's tenuous claims to Christianity."

To Ray, who had no claim to Christianity or any religion, the evangelicals' position seemed backward. The canyon's geology almost forced theology on its visitors. To study its physical and biotic evolution might open an agnostic soul to God's creative extravagance. "Why didn't those church folks see the canyon as a two-billion-year proclamation of God's glory?"

"Please, Ray. They weren't that evolved." Glen finished telling the story. Finally, on the last night, in the midst of prayer, the leader signaled Glen over and took his hand, inviting him into the circle. Then he begged God to forgive Glen for his scientific heresy. The leader implored the rest of the group to spare Glen from the everlasting fires of hell through an extra dose of intercessory prayer. "They offered to baptize me right there, where the Colorado River spilled its wild heart into the captive bathwater of Lake Mead. It was a dirty trick, and they knew I was already baptized. I decided then and there that there really was a hell, and it lived in their twisted, pseudo-Christian hearts."

Duke, who'd been shocked into unhappy laughter by Glen's story, now nodded in solemn agreement. "Yeah, but it's not just Christians. It's amazing how full of hatred religious people in general can be."

"Now, now," Hannah said, accepting Duke's upraised hand to guide her down a boulder. She sighed, her hands on her hips, standing on a ledge overlooking the river's sweep through a narrow, winding chasm. "Just because stupid people make proclamations in the name of religion, it doesn't reflect badly on religion. It reflects badly on their interpretation. Just because some firemen are pyromaniacs doesn't mean I won't call the fire department the next time I smell smoke."

Ray smiled at this vintage Hannahism, delivered in her croaking, salty tones, but Duke was not amused. He stood beside her on the overlook, punching the passionate air of his faithlessness with his lone arm. "Religion promoted intolerance and ethnic murders in Bosnia."

"My point being," Hannah said, easing down the last stretch of trail, "that's not religion. It's political hatred, or bigotry, or something else I don't understand. It's done in the name of God, but all it does is spread evil and destroy His reputation."

"With all due respect," Duke said, pacing carefully behind Hannah, "I don't think religion has much of a reputation left to destroy. Except a bad one."

As the trail leveled, Hannah hooked her arm into Duke's. "I just can't bear for such a smart, beautiful young man to think this way. Muhammad and Jesus aren't to blame for the atrocities their followers commit."

"I always kind of liked ol' Jesus," Jack said, his drawling

voice echoing sharp and clear, but he was nowhere in sight. When the trail bottomed out, Ray finally found him lying back behind an outcropping. He fanned his flushed face with the Greenpeace cap's brim, exposing his balding head to the punishing sun. "I like His tendency to forgive."

Glen and Hannah went to him immediately, inquiring after his health. Jack had expressed an eagerness to join the other hikers, promising to take it slow and easy following last night's nausea after he devoured the remnants of Tess's birthday cake. So he had, making it all the way to the first patch of fossilized nautiloids before he decided to turn back. "I'm only a little wobbly, a little dizzy. Lost my balance on that big boulder up there, and I decided to catch my breath."

Ray and Duke each gave him a hand up and guided him down the short distance to the launch site. Nearer the boats, he broke into a stronger step. "Thanks for your help, guys, but I hate to think of myself so out of shape at the tender age of forty-one." His hand in a defiant fist over his chest, Jack walked the final yards on his own. "I'm not a fossil yet."

❖

RAY turned around to catch Carol's words. He sat in *Last Chance*'s bow, with Carol in the stern beside Jenny. The late morning sun had risen above the mostly flat water since Nautiloid Canyon, growing more oppressive.

Carol flashed her white, toothy smile. "Jack could be faking this particular bout with nausea, since he couldn't hack such a short little hike. He might be ashamed he's in such bad shape compared to you and Jenny, not to mention Duke, Faith, and Glen. And Glen's got a few years on him."

"Twenty plus," Glen put in from the boatman's seat.

Ray glanced over to *Dirty Devil*'s cargo of Jack, Annette,

and Duke. At launch, he'd hoped to share the bow with Duke, but weight distribution, not queer crushes, ruled the guides' seating chart. He glanced back. "But Jack did seem pretty sick at Lee's Ferry."

"He was," Carol said. "What with his smoker's lungs, the altitude, and his lousy attitude. But look at him now, yakkin' away..."

"With his eyes glued on Tess's body, sprawling on the supply raft," Jenny said. "Funny how reviving a young girl in a two-piece can be."

Windless and listless, the canyon seemed to be gathering heat for the deep summer to come. Ray had already joined Tycho and Tess for a plunge into the frigid water. While Hannah rowed the supply raft, the two continued to dunk themselves and sunbathe in the bow.

Faith steered *Dirty Devil* alongside *Last Chance* so that Jenny could point out their entry into the new life zone. "Be watching for the first catclaw," Jenny announced to the volunteers as the dories drifted side by side. "That'll tell us we're in the Sonoran Desert."

"Catclaw's the sign?" Annette asked. "Not this infernal heat?"

"Why don't you put on your bikini if you're so hot?" Jack asked. "Like your young friend over there?"

"Why don't you put on yours?" Annette asked. "You're always so covered up, Jack. What are you trying to hide?"

"I'd never discuss that with a young lady of your character. Just figure it out yourself. When red-blooded men are constantly being stimulated by young girls wearing next to nothin', guess why we like to wear baggy shorts."

"Ohh! You didn't have to say that." Annette rose from her seat beside Duke in the stern. She winked at Duke, then caught Ray's eyes and winked again before she faced Jack. "It's just not nice to reduce women to sex fantasies for whatever little thing wiggles in your shorts."

"Hey, I didn't say anything nasty," Jack said. "It was all in your own mind."

"I don't like the picture you put in my mind," Annette said, dipping her toe into the water. She peeled off her own baggy shorts to reveal her swimsuit bottom. Ray appreciated the melodrama Annette enacted as she shivered in showy gasps. "It's like you raped my imagination, Jack." Holding on to the gunwale, she lowered herself with a scream into the water, then bobbed up for air. "If you weren't such a pathetic invalid," she blubbered, "I'd splash you until you half drowned."

Carol applauded, laughing. "A good drowning with cold water might douse Jack's wiggling little thing, Annette. Let him have it!"

❖

RAY would remember later how their solemn cluster around the ruins of Bert Loper's boat seemed like a premature graveside memorial. It would be their last gathering as a full group of eleven.

"He wanted to die on the river, and he did, but Bert's bones weren't found until twenty-six years later, far downriver," Glen had told the assembled crew. "After he expired at the oars at Mile 24 in 1949, his boat was found washed up here at Mile 41, above the mouth of the side canyon that bears his name." Glen had generated suspense about whether the flood release would finally sweep away the ruins of Bert's boat, but they'd found the remnants still undisturbed above the water line. Though they'd stopped by the beach at Bert Loper's Canyon for a brief data session, they first gathered around the scattered lumber fanning out from the intact, triangular prow.

Glen marveled at all the "flash floods the boat endured before Glen Canyon Dam."

To Ray, what took imagination was understanding how the thousands who'd run the river over the past decades had learned the necessary grace to leave Bert's boat alone. Apparently unbothered on a hillside, it seemed akin to the nautiloid fossils, a carcass carved in wood instead of stone. Like them, its lively illusion of movement was freeze-framed, spilled across time to honor a story of individual life and death.

Now, a short distance downriver at a no-name box side canyon Glen had dubbed Little Bert's, Ray studied the release's mud line in the forgiving tamarisk shade. The area fronted the thrust of the river before it turned sharply south to capture piles of flood release debris. A beautiful, newly made sand beach, cradled among perching boulders, spread upstream from the dry canyon. Awaiting Hannah's call to lunch, Ray followed the caking soil deeper up the dry canyon bed.

Jenny had wanted this to be a quick study, allowing plenty of time at their camp at Nankoweap, ten miles downriver. She only needed a skeleton crew here—herself, Carol, Duke, and Ray—to note mud deposition around Little Bert's. She'd sent Annette and Faith downriver to study seed scatter. Jack had been given more "recovery time" to help Hannah prepare lunch, though Hannah protested that she didn't need his help. Tycho was going to use the time to reorganize his storage area, using the extra space created for the lost phone box, then join Ray to help collect data. Glen decided to soap up, plunge into the side stream, then nap on *Last Chance*. The last Ray heard from Tess, she was going to borrow Glen's shampoo and make herself an "Indian maiden's spa" on the new beach upriver.

Scaling a boulder above the dry streambed, Ray could hear Glen's hearty, echoing laugh. Then, almost in response, he heard the startling, falling whistle of a canyon wren. Now

Ray regretted his foothold, because he mashed a fresh crust of mud, a clue to the elusive water line he'd been finding and losing and finding again for the past several minutes. Scrutinizing the streambed, he found unexpected evidence of the flood release's power even this far up canyon. Dry grasses were flattened, caked in clumped soil, and bent toward the canyon wall rather than downstream. Ray snapped a picture, scribbled a note, then yanked a single tufted stalk sample, scattering its seed pods. He didn't recognize the type of grass but knew it would be of inscrutable significance to Jenny. He looked for her as he started up the sandy streambed.

Instead, Duke appeared. "Have you seen Carol? We were working together when she said something about these grasses bothering her allergies. When I turned around, she'd disappeared."

Ray shook his head. "Do you recognize all this tufted stuff?"

"Sorry, I'm not so good with native grasses." He removed his sunglasses, peering close to the stalk. Then he peered just as intently into Ray's eyes, smiling, shy, but holding his stare. "I've got to get more intimate with them, though."

There it was again, *intimate*. Whatever was going on between them, it didn't seem so abstract now. After the canyon, would Duke carry him off to his ranger cabin where they'd patrol the desert on horseback by day and snuggle in a bedroll all night?

"Jenny wanted me and Carol to collect samples under that escarpment over there," Duke said, pointing upriver. "I guess I better finish by myself."

"Holler if you see Jenny," Ray called after him, faking nonchalance. Had Duke really been there, dark eyes staring into his, or was it an overheated hallucination?

He spotted Carol in the distance, hiking out of the

offending grass. Completely alone, Ray became aware of a phenomenon unknown to this group, peace and quiet. Nature's sounds rose up, the faint breeze stirring the coyote willow, the chittering swifts, and the river's constant plashing rush. Ray plucked a mud clump sample already dry enough to crumble at his touch—which felt wrong, as if he were contaminating evidence at a crime scene.

At that moment, Glen laughed again, followed by Tess's hysterical squeal, faint and much farther upriver. Ray imagined the two of them inventing something funny out of the shared shampoo. It didn't take much to make Tess helpless victim to her own bloodcurdling laughter. Ray crouched to measure the crusty mud edge and continue his notes, juggling tape measure and clipboard awkwardly on his own. Where had everyone gone? And wasn't Tycho supposed to be joining them by now?

After a few minutes of wishing he had three arms, with pencil in his teeth, tape measure under his sandals while he bent to stretch the tape from streambed to mud line, Ray wished Duke had stayed on to help him. As Ray imagined the ranger bending close as they measured the release's reach, Duke's hand grazing his own, he heard a thrashing in the catclaw grove up the side canyon. Jenny appeared, immediately coming to Ray's side and holding the tape to free him to note measurements.

"Have you seen Carol?" she asked. "I lost her way up the canyon. Did she pass by here?"

"She just left the grassy area over there. Allergy attack."

"Ray, I've got to tighten up this crew. We're scattered all over hell this morning."

"Well, maybe it's a good sign. The volunteers are sure concentrating on their work. I know what it's like, Jen, to lose myself tracking all this exciting mud."

Jenny smiled, but it died quickly. "I just worry someone's

going to get injured, especially in this heat, and—hey, what's going on?" Jenny pointed toward the river. "Wasn't that Annette, running like hell?"

"With Faith right behind her. Maybe they actually saw the mountain lion they've been hoping to spot."

"Somebody's yelling. That's Hannah!" Jenny let go of the tape measure, and it slapped back under the metal spool at Ray's feet. "I better check this out."

She was gone, sprinting along the streambed, leaving Ray to gather his scattered field equipment and hurry off behind her. He bounded along the riverbank, noticing the lunch table had been abandoned, a cheese block still uncovered, the knife halted in mid-slice. Glen's paperback mystery, *The Ghost Journey*, was floating face-down like a drowned corpse in the shallow water beside his dory. Ray bolted upstream toward the commotion of voices.

He hustled over the rock outcrop that sheltered the sandy strand and, reaching the top, saw that all the pandemonium had already shriveled to stillness. Below him, all eyes raised, shielding sun-blinded brows to see who was next to reach the improbable scene.

Fifteen feet below a sheer hunk of rock, several yards down the beach, Jack Carne lay motionless, blood still leaking from the gash beside his right temple. Above where Jack's blood seeped into the sand, Tycho stood, arms around a silenced Tess, who buried her face in Tycho's bare chest, her hair wet, her chest heaving, and her face a mixture of tears and relief.

Glen comforted Hannah, who stood farthest upstream. Faith and Annette, just downstream, hugged each other. Between them, Jenny and Carol stood side by side, squeezing each other's hands. All turned as the final straggler appeared. Duke clambered over the talus slope behind the beach, lugging his pack, a pencil still between his teeth. He peered over Hannah's shoulder to punctuate the silence with hard, strangled breaths.

From the impressions in the sand immediately below the outcropping, Ray noticed odd circles of footsteps leading to and from the fanned, scooped shapes that looked like a large child had made a snow angel in soft sand, smooth and fresh from the flood release. From the sand angel, two straight lines plowed several yards down the beach, grooved into the sand, one slightly deeper than the other, twin trails that ended at Jack's sandaled feet.

Jack's sprawled legs were slightly bent, his arms dangling beside his torso. Since the moment his body had been dragged across the beach, his position must have remained as fixed as a fossil's.

CHAPTER 6

Mile 50 to Mile 52

JENNY appreciated Faith's attempt to lighten the gloom when they first rowed into the Bright Angel Shale around Mile 50. It had to do with Glen's briefly losing hold of his oars in an easy riffle, the revenge of heaven's angels, and the name *Dirty Devil*, but Jenny couldn't hear it all. Polite chuckles sank back to dead silence.

Their talk and laughter had expired with Jack's last breath. They'd drifted eight flat miles since they'd set Jack's body on the raft, listening to the oars' slow swash. Jenny imagined her own jittery heartbeat mixing with the rhythm of Faith and Glen's breathing.

Now Glen's voice, drifting over from *Last Chance*, echoed above the river's refrigerated, steady murmur. Whatever he said was lost to distance, the unnatural wall of hushed unease, and the deadening, fake tranquility imposing itself over the entire party. Glen tried to break the spell with a brief lecture about the composition of the Bright Angel shale, its odd greenish tint, and its many fossilized trilobites and worms. Alone in *Last Chance*'s bow, Hannah groaned at the mention of worms, a message more vivid and clear than any of Glen's words.

Jack's death had disturbed Hannah deeply, a fact that

surprised Jenny. Inconsolable, she'd shaken in Glen's arms for long minutes before they shoved off from Little Bert's. With Glen and Duke's counsel, Jenny had gently encouraged Hannah to ride with Glen. She'd assigned Ray to ride with Tycho on the raft, which held Jack's body zipped in his sleeping bag, covered by a plastic tarp. The corpse made a heap in the space left by the lost satellite phone box, two days of meals, and the six-packs of beer Jack had consumed.

After Ray and Duke had carried the body away, the group left the beach at Little Bert's. While Glen urged everyone to help prepare the boats, Jenny had taken time to study the marks in the sand. The formless, sandy footsteps told Jenny almost nothing, the trampling of arriving onlookers eradicating those of Jack's departing attacker. Tess said she saw Jack "diving" for her "from out of nowhere" but probably from the rock ledge above. She claimed to have blacked out immediately. Coming to, she was puzzled to find Jack's body yards from where he seemed to have attacked her.

But Tess was unharmed, just scared and contradictory in her confusion. Jack himself had been attacked from behind. It would have been difficult for Tess to inflict a bloody gash on Jack's temple, supine as she claimed to have been after the attack and armed only with the plastic shampoo bottle. And if Jack's attacker had tried to save Tess from Jack's attack, why hadn't he or she simply fessed up?

The unyielding lemon sky hazing over the ceaseless, overheated afternoon dissolved any coherence in Jenny's search for answers. Glen's voice droned on from slightly downriver, undaunted by few signs of interest from his passengers. Tess and Annette sat in *Last Chance*'s stern as stone-faced as shale.

In the windless heat, Jenny's mind drifted into doldrums of suspended tension. In a chasm defined by its play of light and shadow, the green-gray Bright Angel formation seemed to have lost all contrast. As they approached the steep walls nearer to the Nankoweap delta, the seductive variety of colors, layers, and shapes that defined the canyon grew dreary.

Jenny tried to identify or even find her own feelings, a difficult task in the most ordinary circumstances. Her ex-husband had sometimes complained that she was "like a guy" in her inexpressiveness, except when he complained that she was too self-expressive. "You'll just have to look at what I do, that's what counts," she used to say. "My actions show my feelings more clearly than words." But today this argument doubled back to curse her, since she could not interpret herself to herself, and her actions, the autopilot efforts of a crew leader, felt disconnected from her inner turmoil.

Despite what might have seemed determination and competence in her management of the group at Little Bert's, an unsteady contradiction of numbness and confusion seesawed in her guts. Since Tycho, Annette, and Faith comforted Tess in the immediate aftermath of the attack, Jenny's first impulse had been to take care of Carol's needs, to separate her from the group and provide peace and time enough to absorb the reality of Jack's death.

Yet while Carol had seemed to appreciate Jenny's concern, she also mostly ignored it. Carol had immediately charged into her emergency nurse mode, investigating the gash in Jack's temple with clinical interest, commenting on the probable direction of the blow, wondering at the lack of blood flow, and openly marveling that even such a direct strike to the skull had really been dire enough to kill him. Before Jenny could usher everyone else back to the boats, Carol began to strip Jack's clothing in search of bruises or wounds. Finding none, she helped Ray and Duke cover the body when they arrived with the sleeping bag and tarp. Even after that burst of professional bustle, Carol declined all offers of time apart.

She helped to load lunch supplies and equipment on the supply raft alongside Jack's corpse. Then, after boarding *Dirty Devil*, Carol had slipped into silence, inscrutable under her cap and sunglasses.

The moment Ray and Duke set Jack's body onto the raft, Annette had abruptly bolted from her position beside Hannah on *Last Chance*. Throwing aside her life vest, she scrambled out of the dory. She sprinted beyond the beach at Little Bert's, disappearing into the coyote willow. Jenny loped after her, tracing her path into the brush until she found Annette cowering in a shady clearing. Head hunched over her upraised knees, she sobbed in the sand.

Jenny had crouched beside her, putting her arm over Annette's bare shoulders. She could not understand the phrase Annette kept muttering as she shook her head slowly from side to side. "What is it, honey?"

"I can't…" Annette caught gulps of air, then swiped her tear-dribbled cheeks with the back of her hand. "Jenny, I can't go on down. I just can't."

"Down? Down the river?"

"How can we just keep going like this? As if nothing happened. With Jack's body on the raft."

"I know, Am—" She stopped herself, stealing back "Amelia." "I know, Annette. But we have to. We can't stay here, right?"

"Did someone come down from the rim?" She looked upward. "Like those gun show creeps at Lee's Ferry?"

"That's impossible. This box canyon ends in a jumble of huge boulders. It's all topped by hundreds of feet of sheer wall. Above that, there are hundreds of square miles of roadless wilderness. There's no trail to the rim from here or anywhere nearby. The only way in or out is on the river." Jenny squeezed Annette closer, then let go and stood, extending her hand. "We have to get to Phantom Ranch as soon as possible and report what's happened. It's only thirty more river miles."

"I just feel so bad. I was so mean to Jack. From the very beginning and even just before he died. I never gave him a chance. Preaching about cigarettes. Teasing him about his 'little thing.' He was just being a lech, you know, like most guys. I didn't have to make a federal case out of it."

Annette stood, dabbing at the last of her tears. Her eyes red-rimmed, she stared ahead, fixed straight toward the river's glimmer through the gray-green foliage. "I can be too self-righteous sometimes." She raised her cap and forced her stray, dark hair back into its ponytail, then screwed the brim down tight. "I know I can be the insufferable preppy princess, but I've been trying to change, Jenny. I just want you know. Testing my courage. Working extra hard. Getting my nails dirty." She finally smiled. "Even broken. Look."

"You've been great, Annette." Jenny clasped her hand. "No traces of any preppy princess. And I'm not surprised. I knew you were up to this. That's why I wanted you along for the project."

"Thanks. And I'm sorry about freaking out. I've just never seen anyone dead before."

When Jenny led Annette back to the dories, she seemed to be herself again. Yet when Jenny guided her into *Last Chance*, her bare back felt corpse-cold against Jenny's hand, and her chin still trembled like that of a child fresh from an unexpected plunge into the deep end.

"Jenny?" Faith called as *Dirty Devil* scooted beside *Last Chance* through a calm stretch. Overheated from her efforts, Jenny glanced again at Carol, who appeared to doze beside her in the stern. She tried to concentrate on Faith's question.

"Are we still going to pull in at Nankoweap, then? It's coming up around the bend."

"We still have several hours of daylight. I think we should go on to the Little Colorado."

"What about our rendezvous with the Canadians?" Faith asked. "Don't we need to exchange data and check in, since we've lost our phone?"

"We can't count on any rendezvous." Jenny glanced past Faith for a glimpse of Duke, brooding alone in *Dirty Devil*'s bow. "Nothing was ever definite with the hydrology crew. I'd like to get as far as the Little Colorado River before dark. There's a chance of sending word out with someone who might have hiked the trail from the rim above the confluence."

"But who are we going to send word to?" Duke asked.

Why was Duke being so dense? "Well, to the park authorities, right? Via some sheepherder with a cell phone or tourist up on the rim who's taking a drive back to Highway 89. Then an investigator can meet us at Phantom Ranch." Jenny was amazed at how rational and organized she sounded. Would anyone else share that impression?

It did seem imperative to hurry to Phantom Ranch, where a small tourist settlement promised phone service, a ranger station, and a footbridge to the nine-mile path leading uphill to park headquarters on the South Rim. "And we'll need an expert medical examination of the body."

"Didn't Carol already examine Jack, Jenny?" Faith asked. "Isn't she an expert?"

Was she, really? "I still need to file an official report."

"I'm an investigator myself," Duke said. "Since I'm a federal ranger, you can file a report directly to me. That kind of police work is part of my responsibility, anyway. If I weren't on this trip, I might even be one of the Park Service team coming down at Phantom."

Was that right? Jenny flickered between discomfiture and annoyance. She didn't want to make Duke feel undervalued, but didn't he understand he himself was a suspect just like everyone else was? And surely he wasn't going to pull rank over federal bureau protocols. It just didn't seem like Duke's style. Careful to moderate her tone, she said, "Then I guess I should defer to your plan, Duke."

"I didn't mean to step on your toes, Jenny. You've handled every aspect of this trip well as our group leader, and I think you should continue to be in charge. Just let me know how I can help."

"I'm just concerned that we stand a better chance at Nankoweap," Faith said, "where we might contact the park rangers with the Canadians' phone."

"I understand." Jenny took a deep breath. "But if I'm going to stay in charge, my decision is to go on past Nankoweap. Even if we can't make contact on the rim at the Little Colorado, we can still make a late meal, sleep, and hurry to Phantom Ranch tomorrow."

"Tomorrow?" Faith looked incredulous. "Jenny, we wouldn't reach Granite Gorge until evening. We can't run those rapids in the dark."

"Well, if we don't make the gorge by twilight, we can camp there and run them the following morning at dawn. Which comes at five thirty in the morning these days. As group leader, it's my duty to get to that ranger station as soon as possible. I've got a suspicious death to report."

"*Suspicious?*" For the first time, Carol spoke up, after a cough. "Are you sure? You might say *inexplicable*. But suspicious?"

This inspired Duke and Faith to nod simultaneously, another baffling instance of agreement among these three contentious souls. Jenny was nonplussed by the lack of overt support and confused by their lack of urgency, especially Carol's. But it was Jack, after all, who finally settled the issue.

From the supply boat, just upriver, came a strangled, hawking expulsion.

Seated on the pile of river bags, Ray was gesturing toward Tycho, who had abandoned rowing and was bent far over the raft's outer tube. "He's really sick!" Ray yelled. "Puking his guts out." While Tycho leaned back, gulping in air, Ray hurried to grab the oars and steady the raft. "And Jack's body is bloating up, all gurgly. Unbelievable, just in the last hour. And guys, I'm sorry to say it, but Jack doesn't smell so good, either."

❖

JENNY hovered over the fresh grave at Nankoweap. Along with Jack's body, the heaped earth buried a tactical mistake. She was sure of it.

Still, she understood Ray and Tycho's objection to enduring Jack's rapid decomposition in the relentless heat. When she wondered aloud if room for the body might be made in one of the dories' undersides, naturally refrigerated by the cold river in the cross hatch, she encountered a wall of objection from Faith, Duke, and Glen. Where would they store the displaced food and beverages? What if the body's fluids contaminated the remaining produce and dairy? Even Carol had joined in. "The sooner buried, the safer the perishables."

The safer the perishables? How could Carol be so pragmatic, so blasé? Jenny reminded everyone the trip was essentially over, and that if they did reach Phantom Ranch by the following day, among their many new problems would be the disposal of a two-week food supply. The four oracles fell into silence. So fierce was their sudden solidarity that Jenny kept her own silence about her alternative plan. However bizarre and disrespectful it might seem, it made sense to troll Jack's body in the preserving chill of the river until they reached Granite Gorge's lineup of steep, precarious rapids.

But Carol settled all these issues and halted their descent into black comedy by requesting her husband be buried at Nankoweap. The moment the three craft arrived in the vicinity of its soaring, narrow shale chasm, Carol sighed and announced her widow's prerogative. "Please, let Jack rest here."

Now everyone but Jenny, Carol, and Hannah remained around the disturbed earth of Jack's grave. After Ray, Duke, Glen, Annette, and Tycho took turns digging the rocky granulated shale, bandanas over their noses and mouths, they'd lowered the corpse in haste. Jack's sleeping bag served as shroud and casket. With the damper sand already drying in the blazing heat, the grave's outlines vanished.

In a secluded spot above Nankoweap Creek, a bare oval between tamarisk fringe and a screen of coyote willow, the entire group had gathered to offer their last respects, only to stand itchy and embarrassed by the lack of heartfelt eulogy, fond memories, or generous praise. In their caps, nylon shorts, smudged T-shirts, and river sandals, the mourners looked more like wilted schoolkids waiting for the bus after a field trip.

Staring into the smoothed-over soil, Carol was stone faced, whether in serene acceptance or profound sorrow Jenny had no clue. Glen muttered a valiant attempt at memorializing Jack's eternal resting place. "At least the poor guy's already in heaven."

Hannah, split-browed with irritation at the tongue-tied group, had scolded everyone for forgetting their prayers. She attempted to lead everyone in what Jenny imagined must be some Episcopalian prayer for the dead. All bowed their heads, and a few moved their lips, but Jenny had resolutely kept her agnostic head high, trying to offer Jack's spirit peaceful, soothing passage into the unknown. Hannah interrupted her own prayer with more tears. When Carol shuffled to her side, taking Hannah under her sinewy arm, everyone else gradually shuffled away, as if the distraction had given them tacit permission to ditch the scene.

While Hannah wept, her shoulders hunched in Carol's embrace, warm yet detached, Jenny wrestled with her own devils. The depth of Hannah's feeling sideswiped her, this cascade of sorrow for a man she'd only known for a few days. How often had Jenny sat in various Denver chapels and cathedrals, during funerals for departed members of the complex Pinch dynasty—old, young, cancerous, AIDS-stricken, suicidal, or pulverized in car wrecks—beside a dried-eyed, composed, even crusty Hannah?

Hannah's tears also made Jenny think about her own relative composure. Or maybe the depth of her denial. Despite the rank reality of his corpse, she hadn't yet absorbed the fact of Jack's death. In her numbness, this fresh grave might as well belong to this delta's ancient tribes—a curiosity, a pit stop for archeologists.

Jenny had insisted that the gravesite be several hundred yards above the highest point of the flood release, likely undisturbed by any future artificial or natural deluge. Now she wrestled with her shameful regret that they would never study mud lines or impacts on plant ecology here, in the most interesting spot yet for data collection, where natural floods once formed the wide fan of Nankoweap Creek. Forced back to the reality of Jack's burial by Hannah's renewed sobs, Jenny recomposed herself, dusted by her own guilt. Maybe Andrew Pinch Jr. was right. Was there a dead zone inside her as expressionless as poor Jack Carne?

When Hannah quieted, Carol leaned down to the grave, scooped a handful of the drying dirt and, making a sieve of her fingers, let it slip slowly back to the earth. She smoothed the rough welts left by the small, collapsible shovel with her downturned palm and blew a kiss. Carol linked hands with Hannah and walked away to join the others.

Left alone with what was left of Jack, Jenny wondered why the tenderness of Carol's gesture left her so unmoved. Had she smoothed her husband's grave to honor him or to further conceal its placement?

As Jenny paced back along the creek bed caked and cracked by mud from the flood release, she tried to turn off the data-collecting mode her mind seemed to switch on without effort. She deliberately ignored the mud below for the eventful sky above. The early evening scattered tangerine embers above Nankoweap's steep, wraparound formations. Across the canyon, a red beacon flickered its unintelligible semaphore, the dipping sun reflected in a high glint of quartzite. A strong breeze kicked up the river's chasm, fluting the long, lazy Nankoweap Rapid.

Aware her eyes were brimmed with tears, Jenny first blamed the rising wind. Then she slipped, clumsy and bleary eyed in the creekside mud surges. Damn, she really was crying. She flicked off her tears with her fists exactly as Annette had done upriver at Little Bert's. That was it, wasn't it? The same emotions, Annette's momentary fright and self-disgust, doubled inside Jenny. Half of her was reduced to a skittish girl, scared of being judged as pampered, spoiled, and incompetent, the other half yearning to mother another lost daughter, to be the one who soothed, who kissed the bruise. With the magic of love and comfort, that half would heal broken spirits and protect young girls from the savagery of the human heart.

How had it ever come to this, that she'd had to take flight from wifehood and motherhood in order to prove she wasn't scared of proving herself? Jenny splashed her face with creek water before she eased her way to the docking site. When she reached the dories, expecting to unleash *Dirty Devil* and jump aboard for their evening float to the Little Colorado, she found instead a well-organized kitchen brigade in full progress. Hannah was already unfolding the table, and Glen was connecting the stove to the propane tank. "Aren't we having dinner at the Little Colorado?" Jenny asked their backs. "Wouldn't it be more efficient to set up camp and the kitchen at the same time?"

Then she spotted Tycho tossing river bags onto the beach while Duke hoisted a huge dry sack of sleeping bags. "Oh. I see. Thanks for checking with me, guys."

Glen turned to her, turning off the hissing propane line while Hannah unfolded the stovetop. "Sorry, but it was a spontaneous decision. Everybody's starving, Jenny. We didn't really have any lunch."

"And are you sure we should head downriver now, against this strong upstream breeze?" Faith asked from the end of the brigade, setting down the cookware box.

"Anyway," Hannah said, "pretty soon it would be impossible to get much farther. It's just going to be too dark."

❖

RAY watched Jenny burrow deeper into her sleeping bag, zipped full to the top clasp. She even tried to pull the drawstrings shut, leaving only a burka-like slit for her eyes.

He missed Jenny's company already and wondered if he would ever fall asleep. Clawing under the tarp and blasting sand over the top of his head, the breeze had swelled to a strong, steady wind. It sheared away the last of the day's haze so that the stars blazed, twinkling insanely, impossibly abundant across the delta's wider sky.

"Ray?" Jenny whispered, almost inaudible against the sand blast. "How are you doing over there?"

"Hoping I could smother myself to a welcome death," he stage-whispered across the inches that separated them. "This is the worst. I think this place is haunted."

"Normally, this is one of my favorite camps."

"It's weird, Jenny." Ray shuffled closer, lowering his voice even more. "I keep thinking of the way that dinner just coalesced. The old cliché of life going on. Right under those empty stores of ancient native granaries up the canyon wall. It was so tribal. You know?"

"No. I don't. Not if you're saying it happened because of some programmed neurological principle, just because you've been studying that research for your play. Because if you say it, you'll get that welcome death when I pummel your skinny butt. I'm still pissed off at the way everyone defied me. Even you."

"I'm sorry. We were wrong not to wait for you. But it wasn't neurology. It was mostly plain, honest hunger. What could be more human than that?"

"Don't ask me. It pisses me off when people apologize for indulgence by pleading that it was so *human*."

Ray shuffled again. He could feel her arm poking into his back through the thickness of both sleeping bags. "My butt is not that skinny. Is it?"

"Kind of. But it's still cute, Ray."

Smothered by polyfill, their conversation stopped for good after that. Jenny shuffled farther apart, her back to him. Ray lay still in the disquiet of unwanted solitude, listening to the up canyon gusts, so pestilential and punishing. Alone again with the wind and stars, he wondered where Duke had gone to sleep and whispered to Jenny, asking if she'd noticed.

She didn't answer, probably drifted off into dreams. Or nightmares.

Ray whispered Duke's name, hoping he had settled nearby, but he failed to respond. Under the wind's roar, he thought he heard nearby stirring.

Tonight's camp had gathered closer than usual, compact in the moonless dark across a sandy beach just above the tethered boats. Sharing a single tarp, Annette, Hannah, and Carol slept in a cluster nearby. Faith and Glen, nestled on their rocking dories, would be keeping watch over Tycho and Tess, who slept side by side in the supply raft.

A short hike up the side canyon, the wind must be scattering the sand over Jack's burial site. Ray had a vivid vision of the wind stripping all the soil off the shallow grave. Jack's corpse would mock life itself. In fearsome imitation of gastrointestinal digestion, living bacteria would chew up the guts of the dead host. Exposed to the elemental gusts just as the survivors were, hunched in his sleeping bag in their same wind-driven position, Jack would feel nothing but nothingness.

Okay, that was enough spooky stuff. Ray tried to ignore what sounded like footfalls just above his head. Most definitely audible, even against another shriek of wind.

Someone was hovering over him. Ray could practically count the steady breaths, distinct against the random wind blasts. Then a whisper. "Hey, mind if I join you again tonight?"

Duke didn't wait for an answer. His sleep gear thudded nearby.

"Glad to have company." Ray sat up, watching Duke hurry into his sleeping bag right next to him. He felt grateful to be so snug between the ranger and Jenny. "One of us has got to stay awake and stand guard," he whispered, "and I think Jenny's out for the night."

"Okay. I'll take the first shift, if you'd like to get some shut-eye."

Ray smiled. "It's okay. I reckon I'll be awake for a while."

"I do feel zonked. Emptied. I was down by the river just now, sitting on a rock, trying to think this through."

Really, in this howling wind? Ray kept the question to himself.

"I can't get past the simplicity of it," Duke said.

"You mean that one of our crew whacked Jack in the head?"

"Yeah. It's not exactly complicated."

"Was it an accident?" Ray asked. "Or a fit of rage?"

"Or done to protect Tess?"

"And what else is this person among us capable of? How do we manage this, Duke? I'm sure everyone is feeling endangered. I know I am. Do we just try to keep everyone safe and everything shipshape and get to Phantom Ranch as quick as we can?"

Duke didn't respond. Ray heard only his sleeping bag's zipper. Then he felt Duke's hand, touching his face and slipping down to his neck. Gentle. Ray unzipped his bag from the inside, enough to clasp Duke's fingers in his.

They said nothing. Soon Duke was breathing softly in even rhythm. Bludgeoned by exhaustion, Ray fought the urge to shut his eyes. He squeezed Duke's hand as if it could keep him from sinking into a chasm of sleep.

CHAPTER 7

Mile 62

RAY had no doubt Jenny would trot up the switchback trail to the canyon rim without stopping, even in noon's inferno. Before Hannah set out the sandwich board near the confluence of the Little Colorado River, Jenny began to hustle along the smooth, creamy rocks lining the turquoise tributary, two liters of water strapped like six-guns at her hips.

Trail running was what Jenny did for fun in the San Francisco Mountains above Flagstaff. It was what she'd called her "great escape" from Andrew Pinch Jr. when she lived in Denver, dashing up foothills trails and peaks, paying no attention to summits' altitudes or summer heat. Jenny's physical condition and ferocious determination made Ray feel decrepit in his early twenties, eating her dust on extreme after-work runs.

Making their sandwiches, Faith and Glen continued to debate the wisdom of Jenny's solo attempt to make contact above while the crew awaited the Canadians' approach below. "I told Jenny there's nothing up there," Glen was saying, pointing to the inner canyon's rim, a thousand feet above the confluence. He squinted into the noon sun, shoving back his cap brim for a better view. "She'll be lucky if she spots a stray sheep."

"She's right about tourists, though." Faith paused to bite into her sandwich. "They sometimes wander down from the Navajo reservation's back roads."

"What fool would be hiking in this heat?" Glen asked.

Ray watched Jenny scramble up the faint rim trail, her red T-shirt a bright speck in the bronze sandstone wall. Just before scrambling away, Jenny had squeezed his hand and kissed his cheek, the departing general blessing her lieutenant. Then she'd whispered her instructions. "Help Duke keep an eye on Tycho and Carol, and keep everybody together and safe. I'm counting on you, Ray."

The reluctant lieutenant surveyed his charges, the assembled party arranging itself on the sleek slickrock near the confluence. Only Carol sat by herself, in the shade of a boulder, with the Greenpeace cap pulled down low over her brow. Tycho, Tess, and Annette clustered together on the bank, holding their sandwiches and dangling their feet in the tributary's warm water. Faith, Glen, and Duke stood around the sandwich board while Hannah helped herself to the ample remains. "There's plenty for seconds," Hannah cried out, her gravelly tone reverberating through the side canyon. "We might as well enjoy this now, relax and get some nutrients into our systems, eh? Jenny hurried us through breakfast so fast, it's a wonder no one got sick. And we don't need another sick person on board, do we?"

No one responded to Hannah's call except Tycho, who hurried to replace the sandwich he'd just devoured with another. Hannah's comment struck Ray as supreme bad taste, considering Carol's silent, solitary mourning. The sarcasm echoed a crack Hannah had made earlier, while Jenny had made a sandwich to take to the rim, that Jenny's insistence on "starvation rations" at breakfast in Nankoweap "treated the rest of us just like her poor husband and kid." Though this inaccurate and unaccountable slam had been delivered with a hearty sardonic laugh, Ray didn't get Hannah's so-called humor at Jenny's expense—or where the last vestige of yesterday's weepy, religious Hannah had gone. Acting like the Ex-Mother-In-Law-from-Hell was actually what had cleared the breakfast crowd. Now everyone ate lunch in unresponsive silence except for Duke, who'd brought Carol a sandwich and engaged her in a halting, inaudible conversation in the boulder's shade.

Choosing to stand on a higher outcrop between the youthful cluster on the bank and the older group around the table, Ray decided the silence was not eloquent but stifled. The group's natural humor and sympathy was squelched by the gaseous antimatter of Thoughts Unsaid leading to Conclusions Inescapable. One of their company had committed a murder; one of their company was capable of killing again; and any one in their reduced company could again be either perpetrator or victim. Ray would keep an especially close watch on Tycho, who could easily slip away unseen, unleash the supply raft, and disappear downriver into whatever oblivion he could reach.

Ray had no idea what to say to help the group regain its voice. The Little Colorado sang its dancing gush through its wide, sun-blasted side canyon. The tributary's unworldly, dreamlike blue heightened the moment's uncanny quality. Azure pools beckoned like a fantasy Caribbean. Bleached, soft rocks rippled under the water's light sapphire sheen.

Ray recalled just such a silence when he'd visited the documentary drama project's co-author, a neurologist, at his university hospital laboratory. While Ray got the feel of the study team's environment, as playwright-researcher he observed real-time video close-ups of a dead murderer's brain being sliced. In the video lab, the scientists did nothing more overt than call for better resolution or crack black gallows jokes. At lunch, though, after they'd studied the flesh and blood subject, the team's conversation strangled itself, not really silence but a buzzing disconnection from full feeling. A post-cadaver disquietude.

As if unable to suffer their wordless lunch for another moment, Glen began an impromptu lecture. He bit into the last of his apple and used the core as a prop, pointing it upstream for emphasis. "The Little Colorado maintains this unreal color when the water's low, which is most of the time. With such unreliable sources of moisture, its gets milky from calcium carbonate and shows off this crazy blue that would look phony even in Las Vegas."

"But watch out during a flash flood," Faith said, taking Glen's arm to steady herself on the rock ledge he'd chosen as his lectern. "Then it's an angry, ugly, muddy surge of sheer power." The group overcame its after-lunch torpor, all eyes idly focused now on Faith. "So much silt comes down this side canyon, so many megatons of sediment, that landforms way down river can be transformed forever."

"In full, raging pour, back in 1869," Glen added, "this little creek inspired Powell's men to think it was a portal to hell itself."

"Hey, man, it sure looks like heaven to me," Tycho said, standing, twisting himself as he tore out of his T-shirt, then arched to flip head-first and backward into the impossible blue. Tess squealed, bloodcurdling as ever, and dove straight in, her dark skin shadowlike as she scooted and looped through white shallows.

"Wait for me!" Annette cried, cutting a smooth, elegant dive into a turquoise pool.

Duke and Carol rose from their shady chat to stand on the bank, staring at the opposite shore. "See that fresh water line opposite?" Duke asked, pointing. "Imagine the force of flood release to scour rocks way up there."

"I wonder how far back into this drainage it surged," Glen said, glancing upstream. "Or how long it took for this warm, baby blue tributary to flush out the big, cold, dark green invading river. There's got to be so much the project could learn from the sand and soils that must've boiled up."

It was as if their three days of research upriver had already habituated the crew, all fingers now itching to trace the mudflows and waterlines and altered habitat in every side canyon.

"It's a shame we can't take a few notes here," Faith said, "since we've got to wait for Jenny anyway."

"What's to stop us?" Carol said, rising from her shady retreat. "We've got all our equipment, and we know what to do, don't we?"

"Well, I guess we do," Glen said, a giddy lilt in his voice as he joined Faith and Carol at the supply raft. Duke hopped up to get his measuring tape and notebook from *Dirty Devil*.

Ray didn't know what on earth to do now. How could he keep everyone together if the whole crew was going to scatter up the side canyon to swim or perform improvised research? He might press Duke for help, except the ranger seemed the most eager to start collecting data.

Meanwhile, Tess, Annette, and Tycho were battling each other for "King of the Rock" atop an almost submerged but flat-topped boulder. Tycho pressed his belly hard against the crest, a stubborn lobster pose neither Annette nor Tess could pry away. With great gurgling yelps and squeals that echoed upward into the rocky chasm, the two contenders continually fell, splashing back into the pool as Tycho hunkered down, then lashed out to secure his kingdom, slapping water and howling in triumph.

"Come on, Tycho," Annette cried, paddling back from one of his slapped strikes. She fought for her breath. "Give us a chance. Be a good sport."

"Good sport? *Good sport?*" Tycho screamed out, his tone between fun and outright rage. "Come back here, Annette! I'll show you good sport right across your dainty little bottom."

Ray was so distracted by Tycho's manic antics that he almost hadn't noticed Duke waving him forward from the bow of *Dirty Devil*. When he approached, Ray realized they were alone together behind a protruding rock, out of sight from the supply raft and *Last Chance*. "I'd love to do more research here," Duke said. "But I'm not so sure we should go ahead without Jenny's supervision."

"God, Duke, isn't the research irrelevant now? I could really use your help herding this group. At this point we've got to keep our sights on everybody."

"That's why I wanted a minute alone with you. Do we have a plan?"

"Not really. I know Jenny's hoping to enlist your, like, law enforcement expertise."

"I've had some training in police work for the Park Service, like all rangers, but I'm not exactly a detective."

"Which is what we need, detection. We've just got to get to Phantom Ranch and get in touch with professional investigators. First thing."

"Yeah." Duke sounded distracted, lowering his voice. "I also had another motive for wanting this minute alone with you. They're kind of rare on the river, aren't they?" He reached for Ray's hand and pulled him closer. "May I kiss you?"

Ray lost both his physical and psychic balance. He'd wanted this since their brief clasp of hands the night before, but a kiss seemed misplaced amid the urgency and confusion of their predicament. It felt frivolous, the very thing the moral police were forever accusing gays of being. But what the hell. He leaned in for a quick buss.

Instead, Duke pulled him close and mashed his lips against Ray's. Ray did not resist, losing himself in how his hopes became as real as the hard, slick slide of Duke's kiss—until Glen called from the supply raft, crying "What ho!"

Duke and Ray pulled apart, then hopped around the outcrop. *Last Chance* was tied farther upstream, nearer the confluence, affording a view of the open Colorado.

"We've got company, folks!" Glen shouted.

Ray and Duke scrambled to where Glen peered from a sandstone slab with a good view of two identical, official-looking rubber rafts rowing in silent syncopation on the slow, flat water. The paddlers looked oddly magnificent, mythic mariners arriving at some barbarian port of call. Even from this distance, they seemed organized and harmonious, all in crisp white tops, dark blue life vests, and khaki shorts, their paddles dipping in rhythm.

"Why on earth aren't they using outboard motors?" Faith asked as she approached, squinting upriver beside Ray. "No wonder they're so far behind where we expected them to be."

"They're Canadians," Duke said, smiling as Hannah and Carol reached the viewpoint on the slab. "Dudley Do-Rights, you know. That's what we called them in the Balkans, when they led the international peacekeepers. It's that old Mountie code. Consider all options, then choose the most demanding course of action."

"I wonder if they stopped for a good look around Nankoweap this morning," Hannah said, coming up to the lookout with Carol.

"Aren't they studying hydrology, how the release shifted

the rapids?" Carol asked. She combed back a few long, sun-bleached hairs with her fingers and tucked the strays back under her cap. "I suppose Nankoweap Rapid got all their attention."

"Which is probably why they're in paddle rafts," Glen said. "They've got to experience the big water, study it from inside, not just scoot over the surface on a power boat."

"Well, they're sure to have a satellite phone," Ray said. "We can finally get word to the Park Service."

"I don't know." Disconcertingly, Carol stretched her arm around Ray's waist. "Do we really want to get a foreign team involved in our situation?"

"Good point," Glen said. "We just don't know enough about their jurisdiction, or their chain of command, or their connection to Park Service authorities. They might get the wrong idea."

"Yeah, who knows?" Faith asked as Tess, Annette, and Tycho, wet haired and sleek skinned, crowded onto the slab. "They might question that we buried a volunteer without authorization."

"They might be suspicious," Hannah said. She tiptoed to see over Faith's shoulder as the paddle rafts came into closer view. Now she, along with Glen and Carol, waved and smiled to the Canadian team as she added, "They might wonder if it wasn't an accident."

"Why does it matter what they wonder?" Ray asked. He felt the odd force of their unity, as if they'd all agreed in advance to hide behind this single-minded fortress. "We don't know ourselves whether it was an accident." Ray felt Carol's hand squeeze tighter at his side and forced himself to say, "What's wrong with the truth? We had every good reason to bury Jack where and when we did, and we had Carol's blessing. So what have we got to hide?"

"But, Ray," Annette said, "maybe it was illegal."

"Yeah, this is a national park," Tess added.

"Oh wow," Tycho said. "We're busted!"

"Annette's got a point." Carol squeezed Ray's waist even tighter. "Who knows what federal rules we violated?"

"Nankoweap is an active archeological site," Faith said. "Sooner or later we're going to have to give a full account, but why get the Canadian team involved in it now?"

"Well, are we agreed?" Glen asked. "Now that we can see the whites of their eyes, folks, let's play it cool, in the absence of…"

"What, Glen?" Ray asked. "Reason?" He looked to Duke, expecting him to intervene now, or at least clarify federal lands policy violations. But the ranger, catching Ray's glance, winked. As if that weren't disarming enough, he grimaced in exaggerated exasperation, then turned upstream to the arriving rafts.

"Come on," Glen said, "if we can't explain the mishap at Little Bert's, even among ourselves, how can we expect these Canucks to understand? Here, let's help them dock."

❖

RAY tried not to flinch as Guy Lafever, a managing engineer for Hydro Quebec, slid his tanned arm beside Ray's. "I don't think I've ever been so bronze. Almost as dark as you, boy, eh? Wait till my wife sees this. Back home they're recovering from our most evil winter in memory. Though this research junket isn't supposed to be a holiday." Guy paused, seemingly listening to the echoing laughter and shouts from the upper chutes, where the rest of his men had fled with Annette, Tycho, and Tess to slide down the turquoise cataracts in a human train. "Most of the time it sure has felt like one, eh? The same for your crew, I suppose."

Carol jumped in before Ray could respond. "Even the research is fun," she told him, keeping close, just as Glen hovered practically shoulder to shoulder beside Ray.

He expected Jenny to return soon and dreaded the spectacle she would see. The rest of the volunteers had scattered up the drainage with the Canadians. Even Hannah dog-paddled in the lower pools, while Duke and Faith had taken two of the hydrologists on an investigation of the high water marks on the opposite shore.

"It's been a perfect vacation, blending interesting work, excitement, and play," the Widow Carne told Guy Lafever. "And when the water's flat, we have so much time to relax and reflect."

"Yes!" Guy agreed, holding out his arms to the confluence. "It has been perfect, the long stretches of rowing punctuated by the adrenaline rush of the rapids. Of course, that's where we spend our time, exploring the shifts in the rapids' rock scatter. So much had happened at House Rock alone, we spent extra time. Diving, measuring, photographing, cataloging, comparing pre-release data."

"Really?" Ray hurried to get his question in. "Did you happen to see our satellite phone box?"

When Guy Lafever revealed that he had not, Glen rushed to change the subject. "We were shocked at how much steeper that rapid seemed."

But Guy responded to Ray. "So, you've been down here without a phone? Is there any message you want me to arrange for you? We're behind schedule, so we're going to hurry on past Unkar to camp above Hance Rapid tonight."

"Luckily," Glen put in, "we're all safe and sound. At least for the time being. I just hope nobody cracks their skull sliding down these chutes."

"Yeah, and I've got to get my men back on the river before

they have too much fun with the young ladies, eh? Excuse me." Guy held up the whistle on his lanyard to blow a shrill, reverberating cry up canyon. He turned back, smiling. "They make fun of me for this, call me the overgrown Boy Scout. But it does keep us together when we need to be, eh?"

May I borrow it, then, eh? Ray thought. Better yet, did they have space on their crew for a strong and willing paddle rafter? As disparate shouting and laughter grew nearer, he entertained a flash fantasy of stowing away with the Canadians and leaving this problematic, casually mutinous—and possibly murderous—motley crew behind. Maybe they had room for both him and Duke. Wouldn't that be sweet? "Well, we won't be far behind you," Ray said. "We're picking up our pace, too. We might even see you at Phantom Ranch tomorrow evening, Guy."

"Really? Why on earth would you hurry past so many notable sites? Carbon Creek, and the side canyons in the Inner Gorge?"

"Well, same reason as you, I guess," Glen said, looking out to the main channel. "We tarried too long, enjoyed too much, and now we've got to pick up the pace or we'll never make it to Lake Mead on our supplies. We will probably stop at Unkar tonight, though, and try to give that site its due."

The bare-chested Canadians began to appear around the bend, bearing the life vests they'd used for the human train through the chutes. They pulled on their shirts, massing again, a small harmonious navy in khaki, white, and blue, and passed around paddles at their rafts. The two strays who'd wandered off with Duke and Faith swam across the stream to hop aboard.

"The real study," Carol said, "is how the canyon has been altered without modern man disturbing its solitude. Who knows what we'll see? Mountain lions bathing in the hanging gardens at Vasey's Paradise?"

"I'd love to join you for that, my dear lady," Guy said, kissing her hand, then shaking Ray's and Glen's, before taking giant steps to join his crew and hopping into a raft already paddling toward the main channel. It glided over the lush tributary past a sandbar and out into the chill, roiling dark Colorado, Guy waving as he took his place at the rear.

Ray watched the Canadians until they disappeared out of sight behind the steep, fanning formations of Cape Solitude. Didn't Carol realize their crew was already living her vision of inhuman isolation? About to confront the next deep plunge, inaccessible to all human feet or wheels, their two tiny dories and single raft would brave Granite Gorge in complete seclusion. Without phone and any other parties bringing up their rear, they were utterly alone on the river now.

CHAPTER 8

Mile 73

RAY and Jenny chaperoned from the rear as Faith led most of the crew on an evening tour of the ancient Puebloan settlement at Unkar Delta.

"Not that I'm superstitious," Jenny told Ray, "but I think I've become the target of some powerful curse. Was there a canyon god I forgot to pay homage to? A prayer I forgot?"

A thick, brooding sky roiled over the remnants of the vanished settlement. Just ahead, the volunteers followed Faith from ruin to ruin like obedient schoolchildren.

"I will thank the gods for Dr. Faith Brattle," Jenny said, scanning the clouds and gray whiskers of rain high on the Kaibab Plateau. "She's willing to focus our energies and play tour guide. Thank the gods everyone is together, engrossed, and behaving themselves. This gives me breathing time before nightfall and the prospect of another sleepless night."

Ray fully understood how desperate Jenny had been to make it over Hance and Sockdologer, the steep, complex rapids ahead, before nightfall, then to make camp in Granite Gorge before pulling into Phantom Ranch first thing in the morning. But the gods under whose curse she labored had other plans. After a smooth float through the reddish shales of the Unkar

Formation, they reached new trouble at usually innocuous Tanner Rapid. Its unexpected new channel had misled Glen into craggy shallows where *Last Chance* scraped its chine on sharp rocks. Luckily, the worthy craft did not begin to take in water in any quantity until they reached Unkar. Running its longer and steeper rapid would require some patching.

At this moment, Glen and Duke were setting the marine caulking in place. This broad, hundred-acre delta was where they had to make camp before nightfall, eight river miles shy of where Jenny wanted to be. "It's strange how Glen's story came true," Ray asked Jenny, "isn't it?"

"You mean the lie you said he told the Canadians? That we'd stop at Unkar? A meaningless coincidence, I'm sure. I hope. Unless Glen has decided to become a conspirator as well."

"Conspirator?"

"Ray, how do you think I felt when I came down that steep trail above the Little Colorado, after having seen nothing but yucca and one terrified jackrabbit? Then to watch the Canadians as they launched off, waving goodbye, around Cape Solitude? You even said everyone seemed to band against you."

"I didn't mean they were against me, exactly. They all just formed this insurmountable wall of resistance. They were determined to shut the Canadians out and not let me get a word in edgewise."

"You mentioned the lost phone, didn't you? Why couldn't you just have blurted out that one of us was killed at Little Bert's?"

"Jenny, come on. It was as if our group formed this force field to shut me out. If I went against that, I would've lost everyone's trust."

"Trust!" She lowered her voice to an exasperated hiss. "Who needs the trust of accessories to murder?"

"You're upset, Jen. You haven't had any sleep, and you're exhausted from that crazy noon hike. That's why you're sounding so paranoid now."

"You're the one who just described their 'insurmountable resistance.' Doesn't that add up to conspiracy? What do they all know that we don't? What on earth inspired their sudden togetherness? I've never known Glen to lie in his life."

"It was a white lie." Ray looked ahead to the group, which followed Faith across a grassy hilltop. Above the hilly delta, rusty conical peaks outlined the jagged panorama. After enduring Earth's instabilities for over a billion years, these geologic remains dwarfed the puny human ruins they toured.

Across a broad clearing strewn with ancient foundations, Faith was asking the group rhetorical questions about the old delta lifestyle, circa 1090 A.D. Tycho sat on a boulder, his face hidden in his hands, while Annette stood in the group's center, earnestly fielding responses to Faith's queries. Tess went over to Tycho, petting his hair.

Studying the scene, Ray turned back to Jenny. "They're scared, so they're banding together out of fear. If anything, they probably sense one of them killed Jack in Tess's defense, and they want that person to get a fair hearing before we spread misgivings among a bunch of gung-ho Canadian engineers."

Jenny cast her eyes toward the group, and she took a deep breath. "Okay, I'm willing to concede I'm overreacting. All this resistance has just eroded my confidence, okay? Like I can't trust normally levelheaded, totally reliable people to act rationally now."

"Including me?"

"Baby, I know you've done your best. But I have been turning over what you said about self-obliteration back in North Canyon. I can't have you in that state of mind now. No brokenhearted Mr. Romantic Fatalist. And no Mr. Mellow, going along with the program. And certainly no Mr. Tolerant Drama Guy, open to all facets of human nature. More than anything, I need you to find your strongest self. Because if you don't, buster," she paused, smiling sweetly as she formed a fist, "I'm gonna show you what obliteration is like."

Ray laughed, squeezing Jenny's shoulders. "Don't scare me like that, Big Mama, okay?" But hugging her, feeling her small, still-girlish frame under the bold red T-shirt, he knew her toughness was bluff. She could crack under all this pressure just as easily as anyone if she didn't have support. That was what sent her flying away from Andrew Pinch after almost twenty years of struggling behind her facade of strength and sheer will.

"Don't worry about me," Ray told her. "I'm cold-blooded and objective. Tough as schist."

"Yeah. You can cut schist with a knife."

"Okay. Make that tough as gneiss."

"Yeah, you're too damn nice, which is the whole problem. Forever searching for the humanity in everyone's disgusting little heart. We both need to apply more pure objectivity to this."

"To 'this'? What's 'this'?"

"Look, we're not going to get to Phantom Ranch before I've got Jack's death figured out, even if it's over my dead body. And it might well be. I'm willing to take that chance. We've already got a lot of explaining to do, thanks to the *white lies* Carol and Glen developed for the Canadians. I want to present the Park Service with our man or woman as soon as we dock at Phantom."

"Now you sound like a damn Mountie. Jenny, we're not detectives. Duke is in charge of law enforcement."

Jenny faced Ray, her voice vehement but still hushed.

"I know that, and I don't have any Mountie fantasies or delusions. I feel responsible to get to the truth, and not just as a group leader. As a human being, okay? I've got one of those pumping, pulpy red things in my chest, too, I just don't wear it on my sleeve. This man died on my project, almost certainly by violence. What if, just what if, whoever killed him kills again? Since you're so big on armchair psychology, Ray O'Brien, you've maybe heard the technical term *psycho*?"

"Yes, and I'm aware of whose name it rhymes with."

"Yeah?" Jenny crossed her arms, glancing toward the group as Faith moved them on to a scattering of pottery shards. "Well, I'm willing to explore this from every possible angle. My mind is wide open as this big-ass Arizona sky."

Ray smiled. "Which is trying to go dark on us. But I'm willing to try to find our way. Even through the dark. Let's do it. Let's investigate as best we can. Let's include Duke, too, soon as he's finished helping Glen patch the dory."

Jenny smiled. "And that means the three of us take every possibility, including Glen and every person wandering those ruins, as a serious suspect?"

"Yeah. And the fact that we three were last on the scene gives us the honest advantage of having a lot of questions, doesn't it?"

"Absolutely. We question everyone. One on one."

"So, how do you suggest we start? With the least likely?"

"And proceed on up to the most likely, to—"

"Tycho?"

"No, Carol! Come on. Jack was an insurance agent, Ray, isn't it obvious? She's due for a huge settlement. She can retire in wealthy comfort from one of the world's most stressful jobs."

"You think so highly of your old Society friend."

"I'm learning more every day. Most important, Carol gains all that while she rids herself of one of the world's most embarrassingly horrible husbands."

"God rest his soul. So, Carol plans this, seizing her chance when that other couple had to cancel the trip?" Ray watched as Carol, laughing at something Tycho said, balanced a clay pot shard in her palm. "She was just biding her time until the right moment to kill Jack?"

"Jack was very cooperative, leering at Tess, then molesting her. There's nothing like being married to a first-class jerk to teach you patience. They provide you with perfect moments to reveal their true selves."

"Ah, and now the real armchair psychologist reveals her true self. Chief Investigator Jenny Bridger diagnoses a murder caused by marriage to a first-class jerk."

"I can empathize. No joke. I know firsthand what drove Carol to drastic action, but it doesn't have to be about my intimacy with jerks in this case. It's just the simplest, most logical explanation being the most likely. All things being equal."

"Equal with what? The fact that we have a certified troubled youth with a criminal record and probably a neurological predilection for violence on board? Not to mention he's infatuated with the object of Jack's abuse."

"Yeah, Ray. Lucky for us, we have a fledgling expert on neurology on board, too. While you malign my theory, go ahead and construct a case around your documentary play project."

Ray laughed. "We're not doing such a great job of being coldly objective, are we?"

"I guess not." Jenny smiled, punching Ray's upper arm. "Let's put theory aside, okay? We do have a witness, kind of."

"Tess seems like a less than likely suspect, too."

"Exactly," Jenny said. "Let's start with Tess's version."

"We should probably split up, don't you think? I'll talk with Faith and Annette first chance I get."

Under the evening sky, ignited by the sun dropping straight downriver, a well-worn path led them to a site where the group assembled around Faith. She pointed toward a large clearing, encircled by stone borders. "What do you think it was, folks? Is there any way to tell? A school? A communal kitchen? A church?"

"Or," Carol asked, still fingering the sharp shard, "a graveyard?"

Jenny raised her eyebrows for Ray's benefit before she led him by the arm closer to Faith.

"What would this evidence tell us," Faith asked, as she held a shard of Tusayan pottery, "about the interrelations of these people?"

One thing it told us, Ray thought, was that Faith seemed as passionate about archeology as she was about feminism and river running. Dr. Brattle must be one hell of a force in front of a college class.

"What would it say," Faith went on, "that we could find the same decorative patterns twenty, fifty, or a hundred miles beyond this delta when you know how isolated and impassable this vast canyon is, and how tricky the transportation of people, let alone fragile pottery, must have been?"

Tycho, standing near Tess with his eyes aimed to the ground, fingered a clay fragment. He scuffed the red earth. Ray expected some blurted, off-tune sarcastic response, but instead Tycho caught Faith's question, then her eyes. "They must have cared about the same things. They must have been united."

Faith smiled. "Exactly, Tycho. These ancients must have had an open, widespread, peaceful culture, overcoming physical barriers with common language and art. These pieces of clay may be the shattered remnants of a vanished utopia, where there was harmony, not acrimony. Solidarity and sharing, not division and violence."

"Right," Tycho said. "Vanished." He fingered the fat dagger of a shard before he broke away from the group and roved alone to the next ankle-high pile of ruins. Tess followed, attempting to stroll beside him and take his hand, but he gently batted hers away. They exchanged a few words Ray couldn't hear. Tess smiled at him, but Tycho shook his head and rambled into the next ruin by himself.

Ray watched Tess wander farther off alone just as Glen called, "Jenny, Ray, Faith!" He appeared from the opposite direction, out of breath from his jog uphill from the river. "I think we got her all patched up. But I want to keep her on shore till morning. Just so the bond really cures."

"We'd be crazy not to," Faith said, locking eyes with Jenny as if she expected immediate contradiction. "With Hance Rapid right around the bend." Faith grasped her right wrist as if she'd just lost a bracelet, but Ray knew, via Jenny, what Faith had really lost at Hance years ago. Her confidence. "And nightfall is going to spring on us like a trap in less than an hour."

"And you expect an argument from me?" Jenny said, glancing back where Tess wandered downhill, toward Unkar Rapid, by herself. "Okay, then I'll argue for the other side. Let's take a leaky dory over one of the most dangerous rapids in the canyon in the falling dark."

"So, we'll set up camp here?" Glen said, answering his own question by starting back to the landing.

"Why sure," Jenny called to his retreat. "And, really, thanks for checking, pal. Makes me feel like one of them genuine leader types."

"I'm sorry," Faith said, hugging Jenny's shoulders. "None of us have been acting very rational, and I know what a pain we've been. Nothing like a crisis to show how many cooks you've really got spoiling your pot, huh? I know how anxious you are to get to Phantom Ranch."

"Ah, hell, it'll still be there tomorrow," Jenny said, patting Faith's back. At that point, what was left of the united group disbanded. Hannah called for tonight's kitchen helper, Carol, to join her at the landing. Annette and Faith hurried to help Glen and Duke unload the dories.

Ray realized he should go to Tycho and persuade him to join the unloading brigade. It would be far better than leaving his prime suspect alone, brooding in the ruins of a vanished utopia.

❖

JENNY traced the trail Tess had taken through the ruins, as if searching for a lost daughter through a ghost neighborhood.

More compelling to Jenny than the ancient tribe's architecture or their supposed utopian community life was the agriculture of this vanished village. Here, where the sediments were so ungiving, where torturous winds scraped mesquite bare, today's only crop would be prickly pear cactus. Yet if she had been pursuing Tess eight centuries ago, archeologists believed Jenny would have been hacking her way through cornfields and skirting bean poles.

Jenny found Tess at the barren edge of a delta, sitting cross-legged alone on a boulder above Unkar Rapid. The sun was sinking between the canyon walls downriver, igniting Tess's hair in profile, a sun-bleached aureole. The rapid's swooping roar created an odd pocket of silence in which Jenny could observe Tess close up while she remained unobserved. Tess's gaze remained fixed on the setting sun in the distance.

Tess's beauty seemed exaggerated tonight, exotic. It was as if Jenny had wandered through the high crops and come upon this survivor, a living remnant of those extinguished, golden people, her beauty all the more overwhelming because of her lack of affect. Her silken, resilient skin reflected the honeyed light. The high, almost Asiatic cheekbones of subarctic Finland combined with the full, sensual lips of sub-Saharan Africa gave her the aspect of an earthbound angel stranded on this rock.

But Tess's expression did not register angelic serenity. Frowning, her mouth scrunching as if to surrender to a bout of tears, Tess tried to raise a smile when she finally noticed Jenny's approach. But the smile failed and tears proceeded.

Tess slipped readily into Jenny's open arms and sobbed gently on her shoulder. "Sorry, Jenny. I knew you wouldn't want me to wander off by myself." She broke the embrace, brushing the tears away. "But I just wanted to listen to the rapid for a while."

"I don't blame you, Tess. And I didn't want to bother you, but I was worried." There was Mother Jenny again. How often that tone had escaped from her vocal cords through all the years she'd guided Amelia through bouts of boy trouble. That same, tinny self-conscious strain echoed the mother who wanted to offer respect and freedom as much as she felt compelled to hover and protect. Jenny forced herself to be silent, taking Tess's hand as they sat side by side, sharing the rapid's gush.

Jenny observed a clump of branches straining webs of drying algae a few feet above the lapping water. She pondered their abandoned research. Yet she felt little regret, more absorbed now by the hand of humanity in the canyon—a hand that grasped bludgeons to strike the skulls of its own species. And Jenny was sure nothing had changed about the nature of the human psyche in eight centuries.

In that supposed ancient Eden, skeletal remains would no doubt show traumatic head injuries and speared rib cages. Then peaceful centuries would pass only because the ancients abandoned the canyon. As soon as Americans began exploring it, the murderous impulse returned. The exiled homicidal ferryman Doyle Lee would haunt Mile Zero forever. Above Separation Rapid, three of Powell's men would be murdered either by natives or Mormon settlers. Now one of their little research crew would add to this grisly history their fatal attack on Jack Carne. In the wake of that mystery, Jenny felt ever more ambivalent about the worst currents in the human heart.

Finally turning back to Tess, Jenny spoke as delicately as when Amelia came to the door with another whiskered galoot in stormtrooper boots. "Are things okay with you and Tycho?"

"I think he's just super sensitive, a lot more than any of us realize, Jenny. I think it really got to him when Faith was talking about the ancient Indians' peacefulness. I don't think he's seen a lot of peace in his life."

"And I'm sure he's still upset for your sake, Tess. After the incident, he found you first, didn't he?"

Tess stared downriver, doing her best to appear sphinxlike, her full mouth shrunk to a straight, silenced line. Did her expressive eyes feign blankness?

"Tess, I know this is tough to talk about, but as group leader, I'm going to be asked a thousand questions when we get to Phantom Ranch. So are you. I need your help to understand every detail, as precisely as you can recall."

Finally, Tess returned her gaze to Jenny's, her eyes wide. Even in the sinking light, their pale blue seemed ignited by an inner source, even more alive with a sudden flicker of apprehension. "Precise? Are you kidding, Jenny? That's the last thing I can be. I don't remember anything."

"Then tell me what you recall just before."

"It's nothing. I was standing on that crest of sand, shivering because I'd just dipped into the river enough to get my hair wet. I started shampooing, but it was awkward, holding on to the bottle and lathering with the other hand. I went to set the shampoo on the towel farther up the beach, when I heard this kind of grunt. No, it was more of a groan."

Jenny waited, giving Tess time to collect her thoughts.

But Tess apparently had no more thoughts to collect, or at least any she was willing to share.

"So," Jenny sighed. "Did you see who was groaning?"

"He was already flying at me. Jack, I mean. I know it sounds crazy, but that's how fast it all happened. He must've been crouching on the big boulder that hung over the beach, just out of sight. Watching me."

"Did he seem to be coming at you, then? Attacking?"

"I don't know. I didn't have time to make any sense of it. His arms were out, I think, but maybe that was to break the fall. He knocked me hard against the sand. That's when I blacked out."

"After that groaning, did he scream or yell?"

"No, that's the weird thing. He was totally silent. Like always."

"Always?"

"I mean when he was watching me. He'd been freaking me out since we first got together at Lake Powell, Jenny. The way he'd stare, all big-eyed and dead silent. Then he'd pester me with questions out of the blue, like did my musical taste change after middle school? Who did I like to listen to now? When did my parents let me start dating? Then, after that weird stuff in Redwall Cavern on my birthday, Tycho said Jack must have an obscene fixation on me. But I wasn't sure. I could handle a horny older guy. But I thought Jack's attention was deeper than that. Scarier."

"When he fell against you, did he grab you or bother you in any way?"

Tess shook her head, then briefly shut her eyes. "I don't know. Carol didn't find any bruises or broken skin. All I remember is coming to when Tycho found me with my top down. Tycho must have already tried to fasten my top, but one of the straps was caught under my shoulder. Then Tycho was tapping my face and smoothing my wet hair."

"Wasn't your hair still soaked with shampoo?"

"Yeah." Tess glanced upriver, as if for the answer. "That's weird, isn't it? When I was conscious again, my hair was rinsed, wasn't it?"

"It was rinsed when I got there," Jenny said. "But remember, I was among the last to get to the beach. Tess, do you recall exactly where Jack's body was?"

"Just sprawled there, under that outcrop of rocks on the other side of the beach, a little closer to the river. Near where everyone was standing."

"Everyone? Who do you remember seeing first, besides Tycho?"

"Hannah, I think. Then Annette and Faith right behind her. Then Glen. It seemed like everyone was there before I knew it."

"Including Carol?"

"Well, everybody kept insisting that I not move. Someone asked Carol about it, and she came over and started inspecting my legs and spine. Then she said I was fine, that the sand had softened the impact."

"You were standing in Tycho's arms when I arrived. Do you recall when you got to your feet?"

Tess shook her head, then cradled her face in her hands, sighing. "I do remember when you and Ray showed up. I think I was standing by that point. Everybody turned when we heard Duke scrambling along the talus slope."

"So, you know for sure Tycho was the first person on the scene, and Duke was the last?"

"Jenny, I'm not sure of anything."

"But, Tess, you've been very clear on every other point. Don't disable yourself with anyone else's suggestions. And for God's sake, tell me everything. It's not going to help to cover up for anyone or be shy about anything."

"I wouldn't blame you if you thought I did it."

"If you did, it would be a simple case of self-defense."

"But who knows what I did between blacking out from the collision with Jack and seeing Tycho's eyes looking into mine? I could've knocked Jack on the head if I thought he was going to attack me. Maybe we even fought."

"And you ended up without a scratch after fighting off an ex-football player?"

"Come on, Jenny. Jack wasn't exactly in great shape. If anything, what might've happened was that I knocked *him* out."

"Okay. Let's suppose you attacked Jack. What side of the head would you have hit him on?"

Tess exhaled, then bit her lower lip. She touched her left temple. "Here, I guess."

"Well, you'd be wrong."

"That's no big surprise. I blacked out, remember?"

❖

RAY launched his career as an amateur sleuth in the bow seat as *Dirty Devil* rocked on its tether. He tried some friendly conversation with Faith and Annette before dinner, baiting the hook of interrogation as casually as he could.

"I'm not going to pretend I liked Jack," Faith said as she searched under her boatman's seat for a hairbrush. "I thought he was the biggest horse's ass I've met in a long time, may he rest in peace. But I certainly don't think the punishment for being an ass…"

"Is getting your head bashed in," Annette said from the stern, applying lotion to her legs. "Exactly my sentiments."

After helping the kitchen supply brigade, and with Tycho napping on the supply raft, Ray had followed Faith back to the beach where the *Dirty Devil* was tethered. It happened so fast he didn't have a chance to enlist Duke's help. He hadn't counted on Annette's tagging along, either. She finished Faith's sentences as if they'd rehearsed this routine.

Now, with Faith passing her hairbrush to Annette, who brushed Faith's long, graying blond hair, Ray felt as if he'd crashed into a women's dorm room. Upright in the bow without a single self-grooming task, Ray also lacked a sleuth's guidebook for how to isolate suspects, especially when every individual in the group was a suspect and the group itself acted as if mired in collective guilt. With Hannah and Duke chopping vegetables just up the beach and Tycho lying back in the supply raft's bow, Ray hesitated to ask anything that would not occur naturally in casual conversation.

"Well, ass or no ass, what Jack said after Soap Creek was unforgivable," Ray put in. "He didn't have any right to attack you personally."

"He was just scared," Faith said, arching her neck as Annette gathered her hair to brush out a long clump. "It's typical of a guy. I mean, a certain kind of guy."

"An insecure, unevolved sort of traditional male," Annette said. "We don't mean you, Ray."

"Thanks," Ray said, sighing. *We?* Since when had Faith and Annette become soul sisters? "What do you suppose Jack was so scared of, Faith?"

"First of all, it's not so unusual people, usually men for some reason, show up on the river unprepared for the challenge of the rapids." She glanced down to *Last Chance*, tied just upriver from the supply raft, where Carol and Glen were in deep conversation over cups of wine. "I'm a little surprised Carol didn't do more to prepare Jack for the magnitude of the adventure. She must have had her reasons."

"Like maybe she was afraid he wouldn't come along," Annette said. "I mean, if Jack imagined his life would be in danger."

"Which would be rather ironic." Faith honored the irony with a moment of silence. "Anyway, it's not the first time I've seen a man, surprised by his own fear like that, who takes it out on the boatmen. Especially a boat*woman*. But what the hell? I did screw up on Soap Creek Rapid, didn't I?"

"You didn't deserve abuse for it," Annette said, fingering the ends of Faith's hair, then passing her the brush. "My turn?"

They clambered around each other so that Annette sat in the boatman's seat, unclasping her ponytail and letting Faith brush out her straight brown hair. "Whatever bad blood there was between Jack and me," Faith said, "I feel terrible about what happened. More for Carol's sake, to be honest, and for poor Jenny, who feels way too responsible for this accident."

"Ouch!"

"Sorry, hon. It's getting so dark I can barely see what I'm doing. And you've got a nest of knots here."

"So, it was an accident?" Ray asked, glancing around Annette's fixed stare. Duke lit the lantern in the kitchen area, its faint light igniting the shock of electric blond frizz around

Faith's pleasant, narrow face. "How does a man's skull get accidentally bashed like that?"

Faith creased her brow in response, shaking her head slightly. "I don't know. I wish I'd gotten to that little beach sooner, before everything got so muddled up. But I've been wondering if Jack had somehow injured himself. Tess said he seemed to be flying toward her from those rocks above. Maybe he was already injured? Maybe it wasn't an attack at all, but a fall?"

Annette flinched, but it didn't seem to be in response to another knot in her hair. "You're not serious, are you, Faith?" Suddenly their symbiosis was lost. "Everything points to an attack. Everything! Tess wasn't hallucinating. Jack had been waiting for his moment and took it when it came." Annette checked herself, glancing downriver toward Carol in *Last Chance*. She lowered her voice. "Did I tell you guys what Jack did the night of Tess's birthday? The way he interrogated me for every scrap of information I knew about her?"

"After that creepy episode with Tess at Redwall Cavern?" Faith asked. "When Tycho thought Jack was trying to cop a feel?"

"Yeah, later, at camp. I'd gone to the river for a nice, solitary pee after finishing up the dishes. And Jack startled me just as I finished, appearing out of nowhere. He said he'd been talking to Tycho and Tess just upriver. Jack kept going on about what an *interesting* and *sweet-tempered* girl Tess was, and what was she doing with a hoodlum like Tycho, and so on. I just shrugged him off and started back toward the camp, but he begged me to stay for a minute. He had this, like, pathetic urgency. So I stood there like an idiot and let him ask me all these questions about Tess I didn't have the answers for anyway. I've only known her for the past week myself, right?"

"What kind of questions?" Ray asked.

"Just facts about her life—where she went to school, if I knew anything about her father and mother, what kind of home life she had, what kind of boyfriends she had. It was creepy, like he was gathering material for his fantasies. He kept pressing me for details I didn't have and wouldn't have shared anyway. Like what hour she was born! Finally I just blew him off and went to camp, leaving him there, breathing hard and frustrated. Get the picture? The man was obsessed with Tess, okay? Tycho had every right to challenge him."

"Challenge him where?" Ray asked. "You mean on the beach the next day?"

"No, just that evening in the cavern," Annette said. "Tycho already understood how obsessed Jack was. It's just too bad the rest of us didn't intervene and support him then and there."

Ray glanced over to Tycho, now sprawled on his back on the raft, the cap over his face bunching down his wild curls. With the water carrying their voices, he didn't dare overstate Annette's implication that Tycho must have felt driven to protect Tess the following day. "And if we had intervened in the cavern," Ray said, "how would that have prevented what happened to Jack on the beach?"

"What happened to Jack!" Faith cried. "A question only a male could ask, Ray! Let's just be grateful for what *didn't* happen to Tess."

"Yes. *If* it didn't happen," Annette said, sotto voce. Ray detected a shivering undercurrent of fear in Annette that made him wonder how much of her conversation just now had been bravado, a cover-up. Of what, though? Had she felt threatened by Jack that same night at camp? Or maybe by Tycho?

"You know," Faith said, finishing off brushing with a final, hard sweep, "I guess my thoughts have hardened. It's clear Jack was a calculating son of a bitch, isn't it? He was like a dog in heat, gathering details for his obsessive fantasies, circling around that poor girl until he took his opportunity. I've changed my mind. I'm glad I scared the hell out of him at Soap Creek. And I am too good a boatman for Jack Carne's insults."

"Respect for the dead," Annette said, "be damned!"

❖

JENNY had left Tess alone with the surging rapid and decided to brave a conversation with Hannah at the camp kitchen. Instead, she found Duke alone nearby, seated on a flat stone with an onion balanced on another rock. Steadying the onion in a groove, he managed to chop it easily. Jenny marveled at Duke's one-armed precision with a kitchen knife.

"I volunteered to take Carol's place on kitchen duty," Duke explained, slicing. He nodded upriver to Carol in *Last Chance*'s stern. "It's nice to see her relaxing."

As Duke set up another onion, Jenny surveyed the scene along the docking beach. Ray leaned back in *Dirty Devil*'s bow, looking oddly stiff and tense while Faith brushed out Annette's hair. Tycho dozed on the raft but suddenly turned to his side and buried his head under his arm as if to avoid the laughter rocking over from Glen and Carol's wine-merry tête-à-tête in *Last Chance*.

Yep, the fresh widow sure is relaxing, Jenny wanted to say. She wanted to stay and discuss Duke's role in their improvised investigation, but forced herself to join Hannah while her ex-mother-in-law was still by herself at the stove.

In the lantern's hissing white glow, Hannah's flat, iron-gray hair caught new life, fugitive stray curls that made her seem younger and somehow, wilder. She wore last year's *Invest in Grand River Adventures* T-shirt, the one Andrew Pinch Jr.

had conceived on a napkin at a whiskey-soaked buffalo dinner at Denver's Buckhorn Exchange—the very night, in fact, that had led ultimately to Jenny's new conception. Divorce.

Extra-large, the T-shirt was obviously one of Andrew's, and Hannah wore it cuffed at the sleeves and belted at the waist, as if to strap on her ability to forever clasp her oldest son to the maternal bosom. While Hannah set the noodles in boiling water and began to fry chilies and garlic for the tamarind curry, Jenny took up one of the zucchini arrayed on the folding table. "Chop or grate?"

"Chop. But don't, Jenny. Duke's helping me."

"He's busy with a dozen onions."

Hannah laughed. "I hope not. I said six. But that guy Duke's a go-getter, I'll tell you. Amazing. More and better help than most two-armed folks."

Jenny began chopping the zucchini in tiny, deliberate cubes, and tried just as assiduously to avoid taking Hannah's remark personally. Then, overtaken by a perverse impulse, she removed her left hand from the zuke and tried to hack a section one-handed, as Duke would have. Naturally, the zucchini slipped free of the knife, propelled by the force of the chop toward Hannah's feet. "Damn!" Jenny cried. She attempted a rescue, but fumbled that, too, batting the slippery gourd against Hannah's shin.

Hannah danced away from the attacking vegetable, laughing. "Speaking of two-armed wonders!"

"Okay, okay," Jenny murmured, giggling despite herself. She rinsed the zucchini under the filtered pump. "I know I'm hopeless as a chef, Hannah. But I was hoping I could at least make it as a scullery maid."

"You have other talents. And, honestly, you don't need to help. Duke and I have it all under control."

"I'm sure you do. But I don't mind." At the table, she grasped the zucchini firmly and began slicing. "If you don't mind my company."

"Mind? Why do you think I jumped at the chance to cook my way downriver with you for two weeks? Did you think I wheedled my way in just to torture you?"

Now there was a question. Jenny tried out a Hannah-like tone. "It crossed my mind."

This produced the shocked chuckle Jenny was aiming for. She noticed the half-full glass of red wine Hannah had propped on one of the stovetop's unlit burners and realized she had to seize the cookable moment and sauté Hannah in her own rare openness and good humor.

Reducing the flame, Hannah turned to Jenny, turning down her smile as well. "Although it's so terrible the way our project was cut short. I really can't get over it."

"Yes. I was just talking to Tess about what happened. It's so upsetting for her, she's blacked out even what little she could have remembered."

"I don't blame her, poor thing." Hannah shook her head and returned to stirring. "I guess we'll never know exactly what happened."

"Why do you say that?"

"Isn't Tess the only witness? And she lost consciousness. Isn't it obvious?"

"Nothing about this is obvious to me, Hannah." Jenny set down the knife, gathered up the slices, and took them to Hannah. "You know what? Tess just told me you were one of the first to come running after she screamed."

"Now you're a detective?" She signaled for Jenny to drop the slices into the sauté. "Being volunteer leader isn't enough?"

"I think detection has become part of leadership, not that I ever wanted to be Nancy Drew on a volunteer project. But it's my responsibility to understand the most accurate picture of what happened. For the park authorities."

Hannah stirred in the slices, thoughtful but apparently appeased. "Why don't you chop the cauliflower for me, Jenny? And the mushrooms? I'll tell you what I remember most. Everybody was spread up and down river so much, it was the quietest it had been all trip. Made me realize it was almost high summer. I got that empty sinking feeling like the afternoon is going to burn on forever, too silent. Anyway, the sandwich board was set out and waiting, and I knew I had to round up people for lunch. But nobody was in sight. Or in earshot."

"Nobody? Where was Glen?"

"Last time I'd checked, he was napping on his dory. I went over to ask him if he'd mind beating everybody out of the bushes for lunch, but he wasn't there. When I got back to the sandwich board, Tycho was standing there, picking away at the cheese slices. I asked him if he'd seen anyone, and he just said he'd set out to help Carol, you, Ray, and Duke up in the side canyon, but the four of you weren't in sight. So he'd headed back in search of food."

"But we were all at work, just in different places around the side canyon."

Hannah shrugged. "I'm just telling you what Tycho told me. He kept picking away at my sandwich board, so I swatted his hand and told him to get going."

"Where did he go, then? We never saw Tycho appear in the side canyon."

"The truth is, I didn't pay any attention to where he went. I was just glad to have him away from my buffet. Then I started up the side canyon myself, in search of you four, hoping the girls would be coming back, too. I'd barely set foot up canyon when I heard the scream. Which I thought was just playing, you know. Just more of Tess's fake hysterics—"

Hannah cut herself off as Duke approached with a pan full of onion slices. She directed Duke to pass them on to Jenny for dicing, then reached out to him, touching his armless shoulder and looking into his eyes. "Oh, sweet boy, your eyes are all raw and red from onion tears."

Duke smiled, tear wracked. "Yeah, they sting pretty bad."

Hannah gave him orders to stand still and hurried to rinse her hands at the pump. Hands drenched, she approached him, flicking his eyes. "Does that help?"

"A little."

"Here, this might help more." Hannah filled a plastic cup from the boxed wine. "You go sit down by the river and sip this until you've cried all the onion juice of out your poor eyes." She refused to heed Duke's protests and sent him on his way. "I've got Jenny here now. She's all the help I need."

Jenny wondered. This scene felt so familiar, as if it were an outtake from her old life in Denver, Hannah the super-competent Mother of All Mothers, nurturing and curing in her curious rough way with one hand while she assembled the most delicious meals with the other. And the fussing and scolding and coddling extended not just to her own adult children, but all the grandchildren, and above all, Jenny's own odd child out. Ah, poor Amelia, the victim of a parent who, the Pinch legend went, cared more about biology, ecosystems, and volunteering than mothering.

Even Jenny's figure had been used against her in one of the few conversations she'd been able to endure with Hannah about why the marriage had become intolerable. Jenny had offered the truth to her mother-in-law about Andrew Junior's increasing abusiveness and neglect as Grand River Adventures grew and he raised capital and chased prospects around the West. Andrew Junior had wooed investors in Boise and Salt Lake while coaxing loans and screwing younger women, a project paradoxically matched by his need to have Jenny decorate his arm at Denver business socials. Hannah's assessment? "Was it Andrew's fault that you looked so wonderful in those little black evening things?"

Noticing the odd way Hannah hunched over the pan, Jenny approached with the diced veggies. "Are onions making you cry, too, Hannah?"

"No. No. Damn it, Jenny, there's just something about that sweet ranger that touches me."

"Duke? Is that really it?"

"Yes! Damn it! Why wouldn't it be?"

"I've just never known you to cry over anyone's sweetness, okay?" Jenny touched Hannah's shoulder, trying to catch her teary eyes. "What is it, Hannah?"

"Okay. Okay. Dump those veggies into the pan, and I'll tell you." She reached for her cup of wine. "Duke reminds me of Andrew Senior when he was that young. Considerate, kind, and open as the sky. And I don't have to tell you, Jenny, those days are gone. Especially now. It was a tough winter. Andrew Senior and I had a scare, and I'm glad I didn't tell you. I didn't tell any of my kids either, because I didn't want to upset anyone until I knew for sure. But he'd been terrible, just terrible, drinking much too much. Starting with bloody Marys on weekday mornings before I was up. He'd just keep drinking until he was more bleary and sloppy and mean as the long day wore on."

"Mean? What did he do to you, Hannah?"

"He'd be irritable and silent and petty twenty-four hours a day. Other than to tell me off for prying, he wouldn't say anything until I found out by accident that he was sneaking off to get doctored. All during fall and winter, he'd been afraid he had cancer. Finally, he got some decent diagnosis and he was okay. A benign cyst. But let me tell you, his liver wasn't okay. Cirrhosis, they said."

Soft against Jenny's shoulder, Hannah allowed herself a few more sobs before she straightened herself and turned back to the pan. "So, now you know why I had to get away for a while, Jenny. I jumped at this chance, and I pulled more than one or two strings to make sure you were supplied with dories and any other equipment I could finagle. Andrew Junior was not exactly warm to the prospect. But it was entirely selfish. I had to get out for a while." She glanced at the spray of stars just beyond the dome of lantern light. "I had to breathe again and be absorbed by something beyond Andrew Senior's slow suicide. Now, get me those tomatoes and drain these damn noodles for me, daughter-in-law."

"Thank you for telling me." Jenny did as she was told.

"I planned to tell you at Nankoweap, when I lost my own good sense, you know, at Jack's grave. I think I understand something about the misery Carol went through, married to that poor fool. And more than an inkling about what Andrew Junior put you through. I don't know what it is about the male of the species that makes them absent when they're present, but there's nothing more empty than that feeling you're not wanted as a wife. Only as some kind of old habit."

"Amen. And I thank you again, mother-in-law."

"Don't think I'm letting you off the hook completely, Jenny. I still can't understand your leaving Denver before Amelia graduated high school."

"Maybe you can't, Hannah. But what matters is that Amelia does." After draining the noodles and helping Hannah collect the spices, Jenny knew she had to redirect the talk back to her version of events at Jack's death, or the moment's conversational clarity might never be regained. "Now, what about that scream, Hannah? You thought it was just another of Tess's squeals?"

"Yes." Hannah shrugged. "I knew Tess was bathing upriver, and I figured Tycho had taken a detour in her direction, so I wasn't concerned. I even thought it was just young love, idiot that I was. So I wandered slowly back upriver, giving up on finding anyone. I was ready to send Tycho out as town crier. When I headed over that shrubby crest to the beach where Tess was, I started calling Tycho's name, but he didn't respond. I thought, damn that kid, and yelled again. I figured maybe he couldn't hear me, the canyon does such strange things, carrying sounds every which way, so I walked over the crest and spotted Jack lying there while Tycho hunched over Tess, caressing her face until she came to."

"Why do you suppose he didn't respond to your calls?"

"Who knows?" Hannah raised her spoon from the huge pan, where the concoction was suddenly a fragrant meal. "To tell you the truth, I think Tycho is capable of anything."

"Did you happen to see Carol?"

"Not till a little later." Hannah raised herself on her toes and, cupping her hands to broadcast her voice, called "Come and get it" to the surrounding darkness.

❖

RAY and Jenny took their after-dinner coffee down to the rapids by flashlight, which they promptly extinguished.

Jenny told him about her conversation with Hannah as soon as they were sure the noise of the rapids drowned out any words their voices might carry back to camp.

"Did you ask her if anyone saw *her* before the attack?"

"Oh, great, Ray. Now Hannah needs an alibi? It's not enough that she's a little old lady?"

"Come on, Jen, we have to keep an open mind."

They sat on boulders above the swelling water around the river's bend from camp, the darkness almost total. Hardly able to hear each other over the roar of the rapids, Ray finally felt free to compare his impressions and test even outrageous theories. He'd already unloaded all of his exasperation about his first interview with Faith and Annette. He just wished Duke had joined the effort, to stamp their speculations with an official federal law enforcement imprimatur.

"So, you think Annette and Faith are covering something up?"

"Faith tried to keep it in check, then she let all her anger out. She really does think Jack crossed a line when he insulted her about the incident at Soap Creek. She doesn't seem willing to let bygones be bygones yet."

"No matter how bygone poor Jack is?"

"Nope," Ray said. "But Annette is even more brittle and strangely unforgiving."

"She's become fast friends with Tess. Jack also acted the lech around Annette, and seemed to threaten her friend. Is it possible, Ray?"

"That Annette is the one who intervened, knocking the hell out of Jack?"

"Think of how hysterical she became just as we tried to leave Little Bert's," Jenny said. "Maybe it wasn't just panic over the violence. Maybe it was guilt."

"Maybe that's what everybody is so busy covering up. Our Boston preppy princess lost her cool to save her friend from the slavering lech."

"Meanwhile, Tess all but confessed that she herself probably killed Jack during her blackout."

"To protect Annette?" Ray asked. "But more likely, to protect Tycho. Because she thinks he is a hero."

"Yes, they're all protecting a hero. But her name is Carol Carne. That's why Hannah didn't see her when she started downstream. And that's why we lost track of her in the side canyon at Little Bert's."

"Well, she did say her allergies were bothering her," Ray said. "Maybe she went to get meds from the dory."

"Or Carol was already on the beach upriver, bludgeoning Jack to save Tess from his assault. And what could possibly be more nurse-like, even if the nurse has just murdered her husband, than washing the shampoo from an unconscious patient's hair? Any one of those women could have witnessed the whole thing. That's why Annette and Faith were finishing each other's sentences. To protect Carol. And that's why Tess was willing to take the rap."

"You're right about Tess taking the rap. But she's taking it for Tycho because she's infatuated with him, and now that he's 'saved' her, she's in love. You could see that during Faith's tour of the ruins this evening. It's as clear as Jack's drag marks in the sand."

"*What?*" Tycho yelled from above and behind them atop the sandy ridge, outlined in black against the brighter darkness of the moonless firmament. He had something in his hand. A small pack? A big rock? "I asked you something," Tycho insisted, only slightly quieter. "What's so clear?"

Ray still froze, horrified as he wondered how much Tycho had heard, while Jenny seemed to find her cool. "Oh, we were just trying to put together all these stories, Tycho. Hannah was just telling me before dinner—"

"What?" Tycho yelled. "I still can't hear you. What the hell are you two talking about?"

"Well, come down here and join us," Jenny said, mercifully unabashed. "Here, I'll light the way for you. Just follow the flashlight."

In the flash of illumination, Ray saw him holding a slab-like, triangular chunk of rock in his oversized paw. Ray choked back an exclamation as Tycho suddenly lifted it overhead and flung it, turning at the last moment, so that instead of hurling against his own or Jenny's skull, it dashed unseen into Unkar Rapid.

Jenny continued to extend her invitation with flashlit directions. "See there? To the left? Climb up and sit here."

When Tycho was settled between Ray and Jenny, Ray asked him what his own theory was. Tycho offered each of them one of his precious ready-made cigarettes, then accepted their polite refusals. "I don't have a theory except that I think it's total karma. Jack scared Tess and tried to do the dirty deed, but he got knocked in the head by that rock or whatever he'd knocked loose when he fell. Just like the loose piece I picked up on that higher ledge, up there."

"Well, not exactly like, Tycho," Jenny said. "We're in sandstone now. That was probably limestone, or maybe some transitional shale up at Little Bert's."

"Okay, whatever. So maybe the limestone was more crumbly than the sandstone we're in now. Think about it. That beach was just formed by the flood. But there were chunks of broken rock on the sand around where Tess was lying. I think maybe that's what knocked Jack in the head. Flying rock."

"So, how did Jack's body get dragged," Jenny asked, "all that way, closer to the river?"

"Man, I don't know. That's the part I don't get. Unless he just dragged himself, on his butt, backward. Maybe the knock screwed up his nerve endings, and they stopped sending messages from his brain to his legs. So he was, like, paralyzed."

Lost in Tycho's surreal yet strangely lucid hypothesis, Ray nodded in silence. Those long moments on the beach after Jack was attacked seemed to dissipate now, in clarity of memory, contaminated in the accumulation of competing versions. Ray tried without success to recall any fragments of rock obvious from his perspective at Little Bert's beach, then became distracted by a stream of Tycho's smoke as it merged with the Milky Way.

Ray wondered whether his own brain had ceased sending signals he could decipher while he and Jenny shared the river-spitting air with this volatile young killer.

❖

RAY propped his pillow against a small rock and sat up. In shorts and T-shirt, atop his sleeping bag, he anticipated a night of little sleep under Jenny's orders to trade night-guard shifts. Once again, the volunteers and crew made it easy to keep an eye on everyone, sleeping in close clusters near the boats. Tess and Tycho again cuddled on the supply raft. Carol, Annette, and Hannah shared a big tarp above where Faith and Glen each snored away in their dories.

Ray, Jenny, and Duke occupied a sandy patch just downriver, closer to the rapid. Apparently the only one awake at three dark thirty, Ray feared the whole endless night would prove to be a tormented scenario out of Edgar Allan Poe. He expected to stay awake until first light. That's when he half suspected Tycho would dare to slip away alone. Or worse, lure Tess into joining him for some lunatic escape down the canyon's wildest whitewater.

Their camp faced a bend where the river turned abruptly west, exposed again to the prevailing winds with full force. Gritty gusts kicked up sand, pelting their sleeping bags even more than the night before at Nankoweap. Ravens, taking refuge in the shrubby, boulder-strewn rise above the beach, had amused themselves earlier by dropping pebbles onto sleeping bags. One of them had awakened Annette by rifling through her river bag. The huge bird made off with a credit card in its beak, until Annette and Ray, both giving chase in a jolted stupor, recovered it twenty yards up the beach.

Those wakened in the commotion had cinched their storage bags tight and hunkered down for sleep again. Jenny slept on the edge of the tarp, motionless as a dead woman. Duke seemed restless between Ray and Jenny, wriggling in his zipped-up mummy bag, where he'd stayed during the entire raven-chasing episode.

"Duke," Ray whispered, "you awake again?"

"Kinda," he muttered, muffled in polyfill. "Do you want me to take my shift now?"

"No, I'm fine. Always happy being the Lonely Guy. Don't worry."

"I wasn't worried." Duke laughed, low and quiet. "Every trip has its lonesome loser. It's usually me."

"I can think of several interesting ways we could end our loneliness." Ray kept his voice to a whisper. "But that isn't going to happen when we're all freaked out, is it? Trying to sleep with our hearts stuck in our craws."

Ray could barely hear Duke's mumble-mouth response over the sputter and surge of the rapid downstream. "Yep, my heart sure is stuck in my craw."

Whatever the hell that meant. The wind scoured the sky so clear the Milky Way looked as dense as a cloud, a vast gauzy swath of stars almost captive inside the Summer Triangle. "This is what our Neolithic ancestors must have felt like," Ray whispered, "exposed, terrified under this vast array of random stars. A meaningless hodgepodge of gaseous matter."

"This is no more Neolithic than Sarajevo during the war." Duke stirred, rising up so his head popped out of his sleeping bag, and went on in a hoarse whisper. "The whole city was like this, exposed on all sides, no defense against the Serb snipers. Our situation isn't nearly as spooky and scary, Ray, just so you feel better. I'm sure we're not in any more danger."

"Thanks, Duke. I'd feel even better if you would join our Q&A with the volunteers. Jenny seems to know what she's doing, but I don't."

"I don't either, Duke," Jenny said, wriggling in her sleeping bag, then raising her head. "After Little Bert's, it was gracious of you to defer to my role as group leader. But now we really need your input and involvement."

Ray wondered how much of his and Duke's loopy back and forth she'd heard.

"You're right. I've been reluctant to jump in for sure." Duke sat up so that his face, in silhouette, was even with Ray's. "Out where I've worked for most of my career with public lands, there's very little need for law enforcement. I don't have much more experience with a crime investigation than either of you. I'm impressed how you two jumped into the fray, having the guts to ask tough questions. Look, I'll do my best to take more of a role from here on."

"Great," Ray said. "But how can you be so sure that whoever killed Jack isn't going to strike again?"

"I'm not, but maybe Jack's death was more accidental than any of us realize."

Ray turned, startled by a raven's cry. He watched as it swooped onto the supply raft's tube, its huge wingspan outlined against the river. The raven did not say "forevermore," but as it hopped, flapping its wings so expressively over where Tess lay in Tycho's arms, Ray wondered if it were not yearning to cry out the truth. Jack's death was no accident—no bloody blow to the skull could be—and his killer slept nestled among them.

CHAPTER 9

Mile 73 to Mile 77

RAY watched as ravens reclaimed the camp at Unkar. Just past sunrise, their talons danced across the band of sand as soon as Tycho tossed the last river bag into the raft. Under a pale sky of thin clouds, the huge birds hovered over the beach, screeching to unseen cohorts. Soon an entire raven battalion massed, a jet-black offensive settling with ominous grace.

As Ray strapped on his life jacket in the bow of *Last Chance*, Jenny and Glen fought with a lead line's knot just up the beach. Annette and Tess appeared from the willow brush, bearing the groover to the supply raft. Not yielding an inch of their beachhead claim, the ravens screamed in short, random bursts, punctuated with showy stretches of wingspan. Tycho, tying down the river bags, suddenly whipped a strap in the ravens' direction, slicing the air and crying, in a matching raven screech, "Hance! Hance! Hance!"

"Tycho, stop that!" Battening down *Dirty Devil*'s own hatches, Faith shot Tycho a dark glance. "You don't need to tease those birds."

"Sure it's the ravens you're upset about?" Whipping the mass of bags, he called out across the canyon, each burst echoed and underscored by each strap-slap. "Hance! Hance! Hance!"

Abandoning his effort to untie a stubborn knot on *Last Chance*'s lead, Glen hurried toward the supply raft, where aft, Hannah strapped on her life vest. Tycho, fore, tied down the groover and whipped the river bags in a maniacal syncopation. In one nimble, practiced move, Glen scrambled aboard then restrained Tycho from behind. Ray couldn't hear the verbal scuffle that followed, Glen's voice low and soothing and Tycho's still shrill and wild. Glen's persistence won over, and Tycho released the strap with one last slap and dropped into his oarsman's seat, hiding his face in his hands.

Ray could only continue to serve as dumb witness to the chaotic series of moves that followed. Faith buried her own face in her hands in frustrated response to Tycho's antics as Annette climbed on board *Dirty Devil*, while Hannah cried out, "I've had it!" Using Glen's arm for support, she dragged herself through the shallow, frigid water to clamber onto the *Dirty Devil* herself. "I'm not doing Hance Rapid with that lunatic kid," she said, taking Annette's extended hand to steady herself as she half flopped, half slid into the stern. "And that's final."

"It's okay," Faith said, straightening up. "I understand perfectly. It'll work out. Jenny can ride with the boys on *Last Chance*. Carol, if you'll move to the stern with Hannah, it'll be perfect with Tess and Annette in the bow."

But before Hannah took the stern seat, Tess stood and shouted, "Tycho's not a lunatic!" She propelled herself off the dory and slogged through the muddied water to the supply raft. After Tycho lent her a hand up and on board, she proclaimed, "I'll ride with Tycho if no one else will."

Jenny, still on shore, hurried to Glen's side, halting where her toes met the water. "Tess, you really can't ride the next series of rapids with Tycho. We're going to hit some of the canyon's biggest water this morning. Hance and Sockdolager. Tycho will have his hands full just guiding the raft."

"Jenny, please," Tess said, settling more firmly in the bow. "I can high side and I can swim. And it's my own risk."

"Not really. We went through this before," Jenny said with a desperate sigh. "At House Rock, remember?"

Ray watched the classic furrow dividing Jenny's brow, crinkled in so many similar negotiations with Amelia back home.

"And it might be *your* risk," Jenny said, "but it's *my* responsibility."

"Jenny's right," Tycho said, his head still bowed, barely audible. Then he raised his head, locking eyes with Tess as she turned in surprise. "She is, Tess. I can't have you aboard when I enter Hance. I don't want you to take the chance." He slapped the water with his oars, then turned to Jenny. "But let her ride with me over Unkar. She can switch back to one of the dories when we stop to scout Hance. Okay?"

Jenny dug in her heels, rocking back in the sand, stalling. She pushed her cap back, the brim angled skyward. "Unkar and the next rapid, Nevills, aren't exactly riffles, Tycho. If anyone should ride with you, I'd rather it be Ray. He's got more weight and strength."

Gee, thanks, Ray thought, but raised his butt up to the transom in readiness. "You want me over there?" he shouted.

Glen signaled Ray back down then settled his arm around Jenny's shoulders. "I need Ray's weight in my dory for balance. Let's strike Tycho's bargain. I think he'll do fine. I'll scout him on the next two rapids, then we'll have him do Hance alone."

"Okay, Glen. Just remember it was your idea." Jenny pulled her cap down hard, as if to conceal the smoldering burn Ray imagined in her eyes. She left Glen to unscramble his own knot while she deftly untied *Dirty Devil*'s and slipped with it aboard, to squeeze beside her prime suspect, Carol, in the stern.

After Glen finally outsmarted the knot and hopped aboard, he rowed out first to scout Unkar Rapid from an eddy just above it. A cloud blotted the first feather of morning sunlight. *Last Chance* eddied gently above the rumble of Unkar while Glen called instructions to Faith and Tycho. Ray faced the beach for the last time, where the ravens bounded over their conquered sand, maintaining a silence so total it seemed deliberate, the arrogance of victory.

"Ravens remind me of the Serbs in the Bosnian War," Duke said, following Ray's gaze from his place in the stern, "fighting for every scrap of real estate as their birthright."

"Your first partisan comment, ranger," Glen said, rowing out toward the rapid's tongue. "Up till now, you've sounded so neutral about that war."

"Oh, I'm not neutral," Duke said, strapping his vest more tightly. "I was trained as a peacekeeper, but Bosnia taught me all about taking sides. You'd be surprised how partisan a heart could get over there. Partitioned, just like the country."

"And how did *we* get so partitioned?" Faith called out as they edged past *Dirty Devil*. "We're as segregated by gender as we could be. Glen, you've got all the grown men, and I've got all the grown women."

"Hey!" Tess yelled from the supply raft. "I'm a grown woman, too, and I just had the birthday to prove it."

"That's right, honey," Carol said, looking upriver, beyond Tess. "You left your childhood back at—"

But wherever Carol placed the end of Tess's childhood was lost to the sudden thunder of Unkar Rapid's long, slapping slide through its chute's angling curve. Before Ray knew it, they were in flat water, facing due west, with the raft and *Dirty*

Devil gliding smoothly into place behind them. "I always love Unkar," Glen said, already rowing hard to avoid an eddy. "Curvaceous as a mature woman's hip. Long and gentle enough to enjoy the ride with your eyes open. Nothing like the bastards straight ahead. Certainly not Hance."

"What is the deal with Hance?" Ray asked. "Why was Tycho chanting like that?"

"He was being an ass. Trying to get Faith's goat. She broke her wrist on Hance a couple seasons back. Her last time in the canyon. It was nasty. The most humiliating thing for any river runner."

"So Tycho rubs it in?"

Glen pursed his lips, then grunted in frustration. "Yeah. Which is not kosher among oarsmen, besides being just plain mean." He waited to speak until Tycho and Tess shot by, laughing and waving. "Tycho's still humiliated because he lost the phone box at House Rock, so he's trying to make Faith look bad. He's got a pretty fragile ego."

"Yeah?" Ray asked, trying for nonchalance. "Has his ego problem ever led to this kind of cruelty before?"

Glen adjusted his hat brim against the rising sun. The sudden explosion of light ignited the shale's iron-leached reds on hillocks like the tops of long extinct volcanoes. The canyon here had an aged, broadened character different from anywhere upriver. Ray felt grateful they were taking it so early, before this open stretch smoldered in its shadeless hell. "We're all capable of cruelty," Glen answered at last, "aren't we?"

"Amen," Duke said.

"Yeah, yeah," Ray said. "But rumors are flying about Tycho's background. A criminal record. Some kind of falling-out with his father at an early age. Living under your custody, Glen, as a last resort. You know."

"No, I don't," Glen said with unusual sharpness. "And

you certainly don't, Ray. That boy has been the focus of imbecile rumors and half-baked assumptions all of his short life. His father had it in for him before his kid's own psyche was formed. When Tycho was only three, Pete Bracken took out his failure with Tycho's mother on his only child."

"Failure? Did she leave him?"

"Well, suffice to say she escaped after a breakdown, when she'd suffered her own share of Pete's abuse. I understood her desperation, and I know for sure Pete hired the best lawyers to screw her out of custody, but part of me still can't forgive her for leaving that kid behind to endure Pete alone."

"So, is there any truth about the head injury? That's what I heard. His father 'accidentally' dropped him from a second-story window."

"I did confront Pete about my suspicions. We had a terrible falling-out. But we were estranged by that point, so I never found out the whole truth." Glen rowed grimly on in silence for a few moments. The oars plashed in the still water. Downriver, Tycho and Tess's laughter drifted and echoed. "Pete hid behind his celebrity, you know. He won major prizes for his work on the event horizon, the place where black holes begin to consume energy—chewing up time itself, the way I understand it. And me? The carpenter from Flagstaff? Who was I to question the great man? But I was Tycho's godfather, for God's sake! I felt I had to intervene. Then I found out why Pete was so uncooperative. Yeah, Tycho had new bruises.

"At that point, I wanted to pummel the living shit out of Pete Bracken. We were scheduled to do our annual rafting trip in Alaska. Me along as oarsman, of course, singing for my supper. Fine. When I got him alone, deep in the taiga, I wanted to show him just what a bashed-in skull felt like."

"That's right," Duke said. "Counter the aggressor with aggression. That's the only thing that works. It takes courage and conviction to follow through, though. Most of us let the bullies run the show."

"Well, I never had the chance. Pete wrapped his Jag around a metal post on the Washington Beltway a couple weeks before we were due in Anchorage. I was grateful to that pole for doing what I wanted to do."

"Kill him?" Ray asked.

"Yeah. Maybe. Why not? I've already got a criminal record myself."

"For your environmental monkey-wrenching, back in the day?" Ray asked. "I don't think the penalty for putting sugar in bulldozers' gas tanks is the same as for first degree murder, Glen."

Glen snorted. "They were logging trucks. We were trying to save a stand of old growth right up there." He pointed north. "In the Kaibab National Forest."

"That's no crime, Glen," Duke said. "It's just more humanitarian intervention to protect the helpless."

"Which is all well and good," Ray said, "but hasn't Tycho got a criminal record of his own? Jenny told me years ago about that incident with Outward Bound, when Tycho was sixteen. The boy who was nearly killed? Tycho's partner?"

"I think that story falls into the category of Pinch family mythology. The other kid was embarrassed at his own incompetence, since he almost broke his neck in a bad fall."

"A bad fall? From a boulder where Tycho just happened to be standing?"

"It was a bad fall, like I said. The kid had to be rescued. Tycho was the one who went back for help."

"He was also kicked out of school for possessing drugs."

"A small quantity. For a short time. According to Tycho, he was holding it for an older kid. Listen, no matter how bad the litany of incidents sounds, Tycho is the most genuine case of self-reform I've ever seen. Even during the worst days, when he was seventeen and running with kids who were stealing cars and doing drugs, he stood apart from a lot of their worst antics. And he definitely had no stomach for violence. What matters now, Ray, is that he's a sterling citizen, a decent student at Northern Arizona University. He wants to prove himself on this trip so he can work summers river running for Grand River Adventures. He's not about to do anything to mess that up."

Glen's defense of Tycho intrigued Ray. Maybe it was expected of the godfather who had sympathized with his godson's predicament since birth, and especially of the guardian who had steered Tycho through high school and a successful college debut. Still, there was a whiff of overkill, a scent of overstatement that left Ray wondering about Glen's true motivation.

"We're already passing into the Shinumo quartzite," Glen said, distracted by the landscape and raising his voice as he went into tour guide mode. He nodded toward a yellow-brown mesa rising behind the rusty lowlands. The water was flat here, sun scatter splaying across its azure-tinged surface. Only the plashing of six oars broke the canyon's sudden silence, as if all the birdsong, along with the river's own hurried music, had been absorbed in the antiquity of these tortured landforms.

"We're closing in on stuff that's over one billion years old now," Glen said. "Looks like it, too, doesn't it? A landscape that's been beaten down to its most stubborn surfaces. It's too bad we can't hike up into the bands of quartzite and sandstone. They're like sound waves caught in solid stone."

"Nice," Duke sighed, looking up toward the highest ochre rock face. "A lot of times in the canyon, I get the impression that the rock combines every element in creation—explosive force, fire, water, crystal, violent upheavals that got frozen into place."

"Yeah, and at the same time," Glen said, "don't you get an uneasy sense that the cataclysm happened the night before? It's as far from some static diorama as you can get. The canyon seems organic. Alive! The visible skin of the planet."

"Yeah, perfect," Duke said, lowering his cap's brim against the rising sun. "If the planet's alive, it must be a violent son of a bitch. This must be its exposed face. These old eruptions must be its real complexion."

"Somebody dangled a camera into one of the side canyons during a flash flood and filmed boulders as large as warehouses being spit like olive pits from a giant's maw. Pete Bracken once told us how physicists used Grand Canyon's formation to support chaos theory—volcanism, upheaval, purgation. All random but strangely patterned. It isn't just erosion. It's uplift, too, with blasts of cleansing."

"Yes. Cleansing." Duke sat up. "These were geologic crimes. We're floating through a body of evidence. That's it, exactly. That's what's been nagging at me since Lee's Ferry, this sense of the canyon being some kind of grand crime scene. Like we're doomed to play out the same patterns in human violence as chaos plays out here with rock." Duke grabbed the gunwale, as if steadying himself against his own revelation.

Ray imagined Duke's phantom arm almost visible, stretching in the other direction.

"Think of the long spells of progress, peace, and brotherhood in the ordinary course of a society," Duke continued. "Take Sarajevo, where many cultures mixed, where all religions thrived side by side for generations upon generations. Then *bam*! Civil war and religious hatred, almost overnight. Chaos. Maybe someday we'll have the capacity to look back and understand the real pattern."

"Yeah," Ray said, seizing a pause to jump in. "Look at our own little society of river nomads. I mean, amid all our teamwork and good citizenship, what happened to us? *Bam!* One of us killed Jack Carne."

That produced the abrupt silence Ray expected. He'd brazenly defied the unspoken consensus that had formed, solid and real as any sedimentary layer, that Jack, clearly bludgeoned on the head, had died "by accident." The Nankoweap burial had laid more than Jack's corpse to rest. Any culpability, any curiosity, any insistence on the truth had been buried, too. All of it just as shallow and sure of ultimate disclosure as Jack's grave. It was impossible to conceive of willful violence among so many well-meaning people. But it was also weird for a group of granola-fed environmental humanists to indulge this bougie capacity for polite denial.

"So, Glen," Ray asked, "what's your version of what happened back at Little Bert's? When did you first notice anything unusual?"

"Well, I remember waking up groggy from my nap here on the dory, then strolling around the bend to relieve myself. When I got back, Hannah wasn't at the sandwich board. Her carving knife was hacked through the cheese in mid-slice, so I tried to see where she'd gone. I didn't see her anywhere, so I went back to *Last Chance*, pulled my straw hat back over my face, and tried to fall asleep again. I must have, because I didn't hear any screams coming from that little beach upriver where Tess was attacked. I didn't come to until Faith and Annette called out to me. Then I went running upriver."

"What did you see when you got to the beach?"

"Faith and Annette bent over Tess, while Hannah waved

her cap over the girl's face like a fan. Jack's body had been dragged several yards down the beach, toward the water. By the time I stumbled over that rise, Carol had come running from around the back, across the talus slope and down to the beach. She asked Hannah to move aside and started checking Tess for bruises and whatnot."

"She didn't go to Jack first?"

"No. But it was obvious Jack was dead. There were deep grooves in the sand where his legs had been dragged. And a strange angle to his head. You could tell at a glance. After Carol was sure Tess was all right, she crossed the beach to crouch beside Jack's body. That's when Tycho helped Tess up and steadied her on her feet. By then, Jenny showed up and went to Carol. Then you, then finally Duke, gathered with the rest of us. Right?"

"Right. But didn't Tycho get there before the three women?"

"I guess, Ray."

"Why guess?"

Glen hesitated, rowing on in silence before he answered low and slowly. "There was so much to take in, it was all such a shock. I mean, I'm just about the only person in the story who doesn't have an alibi."

"You, Glen?" Ray asked, suppressing a smile. "What's Tycho's?"

Glen ignored the question. "Not even Hannah can vouch for me during the time I was napping and she'd disappeared. Now I understand that she'd run to the beach when she heard Tess's screams, but who can vouch for where I was? Anybody could say they'd gone off to pee. If I tell you I was dreaming Indian maidens swam up to *Last Chance* and wiggled aboard to slather me in healing oils, would that be alibi enough?"

❖

JENNY strained to hear Glen's final advice to Tycho on how best to angle his way through Nevills Rapid. Faith scouted from *Dirty Devil* standing on her boatman's seat, her oars pitched forward against an eddy's gentle tug.

"Tess," Jenny called from *Dirty Devil*, "you can ride with the guys in *Last Chance* if you want."

"Thanks, but I'm doing fine," Tess called back from the supply raft's bow, where she sat facing the sun, her hair radiating its light, her dark face fixed in absolute calm.

Faith turned to Jenny, sitting beside Carol in the stern. "I'm sure it'll be okay. Tycho's already run more challenging stuff upriver, and Nevills is usually pretty straightforward."

"If only Tycho were," Jenny whispered to herself, bracing for the ride as they pulled out behind the supply raft.

Ahead, *Last Chance* was already bucking the whitewater at the rapid's base. The supply raft was gliding smoothly into the V-shaped tongue at the rapid's crest. *Dirty Devil* would bring up the rear, to sandwich Tycho between the dories just in case. But in hardly the time it took Tycho to whoop in staccato bursts, and Faith to scoot neatly around a whirlpool, they were beside the other two craft, bailing the scant spill in the calm water above Papago Creek.

"About a mile to Hance," Faith said. She was clearly trying to sound matter-of-fact, but Jenny could detect the catch in her throat.

"This is the rapid that broke your wrist?" Annette asked, already putting down her bailing scoop.

Faith, maneuvering the oars, managed a one-note laugh. "No, *I* broke my wrist. The rapid was just doing what came naturally, which is to hurl angry water down the steepest drop in the canyon."

As Faith told Annette the story of her helicopter rescue, Jenny saw her one chance to coax a few facts from Carol. "You know, I've got to get all the stories straight for my report when we get to Phantom ranger station, and I'm still puzzled, Carol." She knew she was being too blunt, but there was no time for subtlety. "When the four of us were working in the side canyon at Little Bert's, I lost track of both you and Duke. I assumed you were working together, marking the mud line along the talus slope, so I was surprised when you arrived on the beach ahead of us. And way ahead of Duke."

"Duke and I did work together for a while, but you know how it is with him." Carol tightened the back straps of the Greenpeace cap, then pulled it snugly so her thick, blond-brown mass sprang out around her ears. "Duke disappeared as soon as I was finished dictating my first measurements. I could hear him bashing branches back through the tamarisk. He headed upriver along the talus slope, studying the track of that mud line, I think. Then I found a little backwater clogged with fresh debris and algae-covered sticks. So I decided to document it and forgot about catching up with Duke. That's when I heard the cries."

"Tess?"

"No. I guess I heard Tess's screams, but they didn't register. Just more playing around, I figured. No, I mean Faith and Annette crying out as they ran to the little beach."

"And that's when you went running? But wouldn't you have had to pass Ray and me?"

"You and Ray had already gone deeper into the side canyon than I did. I could vaguely see each of you through a screen of coyote willow, taking notes. I assumed you'd already heard Faith and Annette, so I just ran on ahead alone along the talus slope, up to the beach. Tess was still lying down, being revived by Hannah, Faith, and Annette, when I stepped in to make sure she wasn't seriously injured."

Carol's composure, certainty, and clarity had a brazen, re-hearsed quality. Vexed, Jenny stole back a breath. "And Jack?"

"Jack's body? It was exactly where it was when you and Ray arrived, several yards away from Tess. After I was certain Tess was okay, I did take Jack's pulse, just to be sure. Do you think it's strange I didn't go to Jack first?"

"I wasn't there, Carol."

"When I got there, I knew he was dead somehow. Maybe I've seen too much death in my career. But everything in my being, in my training, led me to tend to the living victim first. I wasn't operating on rational thought. I was goin' on pure automatic instinct."

"So, Jack's body had been dragged across the beach, and Hannah, Annette and Faith hovered over a semiconscious Tess—"

"And Tycho, standing frustrated off to the side."

"That's right," Annette and Faith said in unison from behind, jolting Jenny.

"Okay, but Carol, come on." Jenny was aware the whole dory was listening now. "What on earth happened? What's your thought on how Jack died?"

"Since it happened I haven't thought about anything else. And I've decided I'm to blame. I should've had a better idea how fragile Jack was. I really do think the added stress of the altitude, the heat, and the sun, plus his panic over the whitewater, all just combined to finish off his poor ol' heart."

That last dose of Texas sounded contrived to Jenny. Was this a goddamn performance, then? "So Jack's ol' heart really was that weak? I didn't have that information on his volunteer application. I mean, if he didn't supply that news, Carol, why didn't you?"

"I certainly didn't mean to deceive you, Jenny. Truth is, I never even thought to glance at his application. I just knew how important it was to get him out of the deep funk he was in back home. That's where I was wrong. I didn't anticipate how stressful this would be for him. I love these river trips and hoped he would, too. I was as surprised as anyone. That's why I'm to blame. I overestimated his capacity."

"Wait. Jack didn't just expire from stress. Let's remember the gash on his head. Let's remember Tess's memory of his attacking her. Let's not forget that someone dragged his body across the sand toward the river."

"That's all got me stumped. But I don't think he attacked that poor girl. I think he was already seizing up from heart failure when he lost his balance and tumbled from that rock above."

"So, Jack was already dead when he almost landed on Tess?"

"I'm sorry if it sounds far-fetched." Carol shrugged. "It's the best I can figure. Listen, Jenny. Can you hear that roaring in the distance? Faith, is that Hance around the next bend?"

"Speaking of heart failure, yes it is."

Clearing her throat, Hannah piped up from the bow. "Carol, are you going to be okay, I mean with insurance and everything?"

"Oh, more than okay, thanks for asking. I actually made more than Jack, especially the last few years. And if there's one thing Jack believed in, it was life insurance. He always said he had us buried under more damn insurance than any life was worth."

❖

RAY and Jenny sat tensely side by side on jagged gray-black rocks above Hance while the guides scouted the rapid. The spot provided their first chance to compare impressions since the night before at Unkar.

"I'm telling you," Jenny told Ray, "Carol has virtually confessed."

The ornery, smacking roar of the rapid drowned out their voices, and no one would sneak up on them unawares. In full view of the blazing midmorning sun, Tess, Annette, and Carol perched on a ledge closer to the river, dangling their legs into flumes of wet, cold air spit by the furious water. Only Hannah remained with the dories, dozing in *Dirty Devil*'s boatman's seat.

Glen, Faith, and Tycho checked out Hance from a higher outcropping farther downriver, where they had a better view of the wide span of whitewater. Duke was just now joining the scouts, hustling up the worn, rocky trail.

"I just wish Duke would join us instead," Ray said, "so we can go over our impressions together."

"He said something earlier about how important it was for him to 'learn the river,' not to act as our law enforcement officer, I guess. Especially when I've solved the crime and don't need his expert backup."

"Duke doesn't claim to be a law enforcement expert. But worry not, Jen, *I've* solved the crime, and Duke's going to make a damn fine boyfriend."

Jenny punched his shoulder. Ray felt glad for the little jolt out of his numb, dumb scaredy-cat apprehension about Hance. The vast rapids matched the buildup and then some. He'd expected its steep plunge and its complex, smashing churning, but he hadn't expected its scale, its broad expanse of white spumes that hid sharp, dark rocks in random array for the thirty-foot dive over its sprawling tumble. In low water, the rocks protruded like fangs, and in high water, they hid underneath to rip rafts and chomp the prows of dories.

The landscape's ancient violence mimicked the water's calamities, a beachhead of debris rising to massive gashes of bright red-orange shale. Dikes and sills fissured by ancient lava walls intruded under slashes of quartzite. Ray turned away, his stomach churning in proportion to Hance's hammering upheavals, back to Jenny's words.

"Carol came right out and said, 'I am responsible,' but in this ambiguous way, as if she still expects us to consider her innocent."

"Then she didn't confess, Jenny."

"She wants it both ways, don't you see? We're all supposed to understand she killed Jack, but still support her excuse that he died of a heart attack. After she finished him off with a whack to the head, of course, then hid out and waited for Hannah, Annette, and Faith to appear."

"Come on. She didn't say that."

"No, but I'm sure that's what happened, though she claims she was diligently documenting mud flows just yards away from you and me," Jenny said. "And she has a batch of willing eyewitnesses to her late approach on the scene. Then she got the chance to act like the dutiful nurse. Who knows how many long minutes after the crime itself? God, if Carol gets away with this, it's the perfect crime. Death by canyon!"

"But it's not perfect, not by a long shot. We've got a bashed-in skull buried at Nankoweap that's not going to decompose for a good long time. And we have a young man with a criminal record, including violence, because he was himself the infantile victim of prolonged violent abuse. The neurological damage to that boy, let alone the emotional abuse he's suffered, provides all the motive we'll ever need. And that's without all the little clues that Glen unintentionally dropped. No one can account for Tycho's sudden appearance in any satisfactory way, not even Tycho himself. He was the first on the scene, according to Hannah and Glen. And Tycho, if I'm correct, is like so many victims of neurological damage. He'll blank out at the crucial moment, completely unable to recall a single detail of his crime."

"That's convenient. You forget that lots of child victims never act out the abuse they've experienced. You, for instance."

"And lots of unhappy wives with spectacular life insurance never murder their husbands. You, for instance."

"Never say never, Ray. Anyway, I'm an ex-wife. Our murder rate is significantly lower. Especially after we put seven hundred miles between our homicidal urges and our well-insured husbands."

"Same for us emotionally abused sad sacks. Soon as we leave our evil stepdaddies in the dust, we find the families we always wanted and live happily ever after."

"I just wish the family you found really was happier." Jenny glanced toward the higher ledge. "Well, I'm going to hike down there and keep my eye on Carol. Can you try to get Duke's version, Ray? Try to separate him from the oarsmen and see if he remembers exactly when Carol left the side canyon?"

As Jenny lowered herself to rock-hop closer to the women, Hannah met her where two rock faces converged.

"Lord, I actually caught a short nap," Hannah told her, raising her voice to full growl while glancing up toward the scouting team. "What on earth is taking them so long?"

As Jenny and Hannah clambered down, Ray headed up to the scouting rock. As soon as he approached, Duke stepped away from the boatmen, lifted the brim of his cap, and smiled. "You ready to ride the rapid?"

"Nope." Ray leaned close to Duke, hoping to hear clearly

over Hance Rapid's tumult. "They can go on scouting all day as far I'm concerned."

"Must be a devil. Glen said there's really only one safe route, but there's no smooth wave train. I decided to hang back, trying not to think too much about it. There's no role for me now but to hop in a dory and try to stay alive. I haven't been this scared spitless since I was crossing a minefield on foot."

"This one's got me spooked, too. I feel like I'm tasting metal, and my stomach's airborne. I just wonder if this is what Jack felt like during those early rapids."

"No doubt. Now we know what the poor guy was going through."

"I thought he was a fool at the time, but now I appreciate his perspective."

"What the hell, though, Ray? Glen's run this devil many times, and he's still intact. We'll probably be laughing about it at lunch. Then you can proceed with your sleuthing."

"I'm still flummoxed. What's your memory of getting separated from Carol when we first heard Tess scream?"

"Like everybody else, I thought Tess was playing around. I remember thinking you and Jenny would be working together as a pair while I went ahead with Carol, scouting the farthest reach of the flood mud line and debris."

"So, Carol must have been working alone at that point."

"I had worked with Carol for a time, then lost track of her and everybody else's whereabouts. Looking back, I should've collaborated with you and Jenny to make our work plan more clear. I'll tell you the truth, Ray. Ever since Lee's Ferry, I've felt kind of inadequate in the supporting role of the federal ranger guy. Especially when I consider Jenny and Glen's combined expertise with the biology and geology. Faith's, too, especially on cultural history. I know I should have been more assertive, but I'm so used to working on my own. It's been great on-the-job training for me, but it's not worth much to all of you."

"Oh, you're worth a lot. To me."

Duke smiled, then needlessly lowered his voice, barely audible over the rapid's growl. "I wish we had time alone together, Ray." He lowered his sunglasses on their leash, staring at Ray, then clutched his shoulder. "Man, we have got to make that happen."

"Maybe we'll have some time alone at Phantom Ranch." Blown away by the intensity of Duke's stare, Ray almost lost his balance on the rock. Recovering, he forced himself to change the subject. "So, what happened after you lost track of Carol?"

"I heard the commotion coming from the beach, but I was pretty far away. I just thought it was time for lunch. I figured Tycho and Carol had already gone down to get lunch, and I was getting some good data, so I just kept working. It wasn't until I spotted the empty sandwich table I realized I needed to follow the commotion to the little beach."

"But didn't you come to the beach from the back along the talus slope?"

"Yeah. I just doubled back in my tracks toward the side canyon, thinking it would be faster not having to climb over that rise. I take it you have some neurological theory about Tycho?"

Though taken aback by the abruptness of Duke's question, Ray welcomed the invitation to sound the theory out. "It's not so much about Tycho individually because I don't have enough details about his physical history. But from what I do know, he fits a disturbing profile, and I mean mostly disturbing for Tycho himself. My research for this documentary drama says many violent criminals have had damage to the frontal lobes. Enough so that their decision-making skills are impaired. Different kinds of injuries—sports, abuse, birth complications—can actually inhibit the growth and development of the brain itself. Many with this condition can't handle physical or moral complexity. They get stuck in destructive patterns of behavior. They apply the wrong rules for the wrong situations. They make hair-trigger snap judgments without the ability to back off. In the midst of action, they can't modify their behavior to fit changing conditions."

"Sounds like ninety percent of the armed forces."

"Maybe," Ray said, after a short, shocked laugh. "It might account for my younger brother's behavior, too. But imagine something even more extreme than on a battlefield. A perceived insult or annoyance sets off an explosive counterattack without self-control—not premeditated, not for personal gain, not out of the survival instinct. Just a sudden flash of aggression out of nowhere, not to be repeated again maybe for years."

"Didn't they find something like that in neglected children, too? Like the Romanian orphans?"

"Yeah. It was that discovery that led to Lewis and Pincus's original study of violent American criminals who'd been severely abused, neglected, and injured as very young children. Their brains just don't organize the right way. The stimuli involved in human attachment don't ever get wired in their brains. Along with the fact that their stress response system is whacked. So, often, these criminals can't remember their own abuse, but whatever they inflict on others. You can actually see the shrunken hippocampus on brain scans. I wonder what Tycho's would look like."

Ray finished as Glen, just above, led Faith and Tycho down the scouting trail, signaling for Ray and Duke to follow.

Glen's bearded, deeply burnished and lined face revealed nothing under his cap's gashed and crooked brim. Ray hoped the rapid's uproar had drowned out his last sentence.

At the docking area, Glen clasped Ray's shoulder and asked him to untie the bowline. Ray hustled on board *Last Chance* feeling relieved.

That was the last of relief Ray would know for some time. Jenny escorted Tess aboard *Last Chance* with proprietary insistence, then set herself in the stern of *Dirty Devil* beside Carol amid a general snapping and strapping of life vests and equipment. Tycho took in great, theatrical gulps of air. Annette, whose face went somehow pale and stricken under her tan, braced his bow line around her waist. Then she and Hannah, who did the same for Jenny, released the lines, tossed them aboard, and jumped aboard themselves.

As she drifted toward the eddyless, tongueless maw of the rapids, Faith broke the silence by asking for everyone's best thoughts. "There's no phone to call the chopper with, so I can't break any bones this time. It's that simple."

"Have a good run, Faith," Glen called, rowing ahead to lead the way.

Tycho would again take the middle position. As he did, he solemnly called out, "Have a great one, Glen. Be safe, Faith!" So, he'd finally learned, Ray thought, to mimic the encouragement river runners graced upon each other at the top of gnarly rapids.

As Glen and Faith returned Tycho's good wishes, Ray tried to brace himself snugly into the stern, gripping the seat hard beside Tess, whose white knuckles belied her sphinxlike expression. He felt Jack Carne suddenly haunting his own nature, a demoralized Ray O'Brien gone blubbery with rank, raw fear.

As Glen steered them out into rocky water, Ray found

himself striking old bargains with a nonexistent God, then abruptly shifting to fatalism. *Oh well, I've had a good life and I'm grateful for everything I've been blessed with.* After one last glance behind to the supply raft, just when *Last Chance*'s bow post rose six or seven feet airborne on the crest of the first great roil, Glen's voice rose up to meet it. "Let's hope Tycho makes it all right. But then, if he bashes his brains out, at least Ray can investigate his shrunken hippocampus."

The dory dove, then rose to meet the next slapping wave crest. Rather than the slow-motion hell Ray had braced for, their descent was actually quick—a stomach-fluttering, rollicking series of drenching whitecaps, more oceanic than riverine. The crew's whoops and cries were hardly audible over the rapid's rumblings.

The knowable world shrunk to the dory's precise dimensions, now lifting impossibly high, rising almost perpendicular to Ray's bottomed-out axis in the stern. The upright dory felt ready to drop its human and material cargo upon him and Tess. It just as quickly reversed, so he gazed down upon Glen, seemingly steering his way through sheer air, and Duke, braced shoulder-to-bow-hatch, far below. This teeter-totter progression, varied by Glen's sudden angling the stern downriver before it angled back to face upriver again, was interrupted only near the rapid's base, when Glen cried out "High side!" Ray flattened himself against the gunwale without flattening Tess. Then Glen was screaming, "Okay! Bail! Bail!" and they were bobbing along in the frothy run-out, up to their knees in freezing water.

Their bailing was so focused and frenzied, Ray did not see the collision until it was almost over. Faith navigated the same churning channel they'd just survived, but she was too close to *Dirty Devil*, the supply raft bucking off on a slapping wave train.

Tycho flailed river left toward a whirlpool, slipping into that same eerie, rubbery slide he'd taken at House Rock. Only here, near the base of this wider, faster rapid, the raft bounced and spun like a plastic ducky.

Faith screamed shrill instructions as Glen shouted the same. Somehow the raft, miraculously spit from the whirlpool, now surged straight toward *Dirty Devil*'s stern just as Faith had exclaimed "High side!" to her own crew. When Hannah leveled herself toward the last great wave crest, the raft's bow ring knocked her backward just as she drew back from the gunwale. Her scream quickly drowned as she flew overboard.

Hannah bobbed up toward the right shore, her bright orange life vest easily visible. Ray bolted to the stern hatch, ready to dive in after her. Though she rode the fast water properly, floating in her life jacket with feet facing downriver, her head was cocked at an odd angle, and her arms seemed motionless. As *Dirty Devil* caught an eddy beside *Last Chance*, Annette hustled into the same position as Ray, shouting, "I'll go in after her!"

"No!" Jenny cried, spreading her arms as if to hold both Ray and Annette back from any forward dive. "Hannah's floating toward shore. She knows what to do."

But Annette was already in the water, her head forward and her strokes frantic, as she tried to swim with her life vest tugging down her torso.

Jenny plunged into the river after Annette, kicking toward the foaming green channel and letting it hasten her to where Hannah passively eddied out, swirling at the water's mercy.

Chapter 10

Mile 84

RAY knelt over Hannah, who lay twisted yet motionless in the sandy shade of sharp rocks, but from her silent lip movements he could see she had survived. Despite the collision with Tycho's raft and her tumble into the rowdiest water toward the sharpest rocks, she had no serious injuries. Ray praised a God he barely conceived of, and thanked Jenny, in whom he most fervently believed.

Powered by adrenaline and raw courage, Jenny and Annette endured the river's hypothermic deep freeze and tugged Hannah toward an outcrop on river right. Ray watched in wonder as Jenny and Annette lugged Hannah's dead weight onto the low, flat granite shelf. Jenny forced the water from Hannah's lungs by pumping her chest, then slapped her to consciousness. The slaps, at least, could fuel enough mother-in-law jokes to ignite Jenny and Hannah's wary reconciliation far into the future.

But there and then, with Glen fighting to pilot *Last Chance* against the downstream current and out to the rightward shore, Ray's relief had turned back to alarm at a closer glimpse of the three stranded women. They were huddled together to bring up their dangerously low body temperatures, the sun sucking vapor from their clothes and hair. Ray had never seen Jenny tremble as violently. For once, the midmorning heat had been merciful, quick to dry them inside and out, though all three re-embarked with obvious reluctance.

"Oh boy," was all Jenny said, "now for Sockdolager and Grapevine."

"Just keep Tycho the hell away from me," Hannah said as her postmortem to the crisis. When helped into *Dirty Devil*, she immediately sank low into the stern, pulling down her smashed, still-steaming cap. Shivering, Annette eased in beside Hannah, extending her arm around her shoulders and pulling her close.

On arrival at Clear Creek, Jenny had said, "Let's just make the four damn miles to Phantom Ranch without another injury or corpse. Okay, Ray? Let's see if we can survive lunch together. That's all I ask." Annette and Tess, who had taken over sandwich board duties, sent Ray to see if Hannah was awake and hungry yet.

Ray fanned Hannah's face with her drying cap. Scanning the beach at Clear Creek, Ray spotted Tycho and Glen seated in the sand at the downriver end in rock shade. Tycho's head was down, his arms folded over crossed legs. Glen was talking to him, but Tycho seemed to be ignoring him, his barely eaten sandwich discarded on wax paper. Farther down the beach, Duke lay on the soft sand, cap over his face, sprawled in a slice of shade no longer than he was.

Under strict orders from Jenny to keep his eye on Tycho during the brief lunch break, Ray meant to get a sandwich and walk over to their spot.

Ray wondered if he could prove Tycho's guilt before they arrived at Phantom Ranch. Could they be ready, all in orderly agreement on the sequence of events, when they had to explain matters to the Park Service? Maybe the entire crew could present the case so that Tycho was not further brutalized by some tabloid circus: *Grand Canyon Psycho: The Trial of Tycho Bracken!* No matter what happened, though, it was essential Tycho got the therapy he needed, clinical rigor as nurturing as Glen's surrogate fatherhood had been.

For now, quieted here on the beach, Tycho seemed so besieged by internal devils, so exhausted he could no longer sustain those displays of apology and self-castigation that had followed the collision at Hance. Ray felt a nick of doubt in his theory's heavy armor. Was Tycho too remorseful and self-aware to be capable of murder during some neural blackout? Was he really that damaged?

Without answers, right now it was essential to assure that nothing more happened to ignite Tycho for the few river miles left.

Ray looked at the sandwich board, trying to conjure hunger. He'd last eaten at dawn and ought to be ravenous, yet his stomach had not really settled since Hance Rapid. After Hance, Hannah had only responded to Tycho's shouted apologies with dazed, sullen silence. Glen had been so preoccupied with guiding Tycho safely over the final rapid, and Faith so freaked by Tycho's battering of her dory, that neither of them could give their usual floating co-lectures on geology and river lore, which ominous Upper Granite Gorge begged for.

Even without their interpretation, Ray noticed this eerie zone, dark and forlorn. Up and down from the narrow beach at Clear Creek, the canyon offered the same stark, lifeless banks of schist. The familiar green tamarisk and coyote willow fringing the water's edge, the eroded tumble of talus slopes, and the pink, orange, and russet bands of exposed formations were stripped away. All familiar colors in the reddish canyon spectrum had been submerged into this ironclad gray black.

Despite the ninety-plus heat, Ray had felt a shivering chill.

These lava-infused, often conical rock formations plunged directly into the river. Shoreless and siphoned, the dark water seemed young, a recent intrusion that had somehow lost its way on its errand to the sea. This was the continent's basement, Ray thought. The very crawl space of hell.

A mere five hundred million years of age, the pink veins of granite the color of butchered beef suffused the two-billion-year-old Vishnu schist like fresh flesh amid rancid meat.

While the river lapped against the slick schist walls, Ray slipped further into geologic paranoia. He was plain spooked. They'd dropped into an epoch that preceded life itself. Gone were the leaf fossils and winged bugs captured as if in mid-flight higher up the canyon layers. Banished were the impressions of coiled nautiloids, the reptile tracks and ancient fish, darting in captive eternity across creamy slabs of limestone at the top of the inner canyon. Just thinking of the Kaibab layer, thousands of feet upward on the rim and eighty miles upriver at Lee's Ferry, flooded Ray with nostalgia. He missed any evidence of that upright biped, that naked, brainy ape who often forgot to use his heart or her intellect to full capacity, whose roads, and bridges, and convenience stores suddenly seemed faraway and precious.

Way down here, in their tiny, vulnerable craft at the gorge's whim, they'd been conveyed through an inhuman landscape. Life had hardly quivered here at all, just bare hints of the epic of biology to come, one-celled stuff too simple to leave an impression in the dark schist—pages unwritten, tales untold. These black crags formed humanity's comfortless cradle.

Ray wondered if the human epoch would even be a smear in Earth's solid, indifferent layering of time. Our fleeting seconds on the geologic clock would only tick-tock a species' slide from grace. Our human crimes would be scrawled in blood no more lasting in the canyon's walls than the echo of a scream.

Uneaten sandwich in his hand, Ray sat on a fragment of Vishnu schist that rose from the beach like a flat black tooth extracted from a pain-wracked dragon. As he tried to muster interest in his sandwich, Ray glanced sidelong toward the shady spot where Tess now dropped into the sand beside Tycho. She offered him half her sandwich, from which he attempted three or four bites. Then, as dessert, he smooched Tess's cheek. Tess made elaborate gestures, her arms poised outward to indicate some destination beyond—Phantom Ranch just downriver, or maybe just the nearly endless future that stretched before an eighteen-year-old girl.

Glen shoved off from the shady wall and crossed behind Ray without comment, on his way to where Hannah still lay. He crouched beside her, offering water from the bottle strapped to his side. She finally sat up, took robust gulps, and engaged Glen in a murmured conversation Ray could not overhear.

Ray stopped even scuffing the sand with his heels, intent on catching some fragment of their words on the breeze. How would Hannah and Glen, acquainted for decades, each bound by ancient Pinch family connections and disconnections, patch this rift? Would Hannah's fury at Tycho overwhelm her sympathy and affection for his guardian and chief defender? Apparently not. The only audible sound carried on the breeze was an abrupt blast of laughter, Hannah's low growl followed by Glen's choked chuckle.

Perched in the beach's center but unable to glean anything from the clusters of lunchtime conversation, Ray felt like the sole audience for a performance piece in which some crucial plot element was kept secret until the final blackout. Down on the river, Annette and Faith hustled beers from *Dirty Devil*'s hull after Jenny and Carol abandoned ship for the sandwich board.

"Ray, will you share your rock?" Annette called, coming up the sandy slope with a beer in each hand. She lobbed one to Ray as Faith did an end run around her, stealing a slab of the dragon tooth's shadow near Ray's feet. Sprawled there, Faith rolled the cold can against her face before she popped the top. "God bless that cold water spewing from the bottom of the dam," she sighed, sipping her beer. "Naturally refrigerated brewskis all the way from Lee's Ferry to Lake Mead."

"Reason enough for us to let Glen Canyon Dam stand forever," Annette said, opening her can as she plopped herself beside Faith.

"Heresy!" Carol cried, but she threw herself into the shade with a short, sharp whoop and opened a beer of her own. "But that shouldn't stop us from enjoying the dam's benefits until Glen and I blow it up."

Jenny, her mouth an expressionless, tight line, sipped only juice from her water bottle. She lay back beside Carol, balancing the bottle on her midriff. "I don't care if you guys take dynamite to Glen Canyon Dam, but we really shouldn't be drinking beer at lunch. If you check your Volunteer Guidelines pamphlet, you'll see it's strictly *verboten*."

"But we've been so good, Jenny," Annette said. "We've waited until dinner every single night until now."

"And it's never been this hot," Faith said. "It's a crime we don't have time to hike up to the waterfall. I'd die for a cold plunge right now."

"Speaking of crimes and dying," Ray said, "I don't see why Jenny should fuss over a regulation about alcohol." He guzzled his beer theatrically. "After all, we've already broken that other silly regulation about not killing each other."

The silence this provoked was deep enough for them to

hear the river's surging rush, along with Tess and Tycho's laughter. Amid the beer-guzzling women, Ray felt again like he'd crashed a sorority party. Even though he had first claim to the site, he no longer felt welcome.

What the hell? Why did no one share his concern about Tycho's condition and culpability? Unless he could rouse it in the others and piece together their presentation to the Park Service, Tycho's chance for therapy and counseling might get lost when the authorities took over the case at Phantom.

He looked at Duke, still napping under his cap. Wouldn't it be swell if his heartthrob, their very own ranger, joined in the effort?

"I'm sorry for bringing this up, Carol," Ray started, "but come on, you guys. We've got to figure out what to say when we reach civilization in less than four river miles. They're going to separate us and dig our impressions out of us, so we might as well get our facts and theories straight."

"What makes you think we have theories, Ray?" Faith asked, sitting up. "It's not like I've got some precious clue I'm keeping secret."

"Okay, I'm at a disadvantage being next to the last at the scene. I've assumed the rest of you know some things I don't. Like what role Tycho played. Like where he was when Tess was attacked and Jack was bludgeoned."

"Well, Tycho knows!" Annette said, raising her sunglasses to her forehead, as if to sharpen her stare. "Tycho has told his version. He was on his way up that side canyon to join the data collection when he heard Tess's scream. Just like you were, Ray. Why isn't his word as good as yours?"

Despite Annette's vehemence, Ray was relieved the narrative was actually being exposed to the free air at the last minute. "Look, that may sound reasonable, but you're ignoring Tycho's past. That poor guy has had a history of injurious abuse to overcome from childhood. And criminal activity to go with it from adolescence. Along with two raft crashes at crucial points—one that left us without contact when the phone box went flying at House Rock, and one that almost finished off Hannah at Hance. Is there any chance Tycho suspected Hannah knew something, since she was next on the scene?"

"And those suspicions are reasonable," Glen said, appearing behind Annette. His tone was tightroped between plaintive and resigned. Ray flinched when he felt Glen's hand on his shoulder, then he turned to see Glen must have been standing just behind the shaded assembly for who knew how much of the conversation. "But that doesn't make them true. And I'll tell you why. Because I'm the one responsible for Jack's death."

With all heads turned in his direction, Glen frowned, adjusted his cap brim, fingered the fringes of his beard, and looked to the river for his next words. "Okay. You all remember I was the only one without an alibi, right? That's because I was already on the scene. I'd heard Tess's scream, and something told me it wasn't just more monkey business. When I reached the little beach and saw her underneath Jack like that, I lost my cool and gave Jack's head a good, sound knock with a piece of limestone that had come off in my hand as I climbed over that rise. It was an automatic response, okay? I meant to knock him out, not kill him. Then I lost my nerve to fess up to it. Then I felt like an even bigger ass for keeping the truth from everyone for so long. So I'm not only a killer, I'm a coward." He kicked the sand, still staring down. "Case closed, okay?"

A shuffling, hunched silence met his question. Each searched for the others' reactions as they tried to absorb Glen's confession. For a fleeting, skittering moment, it clarified so much for Ray. Not only the violence on the beach and the dragged corpse, but also Glen's demeanor, unfitting for this kindly, even courtly man. His seeming callousness, conducting his practiced lectures so soon after Jack's death; his deliberate deflection of the Canadians' attention at the Little Colorado; then the possibly orchestrated way he chinked, then repaired *Last Chance* at Unkar, so they'd miss all further contact with the Canadians downriver. For all Ray could recall, Glen might've shouted Tycho instructions at Hance Rapid calculated to cause the crash, expelling Hannah. That's because she had arrived at the scene in time to witness Glen dragging Jack's body across the beach.

It clarified all that, yes. But it didn't make it true. Ray took a deep breath, stifling the urge to say, "Nice try, Glen," in the least sarcastic tone he could muster. Every single motive could apply to Glen's covering up Tycho's guilt. Ray realized Glen's confession was really an admission that Glen thought Tycho was as guilty as he did. How to get him to confess that?

Carol cleared her throat. "So, Jenny, I suppose I'm not your prime suspect anymore?"

Jenny cringed, folding her head under her crooked arms as if to save her noggin from some psychic landslide. "Good God! I don't know what to believe. Glen, are you really prepared to give that version to Duke, now? And to the authorities at Phantom?"

"It's not a version, Jen. It's the truth. And of course I'm going to tell them, exactly as I just told you. Maybe they'll take mercy on an old fool who tried to save a damsel in distress."

"Maybe," Carol said. "But it could backfire, Glen, and we'd have another innocent man on Death Row. Jenny, I don't want you to cringe like that. You'd be crazy not to suspect me foremost. Especially you."

"Why do you say that, Carol?"

"You know what it's like to be trapped in a marriage that died and yet lived on somehow, contentious and comatose by turns. You knew, didn't you, what it was like to come so close to committing the unthinkable?"

"Well, I had no trouble envisioning myself in your shoes," Jenny said. "Resenting that level of entrapment. And contempt. Especially because I'd just gone ahead and done an unthinkable thing myself."

"Leaving your husband and your daughter behind?" Carol asked. "Living as the scarlet woman in exile? Yeah, but my stigma was around my neck every day. So, I'm afraid I'm the guilty party. Nice of you to take the blame, Glen, but you're not the misanthrope I am. Your false confession proves what an angel you are. No one will have any problem seein' that I'm ultimately responsible, just like Jenny did. And Jenny was right."

"Right, Carol." Glen folded his arms, exchanging a glance with her before he turned his gaze to the sand between his sandals. "Tell these folks who paid for those poisoned farm worker kids' follow-up therapy with her nurse's salary. Tell them who still follows their progress through middle school and will probably pay for their prom dresses and graduation gowns."

"I'm glad you're so confident they're going to make it to senior year, Glen. I pray to see that day, but I ain't gonna hold my breath." Carol reddened under her deep tan, the first time Ray had seen her blush. "Anyway, when Jack's income was up in the good old days, we were doing okay. It's not like I was the heroic single Nancy Nurse. When you've got plenty more than you need, it's easy to give."

Glen raised his eyebrows, then gestured toward Carol as if she were Exhibit A in this beach inquest. "And here is your misanthropic murderer, ladies and gentlemen."

Duke, risen and approaching from his upriver nap,

stopped in his sandy tracks and looked wide-eyed on the scene. "*Murderer?*"

"No, Duke," Annette said, frowning. "Not yet, at least. We've got dueling confessions going on here."

Accepting Ray's raised hand to steady himself, Duke dropped to the sand and sat cross-legged beside him, where he stared up at Glen and Carol as if Tweety birds and stars were circling his waking, sun-dazzled head.

Carol opened her hands toward Duke, as if offering a regal welcome. "At last, a fresh, rational mind to bear witness to the God's truth. Duke, I was just trying to explain to these stubborn people that I bear the responsibility for Jack's death." Clasping her hands prayerfully now, Carol scanned the faces arrayed around her feet.

"Me and Jack were going through a rough patch as big as Texas, folks, I'm sorry to say. And I decided to take Jack along to get his mind off some of that trouble. I knew damn well he wouldn't fit in with you all, just as I knew damn well he wouldn't have much of a good time. At best, I was just hoping to divert him. It didn't take long. That first rapid, when he was such an ass—God rest his soul—about Faith's fine oarsmanship, showed me my plan was not going to work half the way I hoped." Carol pointed toward Tess, who was busy braiding one of Tycho's forelocks. "And the reason was that pretty young girl over there."

"I knew it!" Faith groaned, then fell back, staring skyward. "How disgusting. And how disgustingly predictable."

"It's not what you are all thinking, but that's because I've left you in the dark on this. And that's because I just hate to be the object of anybody's pity, no matter how well meant and kindly. It's just a hang-up of mine, and now I've got to swallow hard, then spit it out, because you all desperately need more information. Okay?" Carol seemed to ask permission of herself and paused to take a deep, slow breath. She looked to the river, for whatever inspiration might churn in its glassy blue greens. "Jack and I were on the cusp of an anniversary neither of us cared to face, much less talk about. It would've been hard to take in any case, anywhere we chose to run from it, but what happened in that Tornado Alley town we told you about earlier just made it unbearable.

"Remember Jack's story about Scots Springs, that little town he investigated, where everything was destroyed? It was our hometown, where we'd been born, raised, schooled, and married. When Jack and I were eighteen, I found out I was pregnant with our first daughter about two weeks shy of our high school graduation."

"Oh, Carol!" Jenny said, biting her lip. "You never told me. Did you have to, well, give her away?"

"Oh no, honey. Both our sets of parents were great about it, and that kind of thing was not so unusual in small-town Texas. But my baby was stillborn. So Jack and I went off to Amarillo to get our educations and start our lives over. When I was twenty-three and all finished with nursing school, we had another, healthy baby girl. Jessica.

"But, anyway, I can't tell you how tough it was on Jack when his folks' home was completely leveled by that twister this spring. He had to handle their claim, and my parents' claim, and their neighbors, and so on down the line to the preacher and the candlestick maker. There was nothin' left of that whole sad-sack burg. It might as well have been a blueprint traced in the prairie dirt. By that point, Jack was pretty depressed about the inherent damn tragedy in his work anyway, and his assignment in Scot Springs just brought it all home, no pun intended. And smeared it in his face.

"But it was even worse, folks, because we were coming

up on this May's five-year anniversary of Jessie's accident." Carol chugged a healthy swig of her beer. "Okay, it goes like this. Jack insisted on buying a damn speedboat with one of his first big bonuses. He was on Lake Meredith with his stupid drunk buddies. They insisted on steering while spotting for Jessie, who was just learning to ski. Jack didn't have any business letting her water-ski anywhere near those drunken bums in the first place, but Jess begged until she wore him down. Well, in no time they dunked and mangled her up so bad she didn't make it alive to the emergency room in Borger. Those drunken fools killed Jessie in our ski boat just before her thirteenth birthday. And Jack never forgave himself for being the main fool."

Carol took a long breath. "Tess and Jessica were born on the exact same day and year, so Jesse's eighteenth birthday would have been the same as hers. Look over at that wonderful girl, growing before our eyes into an independent woman. Maybe you can understand why Jack's fat, clogged ol' heart, which never healed in the first place, broke all over again." Carol's voice remained steady, her accent homey as ever, but now tears slipped from under her sunglasses. She swiped them off, but they kept saturating her cheeks as she continued. "So, my big plan to get Jack away from home during that horrible anniversary, distracted among all you good people and a small, exciting risk, just backfired so bad.

"So, I am the guilty party. I should have withdrawn my application and let some vigorous couple take our places. Because you're right, Jenny, Jack never would have been approved on his own, not in his poor condition. I took advantage of your faith in my judgment.

"And though I'm guilty, Jack himself is my prime suspect, not so much slow suicide as self-sabotage. There had to be some subconscious deliberation to it. This day-long sun and heat and exertion didn't do his weak heart any good at all. Not to mention how he got up there on that rock, spying on Tess. He had no right to do that.

"But I think I know why. Jack was just trying to work up the nerve to talk to her about Jessie. How Jessie might have come along with us on this trip and celebrated her eighteenth birthday at Redwall Cavern right along with Tess. I think Jack just needed some kind of healing. Some communion. For Tess to understand his loss, maybe to extend a kindly hand. He really wasn't leching."

"No," Annette said, crimping her brow in sorrow. "He was yearning."

"But, it being Jack," Carol continued, "even that gracious motive had to end in blunder. He probably scared that poor girl out of her skin when his dead weight fell on her. I'm sure he had a heart attack—probably already dead when he hit the ground."

"Okay. I accept that," Jenny said, leaning in to dab more tears off Carol's face with her bandanna. "But how do you explain the wound to Jack's head?"

"He could've already fallen once. He was determined to have his moment alone with Tess, but he was exhausted and physically overwhelmed. He might've been nursing that head wound from some clumsy accident up on the outcrop, when he got light-headed from the blood loss and fell."

"Then," Ray asked, aware of his boldness, "who dragged his body down the beach? Wouldn't there have to have been a third person on the scene, somebody strong but panicked by what he saw, somebody who bolted when he heard Hannah's cries?"

"*He?*" Glen asked. "Why don't you just come out and say what's on your mind, Ray?"

"Like I haven't done that, Glen?"

Duke cleared his throat and stood. "Look, I've withheld something that's keeping you all in confusion. I need to speak up now."

"Good. At last. Duke, help me out here." Ray glanced around Carol and Jenny, who'd blocked his sightline to Tess and Tycho's shady spot—which was abandoned now. Tycho's T-shirt lay crumpled in the sand. "Hey, where the hell did they go?"

Gazing toward the opposite end of the beach, Jenny pointed toward the empty air mattress. "And where on earth is Hannah?"

"I just passed her upriver," Duke said. "She said she was trying to remember some shortcut to a waterfall. She felt better and wanted to clear her head with a little exercise. I figured you all knew she'd gone."

❖

RAY hurried up the rocky bed of Clear Creek beside Duke. "We shouldn't panic," Duke said between hard breaths. "Tycho and Tess probably wandered off for some private smooching, and Hannah can't be far. Up there." He pointed to a trail angling above the creek. "Her shortcut to the waterfall?"

Duke and Ray jogged their way around boulders in the Clear Creek stream bed, which twisted like a python between the black obsidian Vishnu schist canyon walls. "Do you think smooching is all Tycho's doing?" Ray asked, breathing hard. "Why should we trust Tycho alone with Tess in this snaky canyon?"

"That depends," Duke said, "on whether your theory is true. But I don't think Tycho meant to hurt Tess, no matter what happened back at Little Bert's. I think he was trying to protect her."

"So, you *do* think Tycho bludgeoned Jack?"

"Hey, look!" Duke pointed up, where a figure appeared then withdrew. "That must have been Hannah, trying to find her shortcut to the falls." Duke called her name, but the figure didn't respond or reappear. "And this might be what she's searching for!"

The creek's canyon forked here, the wider, wetter streambed slithering left while a dry, rock-strewn tributary wandered right. A faint footpath led up the rocky jumble. Ray considered the route. "If that was Hannah, she must have decided it was too steep."

Duke was already scrambling up the dry fork. "Hannah shouldn't be wandering alone up here. I'll call to you when I find her, Ray. Meet you at the falls, okay?"

Okay what? Ray didn't know what to think, except that separating now was probably not the best idea. It certainly wouldn't win the approval of that by-the-book Girl Scout, Jenny Bridger. Short of chasing Duke up the tributary, he had no alternative but to press on, boulder-hopping upstream. In the hollow company of his own footfalls and the echo of his hard breaths, Ray tried to suppress the panic in his guts. Was there no way to prevent the tragedy that awaited around one of these serpentine curves?

The next bend was so narrow and severe it doubled back upon itself, a black chasm shutting out even the noon sun. Naturally, it was there he first heard Tess's unmistakable bloodcurdling scream.

A second scream reverberated, now competing with a gushing roar that met Ray as he sprinted into the serpent's very tail, formed where the rock walls whipped upward, boxing the canyon shut with sheer, chunked slabs of granite and schist. Dead ahead, the creek shot over the slabs and along a pink, wound-like flank where it went sideways, an open vein under the artery cascading straight down from the rim. Tycho appeared in the intersection of both water gushes, his eyes wild, actually thumping his chest in triumph. In the cavern behind him, a second figure cowered in the dark.

Ray could move no faster in the deepening pool that formed the distance between himself and Tycho—a lunatic who was in essence his younger brother, an extreme variation on the same biographical script, a shadow self who had emerged from darker closets of cruelty.

Ray hated himself for not acting on it sooner. Now not only was Tess lost forever, but Tycho was too. He would have no chance at rehabilitation, just lifelong punishment in some brutal Arizona prison-industrial complex.

As Ray dragged his legs through the knee-deep pool, hurrying but prowling forward in ludicrous slow motion, Tycho's yelling echoed throughout the box canyon, stupid ape-like howls that took Ray a moment to understand: "Vishnu-Vishnu-Vishnu-*schist*!"

Just as Ray expected Tess's body to float out into the pool, adrift like Ophelia in the hissing water, she popped into view. She shoved Tycho from his place smack between the twin gushes and laughed her hysterical squeal as he struggled, then flopped face-down into the whirlpool. Tess beat her own chest, her foot on Tycho's bare back, woman triumphant, chanting, "Vishnu-Vishnu-Vishnu-*schist*!"

God! They were two overgrown kids playing, exactly as they had done in the shallows of the Little Colorado the day after Jack's death. Just two infatuated kids goofing in the cool water.

After Tess helped Tycho to his feet, she spotted Ray. "Get over here, dude! It is so cool!" Tycho exhorted Ray to come toward the dark cavern behind the twin gushes and dared him to withstand the hard pulse of the falls.

But Ray insisted they head back to the beach immediately. "Guys, we have to get going to Phantom!"

Ray rock-hopped back to the fork in the canyon where, he realized with a hard cold slap to his consciousness, he'd let the real murderer escape unescorted.

Why he had been so ready to take Duke's late appearance on the little beach at Little Bert's at face value? After his aborted attempt to drag Jack's body to the river, Duke had heard Hannah's rough entry to the little beach and must have circled back through the coyote willow under the talus slope, completely undetected. He'd simply waited for the others to gather, one by one, while he lingered and made his well-staged second appearance on the beach. Why had Ray failed even to consider Duke as a suspect?

Because he was the "perfect man," the fleeting object of a gay boy's summertime crush? Because of his sympathy for the perfect man's imperfection—his disability, his sacrifice? Duke had struck Jack with his extra-strong right arm, his shoulder bracing the blow in its odd, glancing angle as Duke rammed the slab against Jack's skull. The muscles of Duke's right arm caused that deeper, rightward groove in the sand trail that led to Jack's corpse.

Ray hustled back to the tributary trail, buoyed by panic's purest blood pumping energy. Ray bounded ahead, weightless with wonder at his blindness to the obvious. Duke was the only one among them who was a trained killer, courtesy of the US military. While Ray had been searching for neurological inevitability, Duke had been seething in his quiet, unassuming way, the crew's foremost candidate for post-traumatic stress.

Ray had virtually escorted Duke here, then sent him off on this errand to eradicate his crime's only witness.

Before Ray could get his bearings under the stark noon sun, he spotted Duke not twenty yards up the rocky path, bent over Hannah's unconscious body.

Chapter 11

Mile 88

JENNY shared a bench with Ray on a shady cabin porch at Phantom Ranch. She stared at the manicured square of lawn that formed a courtyard between the porches of adjoining cabins. The old resort settlement, deep in the chasm of Bright Angel Creek and reachable only by the river, foot paths, or mule trains, had never seemed so civilized on her previous rafting trips or canyon hikes. Phantom Ranch's tidy cluster of one-story cabins, dormitories, cookhouse, and store felt domesticated, even suburban. Had that neat fringe of rock always outlined beds of marigolds, vainglorious in the late afternoon sun? And where had all these pink people appeared from with their tamed hair, clean shorts, and bright pastels, clutching souvenirs and ice cream cones?

Across the lawn, a trio of teenagers who had probably never used a pay phone attempted a giggling conference call. A giant cottonwood offered quaking shade for two young lovers, caught in a mastic kiss while they wrestled from backpacks that threatened to topple them backward. "Amazing that this was once a native settlement, huh, Ray? That poor woman toiled here, in chronic, lifelong pain. Meanwhile, we boogie across her grave site in our three-tone air-gel hiking boots."

"What woman?" Duke asked as he emerged from the darkness behind the cabin's open door. Wet-haired, just-shaved, he'd changed into a shocking clean khaki ranger shirt and matching pants. He sat in an Adirondack chair on the porch's edge, facing the bench, his hair steaming dry in a spot of sunlight. "And whose grave?"

"Jenny was telling me about an ancient skeleton that was found here," Ray said, "twenty years ago, during a construction project. One of the few burial sites ever found in the canyon."

As Duke folded his armless sleeve into neat quarters, tucking it under the shoulder seam, Jenny felt their queasy silence deepen in the wake of Ray's words. Was it her imagination or had a fluky breeze really rattled the treetops at the exact moment Ray said "burial sites," and did each pair of eyes really search upriver in the direction of that fresh grave at Nankoweap? Was this same breeze bound upriver to scour the flinty earth over Jack Carne's body?

"How's Hannah doing?" Ray asked, nodding toward the cabin's open door.

"She must be a lot better," Duke said. "She teased me about my 'sartorial splendor' when I came from the shower in these borrowed ranger duds. Carol's got her ankle wrapped, and Hannah says the painkillers are transporting her heavenward."

"I think it's you who transports her, Duke," Jenny said. She was thankful Hannah's injury on Clear Creek's rim had been no more serious than a turned ankle. When they'd arrived at Phantom Ranch in midafternoon, Duke had finagled access to bunks and showers in one of the hiker dormitories near the ranger station. With Hannah settled and comfortable, Carol had been able to work her nurse's magic with bandage wraps and acetaminophen. "Now we've just got to figure a way to get Hannah the nine miles uphill to the South Rim tomorrow. We'll probably hijack a mule."

"That's a nice problem to have," Duke said, "compared to the scare I had back at Clear Creek. When I came upon Hannah crying out in agony up on that ridge, I was afraid she was suffering a slow-acting concussion from the blow she'd received at Hance. Scared the hell out of me."

"I was just embarrassed," Hannah said, appearing in the doorway, clutching Carol's arm, then hopping by herself to the Adirondack chair beside Duke's. She stretched out in exaggerated luxury, dangling her lower leg outward. "When a handsome young man rescues a distressed damsel, even such an old one as me, howling in pain is the last thing the story needs."

She glanced at her ex-daughter-in-law. "I know, Jenny. You don't have to say it. I didn't have any business searching for that damn shortcut by myself. But I was feeling so much better and wanted to stretch my legs. I didn't bother saying anything because I thought it was just a hop, skip, and jump from the beach. I'd forgotten it was such an overland journey. So my memory plays tricks on me. So I'm getting on in years." She turned to Duke and Ray. "I guess I've already become that troublesome old lady I told you about at Nautiloid Canyon." She turned back to Jenny. "So kill me."

"Not that I haven't thought of it, Mother Pinch," Jenny said, "with heavenly transports of my own."

"Speaking of heavenly transports," Hannah said, "isn't the dory the most obvious way of transporting me? Why on earth can't we just continue on downriver like we planned?" She reached to touch Duke's arm. "I don't see why we need to involve the park authorities and who knows how many other damn meddlers up on the South Rim who don't have any business with us."

"Except my poor husband is buried without authorization in their jurisdiction." Carol perched on the arm of Duke's porch chair. "There's all this nasty unfinished business about death certificates and coroner's reports. But you're right about one thing, Hannah. It's not your business or your problem. It's mine and mine alone. I want you all to go on without me."

"Go on where, for God's sakes?" Jenny asked. "Carol, this trip is over. It's been over since Little Bert's. We've just been floating through its postmortem. We're not going to abandon you to a nine-mile hike and the park officials all by yourself. The longer we put off the full report while we're here at Phantom, the worse it's going to look."

"Worse for whom?" Hannah asked. "Our own personal ranger already knows the contents of any report."

Jenny struggled to maintain her Serious Crew Leader demeanor. Duke stared at her now, half soulful Adriatic hunk, half wounded, guilty child. She decided not to say anything.

"Do we want this war hero to serve a prison term for trying to rescue Tess?" Glen appeared in the doorway, blotting his wet beard with a towel wrapped around his neck. "No purpose would be served by indicting Duke."

"I'd love to agree," Jenny said. "But a man has been killed while I led this group, and I bear the ultimate responsibility."

"No," Duke said, firm. "I do. I'm the killer."

While Duke's words sizzled on the overheated air, Faith and Annette crossed the lawn bearing the remnants of their sugar cones. "It's our turn, now, right?" Annette said, coming up the porch steps. "Did you save some hot water for me, Glen?"

He gave her a gentlemanly nod. "And even a fair dollop of my Green Goop shampoo."

Annette surprised him with a buss on the cheek before she disappeared inside the dormitory. Glen held out his hand to Faith. "Join us, Professor Brattle? We elders are having a kind of council."

Faith swallowed the last of her ice cream cone. "When did I become an elder?"

"Oh, get over yourself," Hannah said. "Ray's an elder too, and he's only twenty-three."

"Wonderful!" Faith cried, seating herself on an arm of Hannah's Adirondack chair. "I happen to be twenty-three myself."

"Aren't we all?" Jenny glanced from face to face, by now all so familiar. Yet here, freed of the leashed caps and sunglasses, they were fresh and exposed. Duke and Ray each looked younger, shorn of bristly whiskers. She'd almost forgotten the kindly, deep crinkles around Glen's gray eyes. And maybe she'd never seen Carol's huge, pale blue irises except by campfire or lantern light, since the entire span of their acquaintance had unfolded behind sunglasses and visors in the glare of Southwestern desert Wildlands Society volunteer projects. And though to Jenny their crew seemed a tribe apart—temporary intruders in this buzzing, well-ordered creekside oasis—in their clean, unfamiliar T-shirts and shorts, hair combed and shiny, they could all pass for any other visitors arrived by the latest mule train.

Except maybe for Tess and Tycho. They were still in their river grungies, Tycho naked to the waist of his baggy camouflage trunks. After the ice cream excursion, they'd crossed the lawn when Faith and Annette came onto the porch. Seated cross-legged in the grassy shade just abandoned by the smooching backpackers, Tess now took a bold lick from Tycho's chocolate double scoop. In return, he licked off the stray chocolate around her lips. Jenny turned away just as the sticky licking led to stickier kissing.

Jenny cleared her dry throat as the others looked at her respectfully and, for once, they quieted. "Duke has something to tell us," she began, "and then we all have a decision to make.

I will need everyone's wise counsel on this. And bear in mind, please, that we all represent the Wildlands Society in whatever we decide. If our decision is the wrong one and word of it gets to the media, we could not only damage the Society but the whole conservation movement." She shrugged. "I'm sorry if that sounds impersonal. And it may sound far-fetched. But this story, an unexplained death in the canyon while it's closed to everyone except a tiny band of conservation volunteers could be exploited by those who despise environmentalists."

Jenny looked again toward the ranger station, its flag catching sunlight in the breeze. Cottonwood boughs shaded the backlit flag, then set it shimmering again, as if Old Glory dispatched some tantalizing secret code. Once she reported this to the Park Service, nothing would ever be the same.

Especially for Duke. He leaned forward, as if aware that his Adirondack chair had suddenly become a witness stand. "It happened exactly as Ray speculated at Clear Creek. At Little Bert's, I was closest to that beach. I'd just wandered there alone, following the flood mud line, absorbed in my note taking, when I heard Tess's scream. I scrambled along the base of the talus slope and through the willows. When I saw Jack on top of Tess, I shouted for him to get off her, but he didn't respond. And neither did Tess. Something inside me snapped. I lost all self-control. I meant to yank him off her, but before I knew it myself, I was clutching a heavy chunk of rock. I don't even remember grabbing it, but I must've knocked it against Jack's right temple, all my strength feeding into my right fist." He stopped, turning to Carol. "I'm sorry, being this blunt."

"It's okay." Carol's hand had never left his shoulder, and she patted it now. "Go on."

"I sometimes forget how strong my good arm has become, now that it has to do double duty for me. And I must've mustered all its surplus strength. Jack didn't resist. I must've knocked him out. Maybe knocked him dead immediately. I just knew I had to get his dead weight off Tess."

Duke looked at Carol, who nodded, calmly urging him to finish. Duke sighed, his eyes cast down. "He was a heavy guy, and I didn't know how much damage he'd done, crushing Tess like that. Once I dragged him across the beach a ways, I hurried back to Tess's side. She was completely out, but her chest rose and fell gently, with soft, regular breaths. This big gob of shampoo was heading down her eyebrow toward her eye, so I took my water bottle and rinsed it away, expecting her to come to. Then I meant to drag Jack's body all the way to the river in hopes it would look like a drowning, but I abandoned it when I heard a sharp snap in the distance, and took off back through the willows."

"That snap was me, of course," Hannah said. "I lost my footing on the first ledge of that rise, so I reached for a tamarisk branch. But it was rotten and cracked off in my hand."

"What did you see, Hannah," Jenny asked, "exactly?"

"Well, nothing *exactly*. But I did hear movement in the brush, and thought I saw Duke running back toward the talus slope. But he was so hidden in the willow brush I couldn't be sure. Then, when I finally hauled my old carcass to the top of the rise, I pretty much had the story figured out. Though when Tycho scrambled around to check on Tess, for a while I wasn't sure if he'd been the one screened in the willows. Returning to the scene of the crime, as it were. But no, I decided. It was Duke after all."

"And you decided to keep this to yourself," Jenny asked, "while we spent three days and forty-some river miles in turmoil? Cooking up schemes? Distrusting each other? Fearing for our lives every sleepless night?"

"Pretty much, yes. I'm sorry, but I wasn't absolutely sure I *did* see Duke, remember? And though I was fairly sure of what happened with Duke and Jack and Tess, I didn't see any reason to get Duke in jeopardy. As we headed downriver, I knew you and Ray were distracted by your suspicions of Carol and Tycho. Just as I was pretty sure that they were innocent." She shifted her injured leg, sighing. "I understood immediately Duke felt he was saving Tess's life. I figured that was something the legal system would never acknowledge, and I couldn't bear the thought of our ranger serving any more time in hell." Hannah's gruff tone had softened. "Now that I know what Jack was really doing, how he was reaching out to Tess, I'm sad he had to die violently. But that doesn't make Duke any more liable."

In the silence that followed, Duke cleared his throat. "But I am liable. It was me, not Hannah, who kept you all in confusion. And unnecessary fear. I didn't have any right to do that. And for no reason, except I was immobilized. Paralyzed like a shame-faced brat. I really hoped, for a while, that I could avoid judgment if I stalled until Phantom Ranch. Especially when it seemed like everyone was satisfied Jack might have been dead before he lost his balance, or had landed on Tess after a heart attack."

"And he probably *was* already gone," Carol said. "That's why he didn't respond to your call, Duke."

"Still, with Ray's certainty about Tycho, and Jenny's about Carol, and with the panic at Clear Creek, I felt so ashamed of what my silence had caused. So, Jenny, you *do* have a report to make. Hell, I'll write it myself and save you the grief." He rose from his seat. "You can help me with the details if you want. All we have to do is cross the path to the ranger station."

Carol got up at once from the chair's arm and intercepted him, pulling Duke into an embrace. He pressed his face against her shoulder, murmuring. "I'm so ashamed, Carol. And so sorry."

"I told you already, it's all right." Carol caressed the nape of Duke's neck. "You only meant to do the right thing. The best thing."

"Excuse me," Jenny said, unable to stop herself. "What did you mean, *already*?"

When Carol didn't answer, Faith intervened. "You've known all along, Carol? Duke confessed to you?"

"Yes, back at the Little Colorado, during all the distraction with the Canadians."

"And you were prepared," Faith asked, "to have us keep believing Jenny was right? That it was you all along?"

"I promised Duke I wouldn't say anything because I am ultimately responsible. Not Duke. Jack was dead before Duke ever picked up that rock, I'm sure of it. Head wounds gush like hell, so I could tell by how slowly the blood trickled from that huge gash on his temple. Jack's poor ol' heart must've stopped pumping blood for a good while."

"So, you and Duke have been very busy," Faith said, "keeping facts to yourselves."

"Believe me, it got very scary with Ray accusing Tycho like that," Carol said. "We just prayed nothing would come of it until we reached Phantom."

"So, when you and I hustled after Tycho," Ray asked Duke, "back in Clear Creek, after your nap, you were really escorting me? Keeping me from going after Tycho."

"Partly, yes. But I was never napping, Ray." Duke winced, trying to meet Ray's eyes. "I've hardly slept since Little Bert's. I was lying there trying to figure out what to say to undo all the confusion, to get us all back to the truth." He moved closer to the steps, indicating the ranger station. "To where we are, right now."

"And right now, just wait!" Faith rose and grasped Duke by the shoulders. "Please, sit back down." She persisted in the standoff until he sank back in his chair. "I'm sure you've got one more confession to make. When Hannah saw that scene at Little Bert's, she was sure you really were a hero, and so am I. You acted out of a reflex, sure, but something much larger than that. Something you left overseas."

"Only old, buried facts," Duke said. "Better forgotten."

"Except that they can't be, and shouldn't be. We're a long way from Bosnia, Duke, but the facts aren't that old. They won't stay buried. Just this spring, when one of those old generals finally went on trial, there was another investigation into the atrocities at Srebrenica. That war was with us, if just for an instant, on that beach at Little Bert's, wasn't it? Remember, Duke, I read the summaries of the rape squad trials for my research. And you took part in the women's testimony, didn't you?" Faith dropped to her haunches, eye to eye before Duke, and grasped his hand. "As a translator, maybe?"

Duke nodded. Annette appeared from the shower, her hair wrapped in a towel. She rested her head on Glen's shoulder as Duke told the whole story, helped by Faith's coaxing.

At nineteen, Private First Class Ivan Dukarić had been in the final weeks of his long therapies in a German hospital, recovering from the land mine blast in Bosnia that had taken his left arm. Duke was looking forward to heading home to California when two US Army officials and two blue-bereted UN operatives appeared, Canadian and British. They surrounded his bed after he'd finished his last hospital breakfast. The UN operatives outlined the desperate need for an objective interpreter, required immediately in the aftermath of violent Bosnian Serb offensives in Bosnian Muslim villages. Dutch UN peacekeepers had been overwhelmed, forced to abandon villagers to the Serbs for the most brutal ethnic cleansing yet in three years of ceaseless brutality. Reports of mass graves circulated, along with certainty that the mostly Muslim townsmen, including the schoolboys and elders, had been shot. After digging their own graves in hillside trenches, all were killed one by one at point-blank range.

The only witnesses might be the villages' women and girls, who had been herded out of town in separate forced marches. Live scenes of the expelled women, the grandmothers and the toddlers struggling across cosmopolitan, humane Europe had been broadcast on cable news worldwide. Fresh rain loosened mass graves, exposing the severed arms of grandfathers. Schoolboys' skulls poked through the mud on satellite video, looped twenty-four hours a day.

The UN operatives hoped some women who might have witnessed the slaughter could be persuaded to give testimony. On the day of his release, they requested PFC Dukarić, permanently disabled from his earlier assignment, to accept an even more special assignment.

"I explained that I had already served for a year," Duke said. "I'd learned to identify likely terrain for ambushes and emergency landings. And I became so damn skilled at finding minefields that I found one with my left arm. But I was lucky to be alive, as everyone rushed to remind me on every possible occasion. Lucky when my nineteenth birthday arrived in a German hospital like a severed arm—gift-wrapped in an ice-packed Styrofoam box but useless to reattach. And I *was*, you know. Lucky."

The uniformed men laid out their case to Duke. They needed an interpreter who knew the territory and the communities involved, and the officials doubted they could get objective translations from Bosnian interpreters. "Even though I was born in Yugoslavia, they knew I'd spent all of my adolescence in California, so for them I was this unique objective being. A semi-American avatar dropped into rural Bosnia to record eyewitness testimony in my native tongue. The language we used to call Serbo-Croatian.

"So, we struck a deal—a deal that made those Lee's Ferry gun nut yahoos more right than they ever knew. Because I am the ultimate affirmative action cripple. I told those Army officials I'd do it if they assured my career in federal lands after I finished college. Preferably an assignment in the desert Southwest. Preferably in the emptiest stretch of national park real estate unvisited by other human beings. The next morning, I was on a huge bombless bomber heading for a secret airfield in southeastern Bosnia.

"It was heat even worse than this, humid and dusty and full of biting bugs. We set up an olive drab canvas pavilion, like a revival tent. The women lined up all the way from our airfield back to their refugee camp. The grammas, the young widows, and the little girls stood all day for all the long hot days in their handwashed print dresses. They'd heard about a nice *objective* American kid. He spoke their language and would record every word they said exactly as they said it. The nice kid would take their words back to the President, who would send planes to protect them from Serb thugs.

"But the women and girls didn't know much about what happened in those mass grave meadows. No more than Hannah knew for sure who was running through the coyote willow back at Little Bert's. They just knew pretty much that their husbands and sons and brothers and fathers weren't ever coming home. When the shooting and live burials took place in another part of the forest, the women were on their own forced march to hell. But these women had their own tales to tell.

"So many of them reminded me of my mother and my aunts back in Croatia. We were Catholic, they were Muslim, but identical in ethnic stock, in the arch of their brow or the turn of their lips. And except for their country cousin mannerisms, they were like the ladies you see at the supermarket or church. And the little girls, well—with their hair pulled back in scrunchies and their *Beauty and the Beast* T-shirts, they might have gone to elementary school down any American street. And after they gave indirect evidence or outright speculation about their husbands' or fathers' or sons' or brothers' disappearances, they would shift in their seats. They'd test the waters of disclosure.

"They told the same story over and over, from girls of eight to women of seventy. Systematic gang rape, usually by men and boys they'd known all their lives. Guys who'd been their neighbors, their students, their teachers. Guys related by marriage. Stepfathers. Second cousins. Last year's date for the Firemen's Ball. Half the armed Serbs were busy attacking women while the other half shot and buried their men, making sure no matter what happened, their lives would be severed forever from all familiar ties. Like an amputation."

When Duke got up from his chair, Faith rose from the porch floor and hugged him. He buried his face against her neck for a long, silent spell. He sobbed a little, and she patted the back of his head, then he was quiet and still again.

Faith kissed him on the cheek, then released him to Jenny, who stepped forward to take his hand. "Come on, Duke," she said, "let's go for a walk. Down by Bright Angel Creek."

Jenny led them silently through a network of dirt paths into a creekside cottonwood grove. She glanced once again at the ranger station, whose flag had fallen into shadow. She searched across the lawn for Tycho and Tess, now napping, arms locked, under a big cottonwood, and felt how much she missed Amelia. Her daughter, too, was almost exactly the same age as Tess.

They stopped at an empty campsite, secluded beside

a gurgling stream in breezy shade. Duke sat at the table, its bench right over the bank of Bright Angel Creek, and indicated the bench across from him. "So, as group leader, you'll be required to make a report. What do you think?"

Jenny sat. "Like those poor Bosnian women? A report?"

Damn, here she had escaped from Denver, ending her horrific marriage and sacrificing her daughter's presence in her life. She'd exiled herself to Flagstaff in hopes of making decisions about her life's course. How had it evolved to her being left to decide the course of Duke's life?

Her mind's eye saw a pretty girl on a beach washing her hair under a rocky outcrop, caught unawares by a man twice her size who—fallen or collapsed—had slammed her to the ground with such force he knocked her out. She saw a messed-up, shapeless man, long drowned in grief for his own daughter, clumsily reaching out to the girl.

Then Jenny tried to see the scene through the eyes of another long-wounded man, once a teenager who'd roamed foreign minefields that were not really foreign to him, gazing into the eyes of hundreds of traumatized women who reminded him of his cousins, his aunts, and his mother.

Report. The word had a stale, officious sound. Jenny hated it. It was a word for tattletales and pompous bottom feeders who worshipped the literal ink of the law and ignored the spirit, the elegance of justice.

❖

RAY stood alone on the footbridge near sunset, watching the Colorado River riffle off to the west, then disappear though the dark, narrow Vishnu gorge. Tycho lay beside Tess on the supply raft far below, sprawled atop the pile of dry bags.

On the raft and the twin dories, all equipment and supplies were still leashed and tied, awaiting Jenny's orders. They hoped they might be able to hitch their bags to a morning mule train, but Glen had been pessimistic at the cookhouse dinner. "There's not a chance in hell there will be room for that. The mules' burdens are planned out way in advance. Plan to carry your gear up on your own back."

Ray stared upward, where the Bright Angel Trail disappeared up a steep side canyon. It switchbacked nine miles to the tourist village atop the South Rim, so distant it could not be seen above the Inner Gorge. Whenever he thought of leaving the river here, the word "aborted" kept announcing itself. As in, they would *abort* now, rather than navigate two hundred more miles into the remainder of the canyon's wilderness.

During these few days on the Colorado River, even amid the crisis, some embryonic change kept kicking toward being born or reborn. Ray knew it would not survive tomorrow's overheated backpacking excursion to the familiar, hypertense world on the rim. After contacting the Park Service, Jenny had arranged to place a call to the chief inspector after dinner, and only after the details were worked out would they know if they needed to stay put at Phantom and wait to be interviewed here or climb out in the morning and meet the officials up at Grand Canyon Village.

The bustling crowd in the Phantom cookhouse unnerved Ray, so he'd skipped dessert and followed Tess and Tycho back to the river. Like a lover suddenly aware of his infatuation's impossible requirements, Ray couldn't keep this blue-green watercourse from his sight for long. Before coming to the bridge, he'd found a deserted trail to the river and sat for long, silent minutes on the bank, letting the water run over his hands. He'd splashed his face with palms full of the cold river as if to say goodbye, wishing that little sacrament could be a baptism, instead of the last rites of his river life.

Ray studied the raft and dories below from the bridge, deploring the waste of all their equipment, food, and research, but much more touched by the inevitable breakup of their tribe, their self-contained floating society. Would he ever see Duke again?

It occurred to him, not for the first time, that their data collection was just a modern form of nature worship. They'd really been engaging in a river cleansing ritual cloaked in the sophistication of science but as primitive and heartfelt as any ancient ceremony.

As if to illustrate Ray's thought, Tess suddenly rose from the raft and hopped to a rock, where she stood with her hands on her hips, having no more specific task than watching the river lap against the boulder's base. Just as abruptly, Ray remembered her story, after the Interior Department ceremony at Lake Powell, when Tess thought Jack Carne was salivating over her while claiming to save her from Jet Skiers. Now he realized Jack had been a paunchy Holden Caulfield, bearing his grief and guilt by appointing himself the catcher in the rye, the catcher determined not to allow violent death on the shore of yet another artificial lake. He'd put himself on the precipice's edge so no other daughters could be lost to drunks in motor craft.

"I'm glad you're still keeping an eye on those two," Jenny said as she leaned on the rail beside him. "They want to sleep down there tonight on the supply raft, to 'guard everything.' Now comes the question of whether I intervene to guard Tess's virginity."

"That's not part of your job description as Lead Campfire Girl. Besides, you're operating on two negative presuppositions. One, Tess is not in control of her own adult self, and two, Tycho is not a gentleman."

"Oh no. After all this, I judge no man or woman for the rest of my days. I presume nothing about anyone."

"Me either. To think, I was ready to have Tycho hauled off to a padded cell under heavy medication for his own good. I was so hung up on my research, so in love with my own theory. I was so sure."

"I was just as ready to believe the worst of Carol. All the while still liking, even admiring, my old friend the murderess. I wasn't prosecuting or investigating so much as cheerleading. Indulging in vicarious husband killing."

"We were reading the situation by the weak light of our own egos."

"And with a distinct taste for the lurid. Which wasn't there, was it? Even the big mystery of Carol and Jack's marriage lacks any prurient juice. She would never have left him, no matter how little of her handsome, athletic high school sweetheart survived. Not in the wake of Jessie's death."

"Nope," Ray said. "In fact, Carol was trying to save Jack. From himself."

"Both Carol and Duke were reacting to years of accumulated pain. They'd remained so pure, so stouthearted."

"Even heroic. But you and I, with nothing to do but figure it out, unleashed the worst in ourselves."

"No, Ray. Not the worst. Just our most vulnerable tendencies based on our own accumulated pain. But look at you now, bud. From a wimpy, self-obliterating basket case of lost love to sturdy crime solver in just eighty-eight river miles."

"God, would I ever love to try the next two hundred. What kind of superpower would I develop by Lake Mead?"

"I can't deal with any far distances right now. I have to contend with the immediate problem of tonight's sleeping arrangements right here at Phantom Ranch. Imagine those lovely bunks tonight, just for a change."

"Well, you'll be sleeping in your own bed after tonight, anyway."

"I most certainly will not." Jenny stared downriver. "After tonight, I'll have a hundred and ninety-one river miles of sleeping bags on sandy beaches, ravens and bugs and ornery, snoring friends."

"Who? You? Me? When?" Ray asked, the sinking sun right in his eyes. Then he laughed. "How?"

"You'd know if you hadn't skulked off by yourself after you demolished that cookhouse special. I told the Park Service folks how our party experienced a death at Little Bert's due to heat and solar stress complicated by the victim's poor physical condition, stress, and coronary strain. He had a fatal fall, in which the victim apparently bashed his head against a sharp jag of Muav limestone. The body was decomposing rapidly, and without phone contact, we had no choice but dig a grave at Nankoweap. You know, Ray. Mostly the truth."

"Okay, Jen. It's truth enough for me. But now what? Do we climb out to answer questions? Or do they climb down to interrogate us?"

"Neither. See that big river under our feet? We float down it, terrify ourselves in humongous rapids every now and then, and continue our research all the way to Lake Mead. If any park official needs to interrogate us later on, they know where we'll be and where to find us when we're done. We're not going anywhere but down canyon for the next ten days."

"Except for me, Ray," Carol said, arriving mid-bridge ahead of Duke. "I'll talk directly to the inspector when I reach the South Rim tomorrow afternoon. I need to make clear how I misjudged my husband's readiness for taking this trip and underestimated the physical strain. If they want to exhume the body, I'll emphasize my widow's prerogatives and try to talk them out of it. And if I can't, we'll have to hope they believe that blow to his head was a result of his fall."

Jenny clasped Carol's fingers. "Did you contact Jack's parents?"

"No." Carol winced. "Still no service on their landline, and no answer on their cell phones. I couldn't very well leave a message on their voicemail, except to say I'm coming home early. Oh God! Jenny, Jack's their firstborn son, and this comes on top of losing the family home in Scots Spring."

"Oh, Carol!" Jenny cried. "I feel like we're abandoning you to this terrible mission. What can we do?"

"Get back on the river tomorrow. It would only make me feel worse if you all didn't go on downriver to finish our research."

Ray reached for Carol's free hand. "I'll hike up with you tomorrow morning."

"Me too," Duke said, easing beside Ray. "We can't let you climb out by yourself. We'll keep you company."

"Thanks for your gallantry, gentlemen. But in the cool of morning, there'll be plenty of hikers on the trail. I'll leave before dawn, and I can use the time on my own with all I have to think about. I won't have any time to myself when I get home to Texas and deal with Jack's family." She nodded toward the dories. "And you all have work to do. You'll need to get an early start, and digest your breakfast before you take on the next big rapids. I hear there's a bunch just down the gorge, boys, and I expect y'all to be big and brave."

Their smiles expired with the last of the sunlight on their

faces. Tycho bounded onto the boulder beside Tess and pulled her into a long embrace. "Look, they're smoochin' way down there," Carol said, "in front of God and everybody."

As Ray glanced at the scene below, he felt Duke's elbow resting against his on the bridge rail.

"Well, it sounds like you've made up your mind, Carol," Ray said. "But I hate to lose you. I hate to break up our little family."

"We have formed a family, haven't we?" Carol said. "And a good one, if you think about it. That's one of the things I need to think over on the trail tomorrow morning. Maybe we humans are more than hungry carnivores after all. I don't know if I was ready to admit that before we started downriver."

Carol looked at them against the bridge's railing. "As much as it pains me to contradict myself, we really are a higher life form. Our little tribe proved that, didn't we? Think of the grace we showed since Jack's body was found. Tess took it like a real woman and refused to jump to conclusions or indulge in her victimhood. Glen was ready to sacrifice his freedom for Tycho's. Hannah held her secret close in order to protect Duke. Annette dove in at Hance and risked her life to save Hannah's. So did Jenny, and with your help, Ray, she never stopped trying to keep us safe and united and still coax us all toward the truth, no matter how unpleasant it got. And we finally got to it, didn't we? A better truth. A deeper connection."

"Jack was reaching for that connection, too," Ray said. "That was probably the last thing he did."

"And I have to connect with the reservations office," Jenny said, "and make sure those bunks really are waiting for us."

"Oh! A bunk sounds heavenly," Carol said, locking her arm in Jenny's as they headed back to the resort.

Easy as that, it happened. Ray was alone with Duke on the middle of the bridge as the sun sank behind the canyon rim. He slid his hand over Duke's forearm and down to his fingers, but felt too shy to say what he was thinking.

Duke clasped Ray's fingers. "Remember when we first met, skinny-dipping at Lee's Ferry? How I said I was ready to rejoin humanity?"

"You've done a pretty good job so far."

"Now I've got one hundred and ninety-one more river miles to rejoin with Ray O'Brien."

"We might even be able to steal a minute or two alone together."

"Like right now? May I kiss you again, Ray?"

His lips sought Duke's, and they met hungrily. Ray lost himself not just in the urgency of this long, slow kiss but in the release of every nerve and corpuscle.

Duke reached around him, pulling him even closer, his body as taut and hard as Ray had imagined though the embrace felt so easy, malleable—giving and given. One arm brought them together, one beautiful olive-toned, muscular arm with the strength of two. Ray didn't think it would take long to get used to that. He broke the kiss, pulled back, took a breath, then promptly kissed him again, looking over his shoulder to the scene below. Though darkness deepened along the bridge, Ray glanced at the canyon mesas still glinting in the day's last light, then at the river surging west into the wild.

About the Author

A native of California's Mendocino Coast, Lee Patton has enjoyed living in Denver—and venturing into the Rocky Mountains—for decades. A recipient of the Colorado Authors League Award for fiction, he's published five other novels, including *Coming to Life on South High* and *Every Summer Day* from Bold Strokes Books.

Patton was a Lambda Literary Award Finalist for Best Mystery. That first novel, *Nothing Gold Can Stay*, and his second, *Love and Genetic Weaponry*, also feature amateur sleuth Ray O'Brien.

Residencies at MacDowell Colony, the UCross Foundation, and the Anderson Center provided time, sustenance, and inspiration for developing his writing. Patton received an MA in fiction from the University of Denver's Writing Program.

Books Available From Bold Strokes Books

Loyalty, Love & Vermouth by Eric Peterson. A comic valentine to a gay man's family of choice, including the ones with cold noses and four paws. (978-1-63555-997-2)

Bury Me in Shadows by Greg Herren. College student Jake Chapman is forced to spend the summer at his dying grandmother's home and soon finds danger from long-buried family secrets. (978-1-63555-993-4)

A Different Man by Andrew L. Huerta. This diverse collection of stories chronicling the challenges of gay life at various ages shines a light on the progress made and the progress still to come. (978-1-63555-977-4)

Busy Ain't the Half of It by Frederick Smith and Chaz Lamar Cruz. Elijah and Justin seek happily-ever-afters in LA, but are they too busy to notice happiness when it's there? (978-1-63555-944-6)

Pursuit: A Victorian Entertainment by Felice Picano. An intelligent, handsome, ruthlessly ambitious young man who rose from the slums to become the right-hand man of the Lord Exchequer of England will stop at nothing as he pursues his Lord's vanished wife across Continental Europe. (978-1-63555-870-8)

Best of the Wrong Reasons by Sander Santiago. For Fin Ness and Orion Starr, it takes a funeral to remind them that love is worth living for. (978-1-63555-867-8)

Coming to Life on South High by Lee Patton. Twenty-one-year-old gay virgin Gabe Rafferty's first adult decade unfolds as an unpredictable journey into sex, love, and livelihood. (978-1-63555-906-4)

Death's Prelude by David S. Pederson. In this prequel to the Detective Heath Barrington Mystery series, Heath discovers that first love changes you forever and drives you to become the person you're destined to be. (978-1-63555-786-2)

His Brother's Viscount by Stephanie Lake. Hector Somerville wants to rekindle his illicit love affair with Viscount Wentworth, but he must overcome one problem: Wentworth still loves Hector's brother. (978-1-63555-805-0)

The Dubious Gift of Dragon Blood by J. Marshall Freeman. One day Crispin is a lonely high school student—the next he is fighting a war in a land ruled by dragons, his otherworldly boyfriend at his side. (978-1-63555-725-1)

Quake City by St John Karp. Can Andre find his best friend Amy before the night devolves into a nightmare of broken hearts, malevolent drag queens, and spontaneous human combustion? Or has it always happened this way, every night, at Aunty Bob's Quake City Club? (978-1-63555-723-7)

Death Overdue by David S. Pederson. Did Heath turn to murder in an alcohol-induced haze to solve the problem of his blackmailer, or was it someone else who brought about a death overdue? (978-1-63555-711-4)

Every Summer Day by Lee Patton. Meant to celebrate every summer day, Luke's journal instead chronicles a love affair as fast-moving and possibly as fatal as his brother's brain tumor. (978-1-63555-706-0)

Everyday People by Louis Barr. When film star Diana Danning hires private eye Clint Steele to find her son, Clint turns to his former West Point barracks mate, and ex-buddy with benefits, Mars Hauser to lend his cyber espionage and digital black ops skills to the case.(978-1-63555-698-8)

Royal Street Reveillon by Greg Herren. In this Scotty Bradley mystery, someone is killing the stars of a reality show, and it's up to Scotty Bradley and the boys to find out who. (978-1-63555-545-5)

Accidental Prophet by Bud Gundy. Days after his grandmother dies, Drew Morten learns his true identity and finds himself racing against time to save civilization from the apocalypse. (978-1-63555-452-6)

Counting for Thunder by Phillip Irwin Cooper. A struggling actor returns to the Deep South to manage a family crisis but finds love and ultimately his own voice as his mother is regaining hers for possibly the last time. (978-1-63555-450-2)

Of Echoes Born by 'Nathan Burgoine. A collection of queer fantasy short stories set in Canada from Lambda Literary Award finalist 'Nathan Burgoine. (978-1-63555-096-2)

www.ingramcontent.com/pod-product-compliance
Lightning Source LLC
Chambersburg PA
CBHW030515020726
47494CB00004B/1111